THE REPLACEMENT

BY RACHAEL WADE

To Jenny.
Be your something.

Rabbit Hole Press
Orlando, Florida
www.RachaelWade.com

ISBN: 978-0-9896304-6-7 (Paperback)

Editor: Susan Miller
Cover Design: Robin Ludwig Design Inc.

ALSO BY RACHAEL WADE

The Preservation Series:
Love and Relativity
(Featuring Carter and Whitney from the Preservation Series)
Preservation - Preservation, Book 1
Reservation - Preservation, Book 2
Declaration – Preservation, Book 3

The Resistance Trilogy:
Amaranth, Book 1
The Gates, Book 2
The Tragedy of Knowledge, Book 3
Unearthed, Novella

The Keepers Trilogy:
Repossession, Book 1
Restitution, Book 2 (2014)
Restoration, Book 3 (2015)

THE REPLACEMENT OFFICIAL PLAYLIST

Criminal – Fiona Apple

Young and Beautiful – Lana Del Rey (Theme Song)

Burning Desire – Lana Del Rey (Elise's Song)

Off to the Races – Lana Del Rey (Masked Ball Scene)

Who Will Save Your Soul – Jewel

9 Crimes – Damien Rice

Breathe Me – Sia

Foolish Games – Jewel

These Boots Were Made for Walkin' – Nancy Sinatra

Just Give Me a Reason – Pink

Hole in My Hand - Benjamin Francis Leftwich

Hands – Jewel

Poison and Wine – The Civil Wars

Society – Eddie Vedder version (Ryder's song)

Landslide – Fleetwood Mac (Thanksgiving Day Scene)

In the Sun – Joseph Arthur

Winter – Tori Amos

Born to Die – Lana Del Rey (Elise and Ryder's Song)

Blue Jeans – Lana Del Rey (Elise's song for Ryder)

Época – Gotan Project

Spark – Tori Amos

Smells Like Teen Spirit – Tori Amos version

Please Don't Leave Me – Pink

Empty – Ray LaMontagne

Jolene – Ray LaMontagne

Thin Line – HoneyHoney

This Year's Love - David Gray

House of the Rising Sun – Animals

Be Be Your Love – Rachael Yamagata

Secrets – OneRepublic

National Anthem – Lana Del Rey (Epilogue)

DEDICATION

To anyone who struggles with what they see when they look in the mirror.

ACKNOWLEDGMENTS

Writing this book nearly killed me. I owe its inspiration to so many different things: old friends, new friends, strangers, people I've met on my travels, people I admire, music, the Northwest, pain, heartbreak, redemption, love, and fear. There's no way I can list everything here, but I'll try.

Thank you, God, for the courage to write Elise's story and for the chance to take painful things and shape them into something beautiful. Thank you Patricia, for letting me read the first few pages to you in our hotel on Bainbridge Island. Thank you for believing in the story and in me, and for letting me have my alone time on the ferry to cry. Thank you to my editor Susan, for helping make Elise's story shine and for your valuable insight on Christmastime in Paris! Thank you to Jodi Ellen Malpas for totally making my year by giving the story a read, and for trampling the cover. Thank you to my wonderful betas: Thessa (my Triple B), Cathy (bestie!), and Rachel (Rach Squared), and all of my book blogger and reader friends—you know who you are. Thank you to my street team and to all of my writer friends for being such an incredible support system. You guys are gold in this crazy industry. A special thank you to Kristina McKillip (Wells) for sending me pics of Seattle when you know I'm feeling homesick, and for tips on Gig Harbor, and thanks to both you and Laura for making me feel even more at home in my favorite city. Last but not least, thank you to my family and friends for your unconditional love and support.

PROLOGUE

INSPIRED BY "YOUNG AND BEAUTIFUL" BY LANA DEL REY

Mom rushes over to me with the long, satin black gloves and a smile that radiates like blinding white sunlight. To her, it's Christmas morning. Those black gloves are like some sort of weird good luck charm to her or something. She made me wear them three times already. Once to the Robinsons' wedding, once to Miss Shelly's funeral, and once to a formal fundraising ball my dad's company threw a few months ago. Tonight will mark the fourth occasion I've worn them.

She squeals a bit, and I can see she's unable to tone down her giddiness. Her blonde, flawless do falls neatly over her shoulders. Her lip liner blends smoothly with her perky pink gloss and the smoky effect she's applied to her eyes is alluring. Each of her lashes is separated with thick black mascara, curled just around the tips to add a final dash of glamor to the look. She's a modern Nancy Sinatra. I don't know if she'll ever escape the 1960s. I sit on the round vanity stool and look up at her as she smiles down at me, and I wonder why I agreed to this, other than to make her happy.

Well, that's reason enough.

There's not a whole lot of happy zooming around this house lately, especially when dad comes home. The scene always starts the same. He walks through the front door with one of those classic honey-I'm-home moments, only his expression is bored and cold, and mom scuttles to meet him, twirling to show him how done up she is for his arrival before asking him whether he'd prefer whiskey or wine with dinner. He always says whiskey. I don't know why she even gives him a choice. Within seconds, she takes his coat, asks him about his day, and follows him to the dining room table, where he takes his seat and busies himself with his cell phone. She rambles and tries to get his attention, but fails miserably, then proceeds to serve him his meal. It's then that he looks up and acknowledges I'm at the table, but he doesn't have much to say to me.

Like my mother, I'm a prop. A piece to a set that is his seemingly perfect life. My purpose is limited. Every now and then, though, my mom catches his eye. It's times like those that she finds that elusive thing called happiness and catches and seals it tight in a little container. I swear, when my father looks at her and likes what he sees, her hands ball up into excited fists and her whole body scrunches inward as if she's suppressing a 13-year-old's girlish enthusiasm. It's no secret my father's love is tainted. If my mother looks beautiful at that moment, her reward is affection. My father misses all the things that make her beautiful the other 364 days of the year, apparently.

It's twisted and delusional and makes me see blood red, but it's how he works, and she's somehow fallen into his toxic web over the years, believing his lies and accepting his conditional love.

Sometime after these tiresome, wordless dinners, my mom puts on a fresh pot of coffee and serves my dad a large slice of whatever she baked that day, while I retreat to my room for homework. My father has never hit my mother. He doesn't need fists. His words do all the work. I hear those words often, after I leave the dinner table for my bedroom. I hear it all, but I never say a word.

"You can't honestly accompany me to drinks at the lounge tonight looking like that, Elena," my father fumed last night at the dining table. I watched from the end of the hall, taking in the weight of my mother's pain. It was all in her eyes. "Do you know how that reflects on me?"

"Darling, I thought this would please you. I bought a new dress and I just had my hair done—"

"You look like a clown, woman. You'll make me a fucking laughing stock." He moved abruptly from the table, throwing his napkin down. "Now fix that goddamn makeup and make yourself presentable. I can't even look at you." He headed for the living room and I remained in the hall, watching my mother. She sat very still at the table, her head down, hands perched neatly on her lap. A tear escaped, then another, but she suddenly steeled herself and wiped them away, smoothing out her features before she stood and collected the dinner plates.

Last night's scene is a common one, but it's one that never gets any easier to witness.

Tonight is my high school prom, which explains my mom's unusual bout of happiness. It's exploding from her tonight, complete with sparklers and firecrackers. It also explains those black gloves she's so eager to slip onto my hands right now.

"Left," she instructs, paying careful attention to each finger, working out each wrinkle as she goes. "Perfect! Right." I relinquish my right hand and sigh, wishing some of her glee would rub off on me. The last thing I want to do is go to prom. Especially with Rick Huntington, captain of the football team. But I'm going to go, because dad insists, and mom…well, mom's happiness depends on it right now.

So I watch as she slips on the black gloves, and I picture all of the things I'd rather be doing than getting dressed to go to prom. Spending a cozy night in with my French indie dramas and a tub of ice cream would be nice. Or dancing like a lunatic with Tee, my best friend, while we drink her dad's beer would be great. It's our usual Saturday night ritual. He's a surgeon and he's never home, so I usually grab an overnight bag and hightail it around the block to her place, where we binge on junk food, beer, and 90s alternative until the sun comes up.

"Remember what I taught you," mom says as she finishes off the gloves. "You're never too young to learn this lesson."

"I know, mom," I say dryly, letting her spin me in the stool to face the vanity mirror. We look at one another in the glass. "Beauty is our power."

"That's right, honey. No matter what the world tells you, no matter what it says about being intelligent and all that, the real truth will always remain: beauty and money make this planet go round. You can get by without money. You can fool people, even. But beauty is a hard act to pull. It takes real effort. A lot of the time it's all mirrors and smoke screens. But look like me," she tilts a hip and plants a hand on her waist, "and you'll always be useful in the eyes of society."

"Beauty doesn't buy happiness, mom."

"Well, now, you're too young to know anything about that, aren't you?" She sticks me with that sickly sweet smile and taps the edges of my blonde curls. "One day you'll see, Elise. The world likes to tell us not to be judgmental. To be kind and tolerant, loving and forgiving. But what they want and what they're actually willing to do are two very different things." Her smile droops a bit on one side, and her eyes glaze with something that stings my heart to see. "At the core, the world is shallow. They want physical beauty, even if it's only skin deep. You have a heart in this world? A soul?" She places a hand on the back of the stool and leans in over me, holding my gaze in the mirror. "It counts for nothing. You remember that." Rising back to full height, she slips behind me and begins to fluff my hair, launching into some frilly chatter about hair products and perfume. I hear her, but her voice is hollow. Each syllable breaks and distances itself from me. I stare at myself in the mirror as she works on my curls, until her voice is a dead lull, and I drop my gaze to my gloved arms resting in my lap. I focus on their color. Black.

I connect with something there, and realize their color reminds me of a small, shallow pit I feel beginning to bloom in my stomach. I'm not sure where exactly it came from or when the seed was planted. I only have the suspicion that somewhere, at one point in time or another, it all began with my mom's little life lesson: Beauty is power. And if you don't have it, the world doesn't want you. And who didn't need to be wanted?

CHAPTER 1

ELISE
23 YEARS OLD

It's five o'clock in the afternoon, and I'm screwing my boss's brother. It's not the first time. He's bald and his name is Tim, and I know he's engaged to be married next summer. I vaguely wonder if his fiancée knows about the things he does with me, or if she knows about me at all. I doubt it.

He's sliding in and out of me slowly, relishing each push and pull, and frankly, it bores me. But he's giving me something I crave and it has absolutely nothing to do with physical pleasure. Sure, I enjoy sex just as much as any man does. Especially when I'm attracted to a man, which in this case I'm not, but my mind usually loves it more than my body does.

Especially when it involves Tim.

It's men like him who give me the greatest mental high. The ones who actually love to cheat. They somehow think they're so smooth, think they're getting away with it—and for a while, they often do—so when they're screwing me, they have this rebellious air about them, as if they wish someone would walk in and catch them with their dicks in the cookie jar. They're half out of their minds with lust, and they're only out for themselves. Obviously, it's quite fucked up that this somehow nourishes me, but it's what I know, and it's what I need.

Tim's looking down at me, with that lost, untamed sparkle in his eyes that I know so well. He's not really looking at me; he's looking at my shell. And as his waist begins to pump harder, I too become lost. Lost in the heady look in his eyes, like for just a few short minutes, I am his whole world. Nothing matters to him in that moment except using my body, his visual of my shell, to get him to where he wants to be. He's relying on me for that, and if I yanked it away from him right this moment, he'd be a crazed, dazed, desperate man. That power sends me soaring, and then the plummeting begins.

This is the best part. It's like a roller coaster. It all begins with that look of his. I ascend, higher and higher, knowing his climax is looming as I rush to the top. Then, as my moans follow in a trail of his own, we both teeter at the top, our bodies enraptured in dizzy anticipation. A few more jerks of his waist and we're tipped over the edge, sent spiraling down in a fiery blaze, our shouts overpowering the sound of the coaster's rickety rattle, until finally, we reach the good stuff.

Once I hit the bottom of the track, I plunge head first into a free fall, straight into an ominous abyss. It confuses me because it's equally dark and light, just as beautiful as it is dangerous. All is cool and still there. So peaceful I could cry. And I often do, which sometimes baffles the men I'm with. Or freaks them out, one or the other. The bottomless void continues to drag me down, farther and farther, and at this point, I'm begging to be swallowed up. And this is where the sobs usually become heavier. Because I can't sink any further. The hole won't drag me down anymore. I hit a wall, and it infuriates me. As if the abyss can read my very thoughts, it cuts the string that was pulling me into it and watches as I begin to float back up, forcing me to ascend back to the place I do not want to be.

I don't want to leave the abyss, I want to drown in it and soak up that peaceful feeling. I want to live there. But I can't, and it's time to go home.

Tim grunts above me as he finishes and then rolls off of me, immediately getting up to walk to the bathroom and dispose of the condom. In my massive quest for euphoria, that is the only thing I always do right—insist on protection, every time. I don't care if it pisses the guy off, ruins the moment, or whatever the hell. I just don't. I might disregard my dignity and tons of other important shit, but one thing I won't consider compromising is my physical health. Not if I can help it.

I ponder that—my dignity—as Tim fumbles around in the bathroom. It's something I think about often. The whole town seems to think I'm in short supply of it, because I sleep around. What they don't realize, though, is I've found my own sort of dignity. It just doesn't match up to their standards. I find self-respect in owning up to what I am and not bullshitting anyone about it. Honesty is self-respect in my book. Granted, I'm deceptive. But if you flat-out asked me if I've deceived you, I'd never bullshit you about it. That's gotta count for something.

"Give me ten more minutes and I'll be ready for round two," Tim says as he steps out of the bathroom, lingering in the doorway. The blinds are drawn and I squint at the clock to get a better look at the time.

"No can do," I say, stepping out of bed and slipping on my jeans. I didn't wear underwear here. I stand there topless in front of him, letting him drool over my tits. Sometimes I think he likes that more than actually having his hands on them. "I work at six. Gotta go."

He stirs from the bathroom doorway and makes a move toward me, but I raise my hands. "Don't, Tim. I can't be late for my shift." He stills and grits his teeth, obviously annoyed. I reach down to grab my tank top and roll my eyes. What's he got to be annoyed at? I just gave him exactly what he wanted, just the way he liked it.

"Tell Jay to cut you a break tonight," he says. "You know he will." I detect a hint of whininess in his tone and I'm immediately turned off. I couldn't fuck him again now even if I tried.

"No. This is my job and I won't screw it up."

He suddenly laughs, and the sound grates on my nerves so badly that it takes everything in me not to run out the front door sans top and shoes. "You screw everything else, what's the difference?"

In a flash, I feel my body leap forward so fast, I'm not

sure where the slap across his cheek begins and where it ends. It just happens, and it feels fucking great. "This was the last time. We're done."

"Oh come on, Elise." He rubs at his cheek, not the least bit surprised by my retaliation. "You know what I meant. You never play by the rules. Excuse me for finding it humorous that you're concerned about a good attendance record all of a sudden." He waves his hands out to the side like he's trying to get me to see some sense. But I only see red.

"You know what I'm concerned about, Tim? The fact that men like you seem to think all women like me don't give a damn about anything. Stop acting like just because I give it to someone else besides you that I'm a worthless slut with no life ambition."

"Hey, you said it, not me." He folds his arms smugly and smirks.

"You know, I think I might stop by after work tonight to give Cheryl a visit when she gets home. She's been in the dark a little too long, don't you think?" I slip on my tank top and snatch up my bag, then start for the door.

Tim's hand snakes out and grabs my elbow. "If you even think about talking to my fiancée, you can kiss your shit waitressing job goodbye." His eyes roll down my body and then back up, locking with mine. "All I have to do is tell Jay how long you've been sucking my dick and he'll toss you right out on the street, honey. Think about it." He lets out a haughty laugh. "You're so ambitious... maybe it's time to find something better than waiting tables, huh? Maybe you can start charging for that fine ass of yours."

I yank my elbow from his grip before spitting in his face and racing out the bedroom door. I have to admit, the son of a bitch has me. I need my waitressing job at Stella's. Not just because it pays my bills, but because it gives me the means to pursue those other ambitions—the ones that Tim clearly doesn't think I have.

I jump in my car and waste no time peeling out into the residential street that I know like the back of my hand by now. The misty rain coats my windshield with a sleek layer of moisture and I flick on the wipers, thankful when I hit the first stoplight. I'm officially off of Tim's property, and I can breathe again. I pop a piece of gum in my mouth and hit the gas when the light turns green.

***

My ride from Tim's house to downtown Gig Harbor is a blur, and I'm suddenly pulling into the parking lot at Stella's for my shift. I park and rifle through my bag to make sure I didn't forget any necessities before I go inside. A clean uniform, pair of panties, bra, and my apron are all rolled up into a ball at the bottom of the bag.

I inhale deeply for a moment before stepping out into the rain, scanning the picturesque harbor view that lies just beyond the restaurant. That harbor isn't the only thing that looks like it belongs on a post card. The grass is an unnatural shade of green—so vibrant I want to snatch up a handful and watch it bleed on my fingers. There are white picket fences that line the adjoining buildings and everyone, I mean *everyone*, is walking a dog, not the least bit deterred by a little Northwest drizzle. On a clear day, this harbor is littered with sailboats and kayakers. Everything in Gig Harbor seems untouched, so pure and sweet that you can almost feel its nostalgia sink you, like sugar hitting sensitive teeth. It's high-end, with a ritzy feel, but comfortable. Like coming home.

I sigh and pull the small bottle of hand sanitizer from my bag and rub a drop onto my fingers, smoothing away the leftover grime from my messy tryst with Tim.

The door jingles as I make my way inside the vintage, classic movie themed diner, and Jay greets me right away.

"Hey, hon." He smiles and glances at his watch from behind the counter. His dark black hair is tainted by a smidgen of gray, and his green eyes are fresh and alert. "You're early today."

"Yeah, just wanted a few extra minutes to change and get myself together," I reply, which is not entirely a lie. "I'll be right out."

I head toward the bathroom and Jay nods, his dark black hair glinting under the counter's lighting. As I strip down in the bathroom to put on the fresh change of clothes, I dampen a pile of paper towels under the faucet and wash off the remnants of my afternoon with Tim. Nowhere near as refreshing as a hot shower, but it'll have to do for tonight. I pull my hair back into a ponytail and wash my hands thoroughly.

The hallway lined with black and white shots of Marilyn Monroe and Lucille Ball greets me when I step out of the bathroom. I pass the old-school telephone mounted on the wall and round the corner to the main counter to check in. Jay has disappeared, but Natalie, one of our newest waitresses, stands there, looking flustered.

"Hey, Elise," she says. "Do you know where Jay put the new dinner menus? I can't find them anywhere and I have three tables waiting, with no menus to give them. Jay ran up the road to give Brad a lift. He's having car trouble again." She bites her lip, knitting her strawberry blonde eyebrows together, and shuffles through a pile of paperwork beneath the register. Brad is one of our waiters and has worked for Jay since high school. The thing about Gig Harbor is that it's homey and tight knit. A family harbor town, where everybody knows everybody. Jay has always treated his staff like family, and Brad is no exception.

"Yeah, here," I say, handing her the pack of new menus from one of the cabinets.

"Oh! Thank you so much!" She jumps around to face me and grabs the menus, sending me a mega-watt smile before dashing off toward the waiting customers. I don't return the smile, no matter how nice it might be. I know Natalie's the new girl on staff, and she is also in the business of looking for new friends. It is bubbly, bouncy girls like her that I avoid at all costs. She seems like a nice enough person, with plenty of girlfriend bonding potential and all; which is exactly why I need to stay far, far away from her. Chances are it won't be long before she catches wind of my reputation around here, if she hasn't already.

The door jingles, calling my attention to the customer walking in. I tie my apron behind my back and veer around the counter toward the guy. "How's it goin'?" I ask, placing my hands on my hips as I approach him. "Take a seat wherever you like and I'll be right with you."

"Oh, that's okay, thanks," he says with a grin. He doesn't move, instead scanning the restaurant as he sticks his hands in his pockets. "I'm just here to chat with my girlfriend for a second. It won't take long."

"Oh?" I scan the restaurant with him. "Who's your girlfriend? Natalie? I didn't realize she was seeing anyone." I laugh. "We know everything around here. Harbor towns are infamous for gossip."

"Yeah," he says, his grin revealing a tinge of shyness. "Uh, it kind of just became official, so..."

"You're not from Gig Harbor, are you?" I give him a knowing look, twisting my lips into a smirk.

"Nope, nope I'm not." He holds out his arms and looks down at his jacket and chuckles. "What, is it that obvious? Do Gig Harbor people have, like, a look or something? I'm from Phoenix. Just moved here."

"Nah, I can just tell. Locals have a sixth sense like that." I shrug and reach over the counter to grab a new menu from the remainder of the stack I pulled for Natalie. "Here you go. She's waiting on those tables over there, so if you want to order something while you wait, just let me know. I'm Elise, by the way."

"Cool, sounds good." He takes the menu and nods, extending a hand. "I'm Nate."

I accept his handshake and let my head roll to the side. "Nate and Natalie. Cheeky."

"Yeah, we seem to be getting that a lot lately."

"Well, Nate, nice to meet you."

"Yeah, you too." Turning on his heel, he gives Natalie a wave across the room and slips into a nearby booth. I stroll over to the adjacent booths and start wiping them down with a washcloth to kill time until the next customer walks in. About two minutes pass and I decide to top off the salt and pepper shakers. I can hear Natalie finishing up with her customers and then a squeal as she walks back to the other end of the restaurant and spots Nate sitting, waiting for her.

"Hey, baby!" she sings, leaning over the table to give him a peck on the lips. I fill one salt shaker, then two, watching their rosy cheeks as they exchange laughter about something under their breath.

The door jingles again and in walks Tim, the bald spot on his head tossing a shiny reflection my way. I stiffen and set the salt shaker down, dropping the washcloth on the seat before I stride toward him. "What are you doing here?"

"Just grabbing a bite to eat, honey. Miss me already?" He shoots a glance at Natalie and Nate, who are still preoccupied chatting, then winks at me. He got here quickly. Must've left his place seconds after I did.

I rush forward, closing the space between us, and glower, lowering the volume of my voice. "You can't waltz in here and say shit like that when you know full well Jay might overhear you."

"Don't get your panties in a twist. His car isn't in the lot. I know he's not here. Give me one of those menus, will you?"

"Natalie," I say, looking over his shoulder, "sorry to interrupt, but I have to run to the restroom. Can you please take care of Tim here?"

"Oh, sure," she pipes up, pulling herself out of the booth. "Tim, you're Jay's brother, right?"

Tim smiles smugly and it makes me even more uncomfortable. Natalie is new here, and the less she knows—the less anyone knows—the better. The community knows most all of my business, but I've managed to keep my fling with Tim on the down low. And I want to keep it that way. This is my job on the line.

"That's me, honey. I'll take a coffee to start, please."

Natalie excuses herself from Nate and scuttles off to fix Tim's coffee, and I slink to the back hallway and into the restroom, dragging in deep breaths as I stare at myself in the mirror. I can't allow this bastard to have the upper hand like this. But I can't lose my job, either. If Jay found out, I guess he couldn't technically fire me over it, but his opinion of me would be severely altered, and he'd probably find some other excuse to let me go, if not for the awkwardness that would surely settle in afterward.

Cheryl, Tim's fiancée, has been friends with Jay for ages, long before they ever got engaged. Jay is possibly the one person in the world I don't want to let down. He is the polar opposite of his brother: honest, loyal, and trustworthy. He gave me a chance with this job three years ago when my mom died. I had dropped out of my first year of college as quickly as I had enrolled, had no place to live, and no job. My dad had sold the house and told me I was on my own. He still technically owned it, even though my parents were no longer married, and I had little say over the matter when my mom passed. Jay had been a friendly acquaintance of my parents over the years. He lived only a few blocks from us and my dad would sometimes pay Jay to help with yard work when he needed to be out of town on business.

My parents split up right after my high school graduation, and my dad moved to L.A. My only other family in Gig Harbor—an aunt and uncle—wanted nothing to do with me, especially after my mom's death. I quickly became the outcast, which made no sense considering I'd never done anything to them to deserve that. So, Jay was really all I had in the way of family. He might have only been my boss, but he treated me like a father would a daughter...like I wished my own had treated me.

Guess I should've thought of that before I started sleeping with his very engaged brother.

There's a knock on the door and I jump, moving to turn the lock and step out. "Yeah?"

"Oh my God, Elise," Natalie whispers, stepping

forward so I retreat back into the bathroom. She carefully shuts the door behind her and I make sure to leave a good two feet of space between us. "Jay's brother is seriously a douchebag. I get super bad vibes from him. He's nothing like Jay!"

"Tell me about it," I mumble, wondering why she's cornering me like this. Did he tell her something? Did she figure it out?

"So, I know you asked me to wait on him, but is there any chance you can come help me? I still have those other tables, and Jay isn't back with Brad yet. I hate to barge in here and rush you, really, but the guy kinda grosses me out and he's so damn picky. He's describing exactly how he wants his lettuce and tomato on his BLT, talking to me like I'm three years old."

I groan. "Yup, that's Tim alright. It's fine, I'll handle him. I was just on my way back out."

"Whew, thank the Lord. He's all yours, girl."

I cringe inwardly at her words as I follow her back out into the diner. I'm not her girl, not her anything. I'm relieved to see more customers have just walked through the door. The more the merrier; whatever helps keep me busy until Tim leaves. I know he just came here to get underneath my skin after our little altercation back at his place.

Showing a family that just walked in to a booth, I take their drink order then waltz over to Tim and top off his coffee, not bothering to say a word. I take my pad from my apron pocket and pop a hip to the left, then click my pen and wait.

He looks at me with beguilement and then shuts his menu, sliding it across the table. I'm vaguely aware that Natalie's boyfriend is within earshot—another reason I won't delve into any conversation with Tim right now. "You are aware that Jay knows you get around, right? It's not some big secret."

My eyes snap from my order pad to his condescending expression. "What can I get for you, *Tim*? A BLT?"

"I'll take another order of what you gave me thirty minutes ago, how about that, honey? You know, I can't tell you how many times I've envisioned taking you right here, over one of these tables. You'd love that, wouldn't you?"

Just like before, back at his place, my hand acts on its own before I can even respond to his scumbag comments. I pick up his coffee and dump it on his lap. He leaps up from the seat, screaming like a little girl. "Son of a bitch! You dirty little whore!"

All of my patience has just been thrown out the window. "You want to play this game?" I ask, disregarding my last drop of restraint. "Too bad, 'cause I'm not playing."

And I mean it.

I need this job, and the last thing I'd ever want is to see the disappointment and disgust in Jay's eyes when he hears the truth, but if he's anything like the man I know him to be, he'll hold Tim just as much responsible, if not more.

"Go on." I jut my chin out at him. "I dare you to tell your brother when he walks through that door. I'll be damned if I let you hold this over my head anymore. And if Jay finds out, Cheryl finds out, too. How will you get your weekly cheating fix then, huh? Who will you run around on? Not everyone will be as oblivious as she is, you jackass. Better start looking for a replacement."

Tim gets in my face. He's beet red and boiling as he hovers over me, drawing every eye in the room to our dispute. "That's all you are, you slut—a replacement. Sloppy seconds and an in-between quickie for every guy in this town who's looking to fill a hole." He speaks through gritted teeth as he leans in closer. "All you're good for is that hot little body. I bet you a hundred bucks you'll be back at my doorstep by the end of next week, begging me to bend you over."

I dig my fingers into his chest and push him back, fueling as much anger as I can into the shove. "At least I know what I am," I spit back. "I don't masquerade myself around this town, pretending to be something I'm not. Now walk out that door, Tim, before you make an even bigger idiot out of yourself."

He shakes his head and swipes his car keys from the table, then turns for the exit, giving me one last glance. "By the end of the week," he repeats, pushing the door open. I exhale when he's gone, but I don't have much time to gather my breath. Natalie and her boyfriend Nate are right behind me.

"Uh…Elise?" Natalie's voice drifts over my shoulder.

It's timid and calm. "Are you okay?"

"Who was that asshole?" Nate asks. I turn to face them, and I'm mortified when I find each customer watching me intently.

"That was our boss' brother," Natalie answers for me, taking a hesitant step forward to hand me a clean napkin. It just hits me then that there are tears running down my cheeks. "Elise, can I get you anything? Is there something I can do?"

I use the napkin she's handed me to dab at my eyes, quickly shaking my head to decline her offer. It's sweet, but accepting anything from this girl would only open a door. One I want to keep tightly shut. "No thanks," I say. "Please just never mention this again, okay? It never happened. That's how you can help." I look from her to Nate to make sure Nate realizes I'm including him in my request.

He nods and shifts his stance uncomfortably. "Oh, of course, yeah."

"We won't say a word," Natalie replies, exchanging glances with Nate. They both back up to give me some space and I hear them whisper as Natalie shows Nate out the front door. Once he's gone, she returns to her tables and apologizes for the scene and for the delay, and I sneak back to the bathroom to ride out the humiliation and to once again pull myself together, so I can make it through my shift. It looks like business might be slow today, but every little bit helps. My head needs to be in the game. I'm still $2,000 away from meeting my goal, and I'll be damned if I let Tim—or anyone—get in the way.

CHAPTER 2

Bacon sizzles in a pan and I wait patiently for my toast, taking small sips of black coffee from my Eiffel Tower mug. Little pink and yellow flowers blossom around the sides of the tower, and cliché French sayings, *oh là là, c'est la vie*, dance around them, reminding me of where I'm headed.

Someday, I'll visit Paris for myself.

Until then, I can only dream about my trip to France and live vicariously through the mug's close proximity to the landmark I want to see standing right in front of me someday—tall, stoic, and elegant. I've been planning the trip since tenth grade. It is a luxury expense, one I've had to claw, scrimp, and save for over the years. I've never been able to explain my fascination with Francophone culture to anyone. Like a passion for teaching or healing the sick, it was just there one day, and since then, I've been unable to think about much else.

My mom gave me this mug when I graduated from high school. After my dad left, she didn't have much money. Helping me get there wasn't an option. She struggled, right up to the very end, when breast cancer took her life. She died alone, convinced that dad left her because she lost all her hair. It was tragic and seemingly delusional—just like my father—but I often wondered just how deluded the theory really was. My father was a material man, after all. Shallow to the bone. Appearance always mattered in his eyes. If it didn't look good, then it wasn't worth his time.

So, the mug was her little way of cheering me on. She wanted me to keep the dream alive, and after she passed, my desire to make it happen bloomed with a vengeance. Dad was well off, comfortable with his new wife in L.A.—a beautiful blonde actress, not much older than me—but asking him for even the pettiest of financial help was out of the question. He didn't call, didn't write. When mom went, he went with her, and it was better that way. I didn't want to depend on his money, anyway. I'd much rather live in this tiny, outdated apartment, where I could at least sleep at night knowing I earned every dime that paid its rent.

My lips still at the mug as I will the toaster to spit out my wheat bread. The bread finally jumps and I slap it onto a plate, lathering it with jam and butter. I settle into my green armchair, the one with the tear in the left arm, nibbling on the toast while opening the paper. My pulse begins to race as I thumb closer and closer to the Sorry Secrets column. It's my favorite column in the Gig Harbor Weekly. Much more entertaining than reading on a hard, impersonal e-reader device. I detest e-books. Give me an old-fashioned newspaper or paperback any day. Give me something tangible, something that gives me paper cuts and leaves my fingers dirty.

I unfold the page that beholds the column and scan each header, ready to pounce on the first one that catches my eye. The column is a collection of short confessions, submitted by readers, all residents of Gig Harbor. Some are downright laughable, while others are so sobering, they're chilling. Most are anonymous, but every now and then, someone decides to be brave and leave a name. The why behind the reason people choose to write these confessions and send them in to a paper for the whole town to read still eludes me, but I find a sort of cleansing in it. I hadn't gone to college long, but when I did, one of my first classes was basic psychology. I remember learning how simply writing down your thoughts or listing your source of anxiety is somehow cathartic. I imagine the sense of relief these people experience, submitting their deepest, darkest secrets. How it strips them of fear.

Once you've cut yourself open and dumped your insides out on the table, what can the world really threaten you with?

My attention latches onto a confession from a daughter to her mother, something about not really wanting to go to medical school. I'm vaguely interested. Before I can jump to the next header to see if it's any juicier, the phone rings.

"Yeah?" I answer, holding the cell limp in my hand.

I'm still restlessly searching the column for my fix.

"Hey, baby. It's almost ten. You coming over?"

I recognize Christian's voice immediately. It's husky and authoritative, which usually sends my libido into overdrive, but today is my day off and all I want to do is curl up with my column and dive into a bag of peanut butter cups after breakfast.

"Can't," I say with a sigh. "Busy today."

"It's Monday."

"I know what day it is."

"It's your day off."

"Very good. You want a gold star for that one?"

"You know I love that smart mouth of yours. If you were here right now, I'd teach it a lesson. Don't deny me, Elise. You know I won't take no for an answer."

"Well, today you're going to have to, because I'm not going anywhere."

"I'll come to you."

"No," I say quickly, sitting up. The paper falls to my lap and Christian has my full attention now. "You can't come here."

"You do realize you're going to have to let me come to your place someday, right?"

I laugh dryly. "You do realize that day will never come, right?"

"What are you so afraid of? You have a husband I don't know about?" His question is full of coy regalement, but I'm not amused. Christian will never see my apartment. None of the men I sleep with ever do. I go to them. This is all on my terms.

"Where's Kylie today?"

"Visiting some friends in Seattle. She won't be back until late tonight. Come on, baby, let me come over and show you a good time. I'll bring lunch."

I almost choke on my coffee. I've grown used to his endearments, but now he wants to eat together? "Lunch?"

"Yeah, you know, that meal after breakfast and before dinner?"

"Christian..."

"Elise, relax. I'm not asking you to have my children. Surely, you can eat a meal with me after I fuck you senseless, yes?"

My earlier plans for binging on peanut butter cups are cast aside by his forwardness. Well, that and the fact that this week's column is turning out to be a letdown. Warmth floods my inner thighs and I fold my legs underneath me in the chair, turning to gaze out the window. Christian is pretty damn delicious. I'd probably count him as my favorite, although Brad from the diner is a close runner up. Brad and I have had an understanding for the past three years now, since I began working at Stella's. He's low maintenance through and through, and he knows my body well. The conversation is always minimal, and he's considerate. Sweet. Kind of like Christian.

I laugh at that thought, watching a blackbird zip past my window.

Christian is far from sweet. In bed, he's as dominant as they come, and he's as charming, persuasive, and seductive as the devil himself. There are times I almost forget about his wife, Kylie—almost. He's that good.

"Okay," I decide, wanting to see his face. "I'll come to you. Give me an hour."

"That's my girl."

"See ya." I hang up and pull myself from the chair, ditching the paper and my mug for my laciest red lingerie. Christian loves me in red, and the day could use a little color. I wash up, curl my hair, apply some make up, and then I'm out the door.

***

What was meant to be a quickie and a bite to eat turned into an all-day romp. Not that I'm complaining. Christian is 30, fit, and maddeningly handsome, with dirty blonde hair and shocking blue eyes. What really gets me is his tan. We're not exactly golden here in Gig Harbor, Washington, but Christian has this perpetual bronze glow. Not the orange, unnatural kind, but the kind that kisses his skin just enough to give him that beach-bum look. Not only is he first-rate man candy, he's phenomenal in the sack. I don't doubt he keeps his wife a very happy woman. Too bad she has to share.

We're launching into another round on his bed, and I go to kick off my black peep toe stilettos, but he grabs my ankle and slides my leg up higher around his waist. "Leave them on," he orders gruffly. My head floats back down to the pillow and I keep my hands relaxed above my head, next to my ears, just where he likes them. I let him do his thing, keeping quiet and rocking my hips up to match him thrust for thrust.

My gaze settles on the corner of the ceiling. It's barren and lonely, and I think there are traces of a cob web hanging there, dusting from wall to wall. I don't whimper or moan for another few minutes, knowing he only likes to hear me on command. "I know," he says sympathetically. He gives me a dazed smile of approval. My obedience makes him happy, and that only serves to make the way he's fucking me all the more satisfying. "You can control it, I know you can."

I bite down hard on my lip, trying to give him what he wants. I'm not sure why I comply with his demands. Maybe because compared to the others, Christian is the most tolerable. Something about him makes me want to compromise. Whereas I need Tim to punish me, I need Christian to indulge me. "Christian," I pant, feeling every spring in my body coil tightly.

"Soon." He starts to pump harder, gathering my wrists above my head to pin them against the mattress. His waist is pushing, his force prodding me on as he nails me to the sheets. "Come on, baby, let me hear you." His arctic eyes hone in on me, never straying from my face. Now that he's given me permission, I let my moans pour from my lips. I can hear his cell ring from the nightstand, but I don't dare let it burst the heady bubble I'm in. He feels too damn good and I'm way too close to be distracted.

"Shit," he mumbles, closing his eyes to push out the intrusive ringing. My gaze falls down to his abdomen, firm and defined, rolling with each thrust. Each one is frantic now, and I know he's close. I allow myself to whimper and my fingernails to dig into the palms of his hands. They're still restraining me, holding my fists in a vise grip above my head. "Tell me you're mine, Elise."

The phone stops ringing and he keeps pushing, smashing me into the comforter, but I let my eyes drift shut and focus on absorbing all of the sensations instead of replying.

"Elise," he barks, stabbing me with a sharp, measured jolt. "Say it."

"*Mmmm*," I breathe, answering him with a buck of my hips. My breasts are tender and swollen with arousal as they bounce against his sweaty chest.

He hammers me with another piercing strike and withdraws, releasing my wrists to flip me over onto my torso. I cry out from the sudden emptiness. In a flash, he gathers my wrists above my head again with one hand, while he lifts my ass with the other. He gives me no warning, slamming back inside of me. The warmth is deep and decadent, just as much as it is possessive. "You like that?" His words ooze into my ear, his head hovering over mine. "You want me to keep fucking you like that?"

"Yes," I say, the word muffled as I answer into the side of the pillow.

"Then say it." He lifts himself up to lean his weight on his hands and peer down at me.

"I'm yours," I lie, pressing my ass harder against him to capture each thrust. I'm about to combust, and the sight of his muscles flexing over my shoulder sends a sinful shudder through me. "Don't stop, Christian."

"Say please." He leans in and bites savagely on my neck, and the pain is numbingly exquisite. Christian has always liked it rough. It's one reason we're so compatible in bed.

"Please."

"Please, what?"

"Please, don't stop."

He growls in approval and lowers himself back down so his chest is pressing against my back, leaning on his forearms. One of his hands fists my hair, tugging my head farther to the side, and he pauses for a beat before powering away. He fucks me mercilessly, pounding me into the bed, and I come hard and gloriously, convulsing against the damp sheets. "So…goddamn…good," he hisses through his teeth, pushing the syllables out in a broken staccato as he comes. His hips slow and our heavy pants fill the air, my body aching in the most delicious way.

Groaning in pure satisfaction, he pushes off of me and rolls me onto my back, sitting back on his heels. He pulls at my legs, propping my knees up, and grasps the tops of my thighs to part them. Before I can catch my breath, his hands slide underneath my knees and he yanks me forward, shoving his face between my legs. His mouth hits my clit, and he begins to suck, setting my body back on fire. “God, I love your pussy,” he mumbles against my flesh, rubbing his nose up and down the slit in between licks. The man has a tongue women dream about, and the way he looks up at me, with the most wicked, gorgeous smile, confirms my earlier musing: He is the devil personified.

The fire he ignited is raging now, like flames doused with gasoline. My entire body tingles from head to toe, the hypersensitive skin at the junction of my thighs blazing with need. My fingers find his hair and push his head down, pressing his mouth tighter against me. He groans as he licks and sucks, moving a hand to tap my calf, encouraging me to hook it over his shoulder. I obey and slide the other one around for good measure, linking them both behind his neck. He loves that, and I find pleasure in giving him what he loves.

My stiletto heels dig into his skin and he groans, moving from my clit to fuck me with his tongue. The bliss sends me into a shout and I start to rock my hips against his hot mouth. Each shot of pleasure he delivers travels from my core to the tips of my fingers and toes, reminding me exactly why I keep coming back to Christian for more. No one screws me like he does, and although I’m cautious today about his sudden interest in sharing a meal together, he’s kind to me, unlike Tim and some of the other assholes I hook up with. Tender, even. The way he leads me into a room, places his hand delicately on the small of my back, and the way he brushes my hair over my shoulder when we talk, leaves me feeling like his lover sometimes, instead of what I actually am.

In seconds, I'm coming again, and he's delighting in every wave of ecstasy that washes over my body. I'm utterly spent, my skin buzzing with a high that only Christian knows how to give. My legs fall lazily from his shoulders and his head rises, his eyes burning as he looks down at me. He watches my chest rise and fall, lets his gaze drift over my curves until it settles on my legs again.

My eyes are shut as I breathe deeply, fluttering open when I feel his teeth graze my ankle. I find him holding my calf up, nipping the skin there, then trailing up to the inside of my knee. The little bites are the perfect dessert for the aftershocks. "You're insatiable," I finally speak, giggling when one of his bites triggers a small tickle.

"You're mouthwatering."

I sigh and smile, rolling my head to the left to find the alarm clock on the bedside table. I move to sit up on my elbows. It's time to go. He's done with me—I've been here all day—and the moment our feet leave the bed and hit the carpet, I know I'll start thinking about how I can get away. I don't ever want to hear a guy awkwardly ask me to leave. Which is why I always beat it to the punch.

"I better get going." I wriggle out of his way and swing my legs over the side of the bed, searching the floor for my dress.

"Wait," he says, moving with me.

I snatch up my dress and begin sliding it over my head, mumbling absentmindedly while searching for my scarf next. "*Hhhmm*?"

"Elise, wait."

His tone causes me to still. I turn to him, and find a determined expression on his face. There's a deep set to his jaw, his blue eyes churning with intensity. I'm afraid to ask. "What is it?"

"Can we talk before you go?"

I sneak a side glance at the alarm clock again, wondering if we really do have the time. That was probably Kylie calling earlier. She could pull up any minute. "Talk about what?"

Christian extends a hand, gently guiding me to sit back on the bed with him, and I feel it—the awkwardness. I let myself sit, but my feet are poised to stand.

"Elise, there's something I need to tell you."

"Oh, God." I jump up, pulling my hand from his. "Don't tell me you have another mistress. Or three. Christian, whatever it is, I don't care, okay? I don't ask questions, you don't ask questions. That's never been an issue, so let's just—"

"I'm leaving Kylie."

"What?" I blink, not sure I heard him right.

"I'm leaving Kylie. She knows I want a divorce. It's over."

"Oh."

The bedroom becomes quiet, his words hanging heavily in the air.

"I know how you feel about me—about this, about us—" he waves his hands in the air, "and you know I respect your position. But I thought you should know. I'm leaving her, and she's relieved. She hasn't been happy, either. I want you, Elise. I want you to be mine."

Shock explodes into little sparks around me, and I suddenly feel the walls closing in. The air in this bedroom is too stuffy, the ceiling too low. He can't have possibly said what I think he just said. "Christian," my voice comes out throaty and dry, "I'm not sure I'm hearing you right." He relaxes with a knowing sigh, leaning forward on the edge of the bed to rest his elbows on his knees. "I'm not trying to put any pressure on you. I just want to be honest, want to put it all out there so you know what's waiting for you, if you decide it's something you'd be interested in. You know I'm a rich man, Elise. I would take care of you, take care of everything. I'd pay for you to go back to college. Anything you want, it's yours." Suddenly, he rises from the bed, carefully approaching me like he knows I'm about to dart at any moment.

I am.

"I want every inch of you, inside and out. And I don't give a damn who thinks what about it. This isn't enough for me anymore."

My mouth bypasses my brain's filter and lets out a laugh, one that I know will hurt Christian if I don't quickly explain where it's coming from. "I'm sorry," I say, half covering my mouth, "I'm not laughing at your offer, I'm laughing at..." I search for the words, turning in a circle to look out the bedroom window. What am I laughing at?

Could it be the fact that aside from being a cheater, this guy is actually a dream? Young, rich, handsome, charming, and amazing in bed to boot? Or could it be the fact that I'm possibly the reason he's leaving his wife? He hasn't mentioned that detail yet, or if I even have anything to do with his decision, but judging by the reality that he sees me often and his wife is not a stupid woman—she's a well-read, educated med student—it's a very real possibility. My mind tumbles through these options, then pauses as it reaches a realization: I'd classified him as someone like me.

Someone who uses his good looks and charm to deceive and take what he wants, then casts aside the object of his interest the second he's accomplished his goal. Granted, Christian had never been a one-night stand or cold lover from a sordid affair, but I'm certain that with each bedroom tryst, he is willfully using me, just as I've been using him. He is unfaithful to his wife with me and who-knows-how-many other women, and he never sees me as anything other than a piece of ass he can call up anytime he is feeling lonely. Each time he touches me, he makes me feel like I am the only one in the universe. The only one he has eyes for. He knows that isn't true, and I know that isn't true, but he has led me to believe it anyway, because he is a wolf by nature. He is wicked like me. Or at least he was, until he started bringing his feelings into the equation.

In this moment, I realize Christian and I are very different.

"You barely know me," I say evenly, fixing my gaze on his. "You know my body. That's not the same thing."

He falters for a second, but he's not the least bit deterred. He's confident, his naked body remaining steadfast and still. "I know a lot about you."

"You know only what I tell you."

"Nothing you tell me will change my mind."

"You can't possibly know that." I shake my head and something in the back of my skull screams for me to find that damn scarf and get the hell out of his house. Right now. "Does Kylie know about me?"

"Our divorce has nothing to do with you, Elise."

"Does she know about me?" I repeat sternly.

"Yes."

"How long?"

"A while."

"Shit." I spin and start rifling around for the scarf, my movements erratic.

"Please don't take off like this. Talk to me." He reaches out to me, but fails to make contact, his open palm hanging in the air.

"There's nothing to talk about. This won't work, I'm sorry."

"I care about you, Elise. I want to take care of you."

I laugh again. This time it's got some bite to it. "You want to own me, that's what you want."

"I want a relationship. With you. No one else. And I want you all to myself, yes. I won't apologize for it. I don't care about the other men you've been seeing. Stop seeing them. Move in with me."

I gasp as I find my scarf, unable to process what he's saying without going completely fucking mental. "Move in with you?"

"I know you have feelings for me, too."

"Whatever gave you that impression?" I gesture wildly in the air, my hands flailing at my sides, the tension building in me like hot lava. "Wait, let me guess...you assume that from the way I beg you to let me orgasm? The way I say your name as I come? Because I say I need you? That I want you?"

That does it. A flicker of hurt flashes over his features, but he recovers quickly. "I see it in your eyes. Every time you look at me, you're searching for something. I feel it in the way you touch me, the way you drop everything to come see me when I call. You think I don't know about the others? Well, I do. I know when you're with them because you don't answer. You take time to call me back. But you're never gone for long. You spend time with me, more time than you ever give to them. I know that much. That tells me something, Elise."

"Yeah, it should tell you that I like sleeping with you. That's all."

"No." He strides forward, placing his hands softly on my arms. "You need something from me and I can give it to you. Something those other dumbasses can never give you."

I flinch from his touch. Not because it doesn't feel good. It always feels good. He's always careful with me, even when he's impaling me like a wild caveman in bed. "What, money and college tuition?" I snicker, stepping back. "You can't buy me, Christian."

"You know that's not what I want. You want more, too. I know you do, damn it. So let's not dance around it."

My mouth goes slack and I'm about to respond, but the chime of his cell phone interrupts my train of thought. "You should get that." I eye the phone, then the bedroom door.

"It can wait."

"It's Kylie, you know it is."

His jaw flexes and his eyes dart from me to the phone, then back. He knows I'm right, and he also knows he can't keep avoiding her calls. Not when she's due home tonight. He may be leaving her and she may know about me, but I'm certain he wants to avoid that potential shit storm just as much as I do. "Damn it," he murmurs, moving for the phone. He answers and stops to give me a silent, pleading look before he slips out of the room to handle the call.

And I take that as my exit cue.

Wrapping my scarf around my neck and collecting my bag, I wait until I hear his voice disappear down the hall. I pull my car key from my bag and count to ten. With a deep breath, I quietly open the bedroom door and peek out into the hallway.

The coast is clear.

I zip through the hall and down the elaborate stairwell, slithering through the front door and making it to my car just in time. I rev the engine and speed off, catching a glimpse of Christian's solemn face in the living room window, through the rearview mirror. He's standing there, pulling the curtain aside, the phone still held to his ear. I watch only for a second, turning to give my attention to the road. My foot powers down on the gas pedal, and I don't want to imagine what Christian must be thinking, watching me drive away like this. But I know what I'm thinking.

This will be the last time I ever see Christian Walker.

CHAPTER 3

The red, white, and blue ad stares back at me, glamorous and elusive. Entirely untouchable for someone like me, someone who lives off of tips and a small hourly wage. If it weren't for the money my mom left me when she passed, I wouldn't have even been able to pull off this one-bedroom apartment. The money wasn't much, but it had helped me get on my feet while I searched for a job and put a plan together.

My mom's money ran out quickly, but Jay's generosity has helped me get by on what I make at Stella's. He's always given me the boom shifts, as he calls them—early a.m. and late p.m. Between those shifts and the doubles I pick up as often as possible, I sometimes luck out and bank. It also works to my advantage that Stella's is in a prime location on the harbor, and that it is one of the oldest establishments around, voted Best Food in Town by the locals year after year. Business is even better during the summer, when tourists roll in. Gig Harbor is an expensive place to live, especially doing what I do, with no roommate, but it is important to me to stay put. This is where the memories of my mom live, and I grew up with Tee here, too.

Tee moved away after high school. She went to school in Portland and we eventually lost touch, something I never thought would happen. She was family to me, not some casual friend I'd shared a biology class with. The idea that we simply drifted apart was unnatural for two people who were so inseparable. When she stopped calling and her visits to Gig Harbor lessened and lessened, a little part of me died. I'm not too proud to admit that.

Tee is the only person I've ever truly trusted. I was there when she came out to her parents, there when her heart was broken by her first girlfriend, and there when a group of hateful dumbasses jumped her in the high school parking lot one night. We were outnumbered that night, and I took the brunt of their anger too, so she didn't have to bear it alone. I could've run, but I would never run from Tee. She'd never run on me.

Except maybe now.

I didn't always sleep around. That didn't start until college. My mom might not have needed me anymore, and my dad might not have wanted me, but that was easily remedied. The world was full of needy people. Like Brian, a guy I hooked up with at my first official college party.

He said his girlfriend, Joanna, was making him wait for a year to have sex, and he told me he couldn't wait anymore. He threw in a few compliments about how gorgeous I was, and three shots of tequila later, I let him take me back to his dorm. I knew I'd crossed over that night, sleeping with someone else's man. It wasn't long after that I met Tim. By then, I was an expert at making myself pay for hurting the Joannas of the world, and Tim was the perfect source of atonement. I never let myself dwell too long on atonement, though.

The reality was the Joannas of the world didn't share the plight that girls like me shared. They didn't have to degrade themselves for a little attention or affection. They didn't have to prove their worth, show the world there was more to them than just skinny legs and a pretty complexion. They were awarded love on a silver platter. Girls like me had to fight dirty.

After Tee was long gone, I graduated from campus floosy to town whore, but the memories of the closest women in my life kept me rooted to this town, no matter how much of an outcast I'd become. You couldn't pay me to leave this place. Unless it was to travel to France.

I tap my pen over the newspaper ad, reading it for the thousandth time. I see the same one every other week, when the Gig Harbor Weekly runs it for the French school. It's a tiny, private school up the road, run by three teachers who offer one-on-one and group lessons. I've heard that people of all ages, from all walks of life study there. Students, widowers, and businessmen alike. Since withdrawing from college, I've given up on my goal to earn a French language degree. There is no way I'll ever be able to afford school. Not anytime soon, anyway. Unless I take Christian up on his offer.

Yeah. Not happening.

So, *Les Trois Enfants*, as the school is called, is the next best thing to earning a degree. I'd be happy just to learn to speak, maybe even be conversationally fluent one day. I've been teaching myself here and there over the years, and I took French instead of Spanish in high school, but I don't remember much from those classes, and I can only make it so far learning on my own.

I stare at the ad for another second, then force myself to my feet to pour some coffee. I have to be at work by 6 a.m., and I'm really dragging this morning. After escaping Christian's yesterday, I came home and showered, then paced my living room for two hours, reciting verb conjugations with my audio lessons.

Christian never called. I don't blame him. He probably wised up and realized just how out of his mind he'd been to even entertain the thought of being with me. I'd miss his kindness, miss the sex. But in truth, that's all I'd miss. How else could I miss him? I knew nothing about the guy, other than the basics he'd shared with me over the course of our time together, but I knew enough to know he wouldn't be good for me.

And I sure as hell wouldn't be good for him.

After I finished listening to my lessons, I read for a while and attempted to sleep, but had no luck. I tossed and turned all night, replaying my conversation with Christian over and over again, wondering how my time with him went from what it was to what it is now in a matter of a day. The fact that I lost sleep over a man is surprising, even to me.

I finish my coffee and head out the door, happy to see cars in the parking lot when I roll up to the diner. It's going to be a good morning. Maybe I'll make enough to put a few bucks in my dream jar when I get home. It's a large, decorated mason jar—my version of a piggy bank—that I've been using for the past few years to stash extra cash away for my goal to get to France someday. I've been close to filling it up a few times, but something always happens. Last month, I needed new tires. Six months ago, I was late on rent. Then there was the unexpected medical bill, when I sprained my ankle over the summer.

Each time I make progress, I take ten steps back.

"Morning," I greet Natalie, who's been working the early shifts with me lately. My voice is still as tired as my body, but my mood is oddly peppy despite the lack of sleep.

"You're way too pretty in the morning," she whines, rubbing at her eyes as she begins to tie her apron. "It's so unfair."

I smirk, clocking in and grabbing a notepad. "I'm beginning to get the impression you're not a morning person."

"There is something ungodly about being awake before the sun is up. It's just wrong on so many levels."

"You'll get used to it," I assure her, smoothing back

a stray strand of hair. "And it's good money." I smile and stroll around the counter to the first table needing service. I hear the radio break the diner's silence with some Golden Oldies, and I know Jay is here, firing up the radio in the back.

"Morning, hon," he says as he saunters past me while I finish taking the table's order. "You look awfully bright eyed and bushy tailed today."

"Do I?" I chuckle, shaking my head. "I'm hurting this morning."

"Rough night?" He moves from table to table, making sure the napkin holders are full. These are the little things his waiters normally take care of, but Jay is always on the ball. He's the kind of guy to go above and beyond, especially when it comes to his business. This place is his life blood and his legacy, and the fact that he sees himself as equal to his staff has always been admirable to me.

"Nah, not that kind of rough night. Just didn't sleep much, that's all."

"Sorry to hear it. Good news is the rush will hit soon, and you'll be so busy, you won't have time to think about how tired you are. You'll be home before you know it." He smiles brightly and I find myself smiling, too. Jay has that affect.

Thankfully, he's right about the rush. The morning flies by, and in a few short hours, I'm heading outside to my car with a pocketful of cash and a dizzy head.

"Hey, Elise?" Natalie calls out, rushing out after me as I open my car door. "I know you're probably beat, but do you want to go grab an early lunch? I was thinking about checking out that new nail salon around the corner afterward. You up for a mani and pedi?" She asks me so casually, I find myself fixated on her face for a moment. Her expression is so honest, so innocent. I study the smattering of freckles on her nose and cheeks, and the way her red hair parts neatly on one side.

I duck and slide into the car.

"Sorry, Natalie. I've got errands to run today, and I really am exhausted. Plus I told Jay I'd like to pick up a double tonight since Jane took the day off. I need to get home and get some sleep before I go back in. Thanks, though."

She smiles sweetly and keeps moving toward me. "Okay, I understand. But just so you know..." She stops when she reaches my car door, watches as I roll down the window. "Well, I just wanted to say that I don't care about the things this town says about you. And that guy Tim is a prick. You deserve better than that."

I gaze at her through the open window and grip the steering wheel. "Is that so?"

"Yeah." She rolls a shoulder. "I mean, I just wanted to put that out there. I know I'm still new around here, but I've worked with you for a while now, and that gossip doesn't mean shit to me. I'm game for hanging out any time. Just say when."

I fall back against the driver seat, letting my hands drop from the steering wheel. "Glad to hear it. Thanks," I say numbly, waiting for her to scurry off. She's wasting her time here.

"I'm serious," she insists, leaning on the edge of my car window. "People should just mind their own damn business, if you ask me. You should come hang out with me and Nate sometime. Maybe do a double date. You seeing anyone right now?"

A small laugh escapes me and I snort, knowing damn well she knows I'm seeing someone right now. I roll my eyes up to hers, then narrow them.

"Okay, okay," she laughs and pushes herself off the car door to raise her hands in defense. "Look, I'm just saying the offer stands. You're welcome to join us any time."

"Cool. I'll think about it." No, I won't. "See you later."

"See ya."

She waves and I drive off, wondering if she'll ever get the hint.

***

I make it halfway home before realizing my errands aren't done yet. I've already swung by the bank and post office, but it hits me that I need to grab a few things from the grocery store. I meander down the shampoo aisle, picking my way through the five different shampoo products. I settle on my favorite, one with a strawberry scent. Christian likes this one. I don't linger on this thought.

"Hey, don't I know you?" a voice drifts toward me and I turn, finding a cute, boyish face I recognize. His blonde hair is messy in a stylish way. His smile forms little creases in the corners of his eyes. He's standing in front of the soaps, giving me a friendly grin.

"Yeah, we just met at the diner. Natalie's Nate, right?"

"That'd be me," he laughs. "It's Elise, right?"

"Yup."

"We were just talking about you, actually. I was on the phone with Nat before I came to the store."

"Oh, yeah?"

"Yeah, she mentioned something about all of us hanging out. She said you're seeing someone? I guess she thought maybe we could all do a double date soon."

I give him a tight smile, tossing the strawberry shampoo into my basket. "She did mention something like that, yeah."

"Well, I say we do it. I mean, I'm always up for meeting new people. Especially since I'm new to town."

I clear my throat and decide to redirect the conversation instead of brushing him off entirely. It's not his fault his girlfriend is dragging him into her quest to befriend me, and it doesn't hurt to be polite. This dude is so sweet, he makes my teeth hurt. "How are you liking Gig Harbor? Do you feel like you're settling in?"

"I like it," he says thoughtfully, shuffling a package of soap back and forth, from one hand to the other. "It's been taking some getting used to, but I'm starting to feel at home."

"Good. Well, if you ever want me to show you around, you should give me a call." The words are out of my mouth before I can stop them. I watch him carefully, eyeing him as he digests my offer.

"Really? Wow, I'd love that, thanks." I'm waiting for him to say "golly-gee," or something. His naivety is hard to resist.

"Definitely. Here," I say, stepping toward him in the middle of the aisle. I dig in my bag for a pen and grab an old receipt at the bottom of my change purse. I scribble my number and hand it to him, catching a snide look from Bridget Waldorf as she passes by with her shopping cart. I went to high school with her, and she's just as nosey now as she was back then. She leers at me and then gives Nate a long, immodest stare as she saunters along. "Call me any time," I finish, speaking to Nate but keeping my glare on Bridget. She disappears to the other end of the aisle and I roll my eyes.

"That was...weird," Nate says under his breath, his brows furrowing as he glances over his shoulder at Miss Nosey.

"Ah, you'll see a lot of that around here." I shrug, slipping my pen back into my bag. "Especially when I'm nearby."

"What do you mean?" he asks, looking genuinely lost. I wonder if Natalie has mentioned the things she's heard about me. I wonder if he's already heard them himself, and he's just playing dumb.

Nah, he's too pure for that.

"Haven't you heard?" I give him a sly smirk and cross my arms smugly across my chest, my basket knocking into my side. I crane my head forward slightly and tip my chin down, as if I'm about to unveil my deepest, darkest secret. "I'm dangerous."

He's still confused. "You're…what?" He speaks in a hush, too, almost a whisper.

"I make good people do bad things." I also make bad people do worse things, but I don't add that little detail. Mr. Boy Scout here needs small doses.

His lips tip up at the corner, as if he's trying to figure out whether or not he should smile at my words, and his eyes narrow as they dance from left to right. "Okay…"

"Stick around long enough," I say louder, dropping my arms and straightening up. I strut past him, tapping his shoulder playfully, then give it a light squeeze. "You'll see. Bye, Natalie's Nate."

"Uh…bye?"

I glance back coyly, flipping my long blonde hair over my shoulder and make sure to let my hips sway subtly as I stroll off. That's when I see it. His eyes are wide, alive with realization.

Ah, Mr. Boy Scout's caught on.

I snicker and break eye contact, leaving him standing there, frozen, with soap dangling from his limp hands.

Check out doesn't take me long, and soon I'm back home, unloading my bags and checking my messages. There's one from *Les Trois Enfants*—one of the teachers informing me of the upcoming class schedule. It doesn't begin until after the New Year. I'm too late to join the fall session, but that's okay because I don't have the cash yet, anyway. I'd have to dip into my France travel fund, and that's not going to happen.

Glancing at my dream jar on my bedside table, I release a sigh, feeling my shoulders slump. I finish unloading my bags and give in to the need for a long, hot shower. All I want to do is crawl into bed and take a nap before I have to go back in to work this afternoon.

I'm just about to retreat to the bathroom, but my cell phone vibrates on the dresser.

"Hello?" I answer after three rings.

"Elise," Tim's voice reaches through the phone and grabs me, and I still. I'm so not in the mood for his shit. Not anymore.

"What do you want?"

"You know what I want."

"I'm sorry, was I not clear enough when I dumped scalding coffee on your crotch the other day? Don't call me again, Tim." I go to hang up, but the anger in his voice alarms me. I've never heard him like this.

"You listen to me and you listen to me good," he seethes, his breaths broken as he pushes out the words. "Don't you ever humiliate me like that again in public, do you hear me?"

"Who do you think you are?" I scoff haughtily, shaking my head. Damn, this man makes me so indignant. "You don't get to tell me what to do, Tim. Back off. This is the last time I'll tell you to leave me the hell alone."

"Elise," his voice quivers, some desperation seeping through. "Don't hang up. Look...I'm sorry. Just come see me. Please?"

"Are you out of your mind?"

"Yes! I'm out of my fucking mind, alright? I can't stop thinking about you. I was an asshole. I said things I didn't mean. Please, come over. Come on, Elise."

I'm suddenly grossed out, picturing a balding, sweaty Tim pacing back and forth in his room with a raging hard-on. I've never found the guy attractive, but something about the neediness in his voice really sends me over the edge into no-way-never-going-to-happen-again territory. This one has definitely run its course.

"I said no, Tim. I'm done. So stop calling me, or I'll call the police and report you for harassment." I hang up and shove the phone in the dresser drawer. I can't face another call. Not from Tim.

I groan and start for the bathroom, but there's a knock on the door.

"Seriously?" I blow out a breath and storm toward the front door. If it's a Jehovah's Witness, I'm going to strangle the poor bastard. At this rate, I'll never make it to the shower and I certainly won't get a nap in before my next shift. I swing open the door with a scowl, finding a startled guy with a tool kit in his hands. "Yes?" I snap, impatiently placing one hand on my hip.

"Uh…sorry, I was sent to look at your garbage disposal?"

I squeeze my eyes shut for a second then blink, shaking my head. "Huh? Sent by who?"

"The landlord?" He looks at me like he's trying to jog

my memory, pressing his lips together. "You reported a problem with your garbage disposal?"

I move my hand from my hip to my forehead and blink again. "Oh. Yeah, yeah. Sorry, I completely spaced out. Come on in." I step aside and wave him in, my focus returning. My gaze falls on his gray utility shirt. It's rolled up at the sleeves, revealing two other kinds of sleeves—intricate, colorful tattoos, one wrapping around each forearm. My eyes are drawn to the works of art, but quickly flick up to his chest, settling on the name patch sewn to his right pocket: Ryder.

"You're maintenance?" I ask, sure I've never seen him around the building before. "Are you new?"

"Yep. Just started a few weeks ago." He shifts his tool box to his left hand and extends his right for a shake. "Ryder Jacobson. Nice to meet you." It's then that I look at him—really look at him—and it dawns on me that he's really fucking good looking. The maintenance department has been taking recruits from a new, very blessed gene pool, apparently.

He's tall, dark, and handsome, but there's nothing flashy about his good looks. He is no star athlete or pretty, squeaky-clean model. Just careless, comfortable sex appeal wrapped up in an easy boy-next-door package, complete with grungy maintenance man khakis and kind, brown eyes to match his tousled chestnut hair. His eyes might be soft, but there's certainty there, like he knows exactly who he is. It's unnerving.

"Elise," I say, taking his hand. The dark stubble over

his cheeks and chin distracts me for a second, but I quickly recover and show him over to the kitchen sink. "It's all yours."

"Thanks. Is it running at all?" He moves to the counter and sets his tools down.

"Nope, I think the motor's completely fried."

"Huh." He studies the sink for a moment before reaching to flick on the switch. "I think you may be right. Is this a good time? Do you mind if I take a look at it?" He turns his gaze on me, and I shrug with a half-smile.

"Sure. Now's good."

"Okay, cool. It shouldn't take me long to figure out what's going on here."

"No rush." I leave him to it and turn for the fridge, pulling out a bottle of water. "You want anything to drink?"

He starts tinkering with the disposal, glancing over his shoulder. "Nah, I'm good, thanks."

"I have something stronger." I grin and retrieve a cold beer, offering it to him. He stops what he's doing and swivels to face me. It's then that I see it. He notices me now.

I can tell by the way his jaw goes slightly slack, his gaze doing a quick once-over, dropping to my tits and snapping back up, lingering just long enough to get a good eyeful. His mouth closes and he looks down, like he's just been caught ogling me.

He has.

It's the same deal every time a man notices me. I've

come to recognize the signs well. I humor him, letting my eyes travel from the toes of his boots, over his liberal dose of ink, and up to his broad, strong shoulders. Resting a hip against the counter, I twist the cap off the beer and wait.

"I probably shouldn't drink on the job," he says warily, a grin sneaking onto his lips. One of his front teeth is slightly crooked and perfectly imperfect. "Eh, what the hell. Thanks." He accepts the offer and kicks back a swig. He makes a satisfied sound deep in his throat and sets the drink down, turning back to the task at hand.

"I won't tell if you won't tell." I smile and turn for the bathroom. "I'm jumping in the shower," I say with a yawn. Sleep is calling to me, and I'm going to need it if I expect to make it through tonight's shift. We're going to be slammed. "Thanks for stopping by to fix that."

"No problem," he calls out as I disappear around the corner. "Thanks again for the beer."

"Anytime." I shut the bathroom door behind me and prepare myself for the hot spray of water my tired muscles so desperately need. As I turn on the faucet, an image of me and Christian tangled in a passionate embrace in his luxurious, tiled shower pops unbidden in my mind. I chase the memory away and scold myself for thinking about him, knowing damn well I have no business doing so. But I still see his face, and I still feel his touch.

I feel him in every part of me.

CHAPTER 4

A week passes before I get the courage to call the French school back. I'm still unsure whether I'm ready to commit to the financial obligation. Tuition for the new session after the New Year would be due just before Christmas, and I have no idea if I'll be able to swing it then.

I have no idea if I'll be able to swing it at all.

I brush my teeth a little too roughly, sneaking a side glance at my dream jar from the bathroom. It sits there on my bedside, taunting me. It'd be all too easy to withdraw just enough cash to pay for the classes. I drag my gaze away from the jar of cash and lean down to spit in the sink.

I can't bring myself to do it. Not when I can keep teaching myself the language at home, and not when I know that cash has and should continue to have one purpose and one purpose alone: getting me overseas. Not to mention, it will likely continue to act as my emergency fund when the next unfortunate mishap seeks to drain me.

Rinsing my mouth out, I decide to close the lid on those thoughts and hurry to make the phone call before I lose my nerve. Or my mind. Or both.

A polite woman answers and takes my name, then proceeds to give me enrollment instructions. It's a small, laid-back organization, so they seem pretty flexible. She tells me to come by anytime between now and the end of December to drop off the check, and then adds a few more details about books and what to expect the first session. I thank her for her time and breathe a sigh of relief the second I'm off the phone.

Hurrying out the door for my evening shift, I make sure to erase the texts from Tim before I leave the parking lot. He's bombarded me with them all week, and I know that if I don't delete them now, they'll only stress me out. I don't want to see them each time I rifle through my messages. By now, he's obviously taken my threat to report him to the police with a grain of salt, and I hate that he's right.

I won't go to the police. Not because I'm too chicken shit to do something about the persistent bastard, but because I don't want to stir the pot any more than I already have. He is Jay's brother, and word travels fast in this town. I don't give a rat's ass what these people think of me around here—they've already formed plenty of theories about me, most of which are 100 percent true—but I'd like to keep my place in the spotlight to a minimum. My reputation might be full of noise, but that doesn't mean I don't enjoy a little peace and quiet, just as much as the next girl. Besides, aside from being a total douchebag, Tim's harmless.

I turn off my phone and chuck it into my purse, and my mind starts to wander again, wondering what would really happen if Jay found out about me and Tim. For a while there, I was so sure the news would harm Jay's trust in me, but now I'm not so sure.

Would he be disappointed in me? Absolutely. Would it crush me, knowing I'd let the one man I respect down in a truly horrible way? Hell yeah. But could I get past it? Could he get past it, and would he stand by me anyway? Probably.

Casting my worries aside, I reverse and pull out of the parking lot, directing my mind back toward more important matters, like the money I need to make tonight. I need to add to the dream jar soon. It's been a few days since it's seen any action, and that trip overseas and those French lessons aren't going to pay for themselves.

***

Natalie talks my ear off as we clock out that night, rambling on about something to do with her goldmine finds at the mall yesterday. I vaguely take in the conversation, which is entirely one sided, but become very alert the second she begins harping on the double date topic again.

"So, what do you think?" She smiles widely, twisting a red ringlet between her fingers as we walk to our cars. "You, me, Nate, and the mystery man you're seeing, tomorrow night? The holiday festival begins at 7 p.m. and runs through the weekend. It'll be fun!"

"*Mmmm*," I swish my lips to the side, pretending to consider it. "Don't think I'm free this weekend, sorry."

"Come on, Elise," she whines, nudging me in the shoulder like we're best pals. Where does she come up with this stuff? "You should get out and have some fun. You've been working hard." I pretend to cough, choking on a laugh. This girl has no idea how much fun I have off the clock. She must really have selective hearing when it comes to rumors.

"I don't know…"

"Is it because you want some alone time with your boyfriend? If so, then I totally understand. I don't want to intrude on your time together. It's just…well, I think we'd all have a good time. Nate and I don't know many other couples our age around here. And Nate is new in town and all, so—"

"Natalie," I raise my hand to stop her, "you're not going to quit asking me until I do this, right?"

Her cheeks puff up with a breath of air she's holding, and her eyes are bursting with excitement. She looks like a 5-year-old who's about to be served a banana split, with extra whip cream and cherries. She remains silent, nodding enthusiastically.

"Fine," I say. The decision comes out so simply, the

ease of it surprises me. "What time do you want us to meet you?" Never mind the fact that there is no "us." I'm sure I can cart someone along. Maybe Brad. We haven't hooked up in a while and I know he's down for it anytime.

"How about 8 p.m.? We can grab a bite and just mosey around. Sound good?"

"Yeah, sure."

"Yay!" She squeals and leaps forward, wrapping me in a quick hug. My body stiffens. "Let's meet out front of Stella's. We can just walk from there."

"Okay," I say, relaxing the second she releases me. "See you tomorrow night."

"Yes! I can't wait! And I can't wait to meet this guy of yours. You've been so tight-lipped about him." She turns for her car and gives her shoulders a shimmy, again, like we're best friends sharing some super-scandalous secret. There is nothing super about our conversation, but my secrets are quite scandalous.

I give her a phony smile and wave, making a dash for my car. I have a date to wrangle up. Shouldn't be hard, but I know one thing: Christian and Tim are definitely off the menu.

***

I'm awakened the next morning by a knock on the door. I fumble my way out of bed and scamper to turn up the heat in the hallway, shivering from the temperature drop. November in this part of the world is mostly cold and wet, the kind of dampened cold that cuts straight to the bone.

I yawn and stretch as I hobble over to answer the door. Ryder, the maintenance guy, stands there, looking a little pale. His rich, mocha eyes are wide, and he swallows hard, looking all sorts of uncomfortable. “Hey,” I greet him, my voice groggy with sleep. “Come on in.”

“Would you rather me…uh, you want me to come back later?” He shifts and runs a hand through his disheveled hair, his jaw muscles flexing. If I’m not mistaken, he’s grinding his teeth.

“No, why?”

“Well, you know…” He casually waves at me, his eyes dropping down my body, then off to the right, like he’s searching for an exit.

I shiver again and cross my arms over my chest, glancing down to find whatever’s making him so uneasy. I’m wearing nothing but a sheer white tank top and lace panties. Well, that could be the cause for his frazzled state.

I laugh and let my arms flop to my sides, gesturing to my near nakedness. “Sorry. I should put something on. Come on in.” I turn and let him follow my lead, feeling his eyes on me. I reach for the terrycloth bathrobe hanging over the back of one of the dining room chairs.

“Call me crazy,” he says as he closes the door behind him, averting his gaze until I have the bathrobe secured tightly around my waist, “but most people in November wear things like thermals and long johns. You know, warm clothes." He laughs good naturedly and two incredibly adorable dimples form on his cheeks. Damn. How did I miss those before? They make his smile all the more charming, and I find myself staring for a moment, wishing I hadn't seen the blasted things.

"Ha-ha," I say mockingly, rolling my eyes.

"So, how's the disposal been working?" He walks to the kitchen and begins sizing up the sink, moving dishes around to get a peek down the drain.

"It's been good— no other problems." I walk over to the kitchen and hoist myself up onto the counter to watch him work. He'd discovered that a peach pit was jammed in the flywheel the other day. It was an easy fix for him to remove the pit and get the blades moving again. I'm happy to see him stop by to double check and make sure it's working properly. The old maintenance guy never followed up like this. Sometimes he didn't show up at all when I needed him. Guess that explains why he's the old maintenance guy.

"Glad to hear it." He runs the disposal, then switches it off when he's satisfied. "Anything else you need help with while I'm here? I won't be back around for a few weeks, unless you need something else." He leans a hand on the counter as he turns to face me, propping his other hand low on his waist. My gaze floats down to his arms, and curiosity gets the best of me. I have to ask.

"What do your tattoos mean?"

His brows lift for second at the change of subject and

he follows my gaze, holding out his arms to take a look. "Hard to explain, really. They're kind of personal." He points to the expressive sleeve on his right forearm. It's full of swirling, black Old English text that I can't make out, and an arrangement of leaves and branches. A tree, I think. There are words carved into the wood of the trunk, but I can't make those out, either. "This one is kind of my version of the tree of life. The text is just a combination of things that mean something to me. Song lyrics, quotes, old proverbs…mostly stuff about nature."

"Oh, yeah?" I hop down from the counter and move closer to him to get a better look. As I lean in, I get a whiff of him. Pine and cinnamon. Like rich tree bark and the topping on a pumpkin spice latte. It brings all of my senses to life. "What does that part say?" I touch a line of text wrapping around the tree, tracing the words. I hear him swallow and feel the muscles in his arm flex.

"It's, ah, it's a part of this poem. By Lord Byron. 'Childe Harold's Pilgrimage.'" I don't wait for him to read it to me. I can see it clearly now. The line mentions loving nature more, but not loving man any less.

"That's beautiful," I say, lifting my head when I feel his eyes on me. "I only have one tattoo."

"Oh, really? Where is it?"

"Nowhere you can see." I smile unabashedly and hold his gaze, liking the way he turns a little crimson when I indulge him with an eyebrow wiggle.

He laughs and shakes his head, sticking his hands in his pockets. "Like I said, ink is very personal."

"I'd agree with that. I love yours. Who did your work?"

"This chick Tracy, over on Bainbridge Island. She owns this little shop downtown. She's pretty rad. I won't let anyone else color me up."

"I'll have to pay her a visit next time I want to get some work done."

"You should. I'd be happy to hook you up."

"Cool, thanks."

He nods and hesitates for a second, settling on the decision to grab his tool box. "Well, looks like you're all taken care of here. Guess I better be on my way."

I watch him as he starts to make his way through the living room, allowing my eyes to travel the length of him as soon as his back is to me. The man has an ass to die for, narrow hips, and broad shoulders. The kind of shoulders girls like to hold on to. He can't be much older than me, and he's got no ring on his left finger. Not that that's ever stopped me before.

I chew on my lip and follow him to the door to walk him out, stopping him when he goes to reach for the door knob. "Hey, Ryder, what are you up to tonight? Anything?" My plan to call Brad this morning to ask if he'd come with me to the festival tonight just got tossed out the window.

"Tonight?" he stills, brushing his palm over his cheek. My eyes hone in on the light shadow there. He's handsome in a rugged way, like the tree on his arm. A clean shave would probably look unnatural on him. "I'm free, actually. Why, you have plans to get some more ink?" His crooked grin appears, coaxing those dimples out from wherever they've been hiding. I'm happy to have them back.

"No, but I do have plans to eat a ton of cotton candy and as many funnel cakes as possible."

His smile brightens, bringing light to his whole face. "You're going to the holiday festival, I take it."

"Busted."

"What time?"

"Around 8 tonight. I'm meeting up with someone from work. You wanna join?" As I watch a glimmer of interest appear in his eyes, I can't help but wonder if he knows me. If he's a local, there's a good chance he does. Most of the women know me. The men know they know, and it hasn't stopped them from trying their luck at least once.

Suddenly, I feel like playing coy, although I get the faint impression that he sees straight through my act. "I mean, unless you have a girlfriend or something…" I can't stop the mischievous smile that springs up on my lips. Why would I want to? It's too much fun.

"Ha," he huffs, his lashes lowering as he looks down at his shoes, "you don't have to worry about that."

"Really? No girl at home?"

"Nah. She couldn't deal with my gypsy ways and modest income. New York business men with cozy 401ks were more her style."

"Sorry to hear." No, I wasn't.

"Don't be," he shrugs, moving to lean against the door frame. "You know what they say. When one door closes…"

I smile playfully.

"What about you?" His eyes narrow and his brow creases as he smirks. "You're not hiding a man in the oven or anything, are you?"

"I'm free as a bird," I answer with no hesitation at all.

"That's…interesting."

I feel my shoulder muscles tighten. Maybe he knows exactly who I am. Elise Duchamp, the notorious, antisocial home wrecker. "Why do you say that?"

He focuses on the doorframe, picking at the beveled wood. "For one, you're hard to miss, with that beautiful body and all. Most men try and lock that sort of package down pretty damn quick. But you know that already, don't you?" His gaze lifts to mine again, rooting me to the carpet.

I expect my muscles to relax, but they don't. They tighten further, and the next question I ask is crucial. I'm desperate to hear his response before I've even asked it. "And for two?"

"Well, for two, you're good company."

"Good company?" I blink, not sure what to make of that. What do I make of that?

"Yeah, good company. I like talking to you. You're down-to-earth. Open. I like that."

"You do?"

He lets out a laugh, and it's husky and hearty. It's a

warmth-inducing, toe-curling sound. "Uh…yeah, yeah I do. But I bet you know that already, too."

I race to cover up my genuine surprise, playing what I play best—the cool façade. "Maybe a little." I grin up at him, subtly arching my back to draw his attention to my breasts.

He takes the bait.

Licking his lips, he breaks the stare from my cleavage and opens the front door. "And modest, too." He locks eyes with me for another second, letting me know he's on to my game. "Okay, so… 8 tonight?"

"Yup. We're meeting in front of Stella's. Do you know the place? The retro diner down on the waterfront?"

"Yeah, I know the place. Never eaten there before, but I see it when I drive down that way."

"Cool. See you tonight."

"Later."

I close the door behind him and slump against it. Something strange unfurls in the pit of my stomach. Strange, but not unpleasant. I don't linger at the door long. I have a lot to get done by tonight, and there's one thing that absolutely has to happen before the festival, one thing that takes precedence over everything else. I need to see Christian Walker, and I need to see him right now.

CHAPTER 5

Christian's sleek black Mercedes gleams in his driveway as I pull up next to it. My fingers have had a death grip on the steering wheel the whole ride here, and that buzzing in my stomach that sparked the second Ryder left my place is now churning with anxiety.

Oddly, this anxiety has nothing to do with the way things ended with me and Christian. Clearly, things never really ended if I'm showing up at his house like this. He didn't hesitate for a second on the phone when I called him. He simply told me to come over right away, adding that he couldn't wait to see me. Still, I can't help but feel I'm crossing over to the dark side. Robbing a grave. Resurrecting something that has no business being resurrected.

A wry smile pulls at my lips as I shift to park. The dark side? I already made that jump long ago. This is child's play. For once, though, I'm here not to screw Christian, but to talk to him. His reaction to that should be interesting, but I'm determined to do this. I'm not even sure I know what this is, but whatever it is, I know it needs to be done.

"Hey baby," Christian greets me at the door, immediately pulling me to him. He doesn't look around outside to see which neighbors might see us, doesn't think twice about holding his intense gaze on me, just takes me into his arms and lets his hungry eyes drink me in. "I've been so worried. When you called, I didn't know what to think."

I open my mouth to speak, but I'm yanked into the house and shoved up against the wall before I can blink. Christian's mouth buries into my neck and he knocks the door shut with his elbow, breathing hard against my throat as he fumbles with my blouse buttons.

"Wait," I pant, already feeling his magic consume me. I haven't forgotten how perfectly his hard, strong body melds to mine, how the sting of his teeth on my flesh instantly makes my clit throb. The man is an animal, and he touches me like I'm the last drop of water on Earth. But feeling it again reminds me how deprived I've been. When I'm with him, I'm a goddess and he's my master, and that's a hard habit to break. "Christian, that's not why I'm here."

His lips roam upward, to the space just below my ear, and he laughs as he dips his tongue there. "You're talking crazy talk, baby. That's exactly why you're here. You've missed this." He lifts up my skirt and skims his thumb over my panty line, sucking in a sharp breath. "I've missed it, too. Don't ever leave me like that again."

I moan as his fingers slip into my panties, rolling over my slick wetness. "Oh, God." My head hits the wall, and my eyes snap shut in pure pleasure. "Christian, we need to talk."

"After," he growls into me, rocking his taut hips and straining erection against me. "Fuck, you're so ready. Always so wet for me." He withdraws his hand and slides his index finger into my mouth, letting me taste myself.

I bite down, heady with wild need, need for this man to own me like only he can, but I release his finger and shake my head. I need to break the spell right now, or I won't get what I came here for. "No, we need to talk now."

"Oh, yeah?" He bites a trail down my throat, moving south. He sounds amused. "What about?"

"I'm not sure exactly," I pant, answering honestly.

"*Mmmm*," he groans when he reaches my breasts, his mouth sucking straight through my bra. My nipples harden and my back bows. I'm losing control fast.

"I want to talk about me and you," I say more evenly this time. His head continues to move downward. It's over my belly now. "I need to know if you were serious about me moving in with you."

He pushes my shirt up and bites just above my navel, his hands dropping down my hips to cup my ass. "Of course I am."

"Why do you want to live with me?"

He laughs, but it's cut off by a moan when he hits the apex of my thighs. The heat swells, sending me closer to the edge, and I involuntarily buck against his mouth.

"You're a dirty, filthy girl, and I fucking love you for it, baby." He nuzzles his nose against me, blowing hot breath between my thighs. I nearly convulse on the spot, but I steel myself up and focus.

"Christian, answer me."

"What kind of question is that?"

"An important one."

He seems to realize I'm not giving up on this and his movements finally slow. He exhales and tilts his head back to look up at me. He rises and his chest is heaving as he stares down at me. "Doesn't this answer it for you?"

"Doesn't what answer it for me?"

"This." He removes his hot hands from my body only long enough to wave between us. "Us. You and me. The way you respond to my touch. Have you ever felt this way with anyone? Because I sure as hell haven't."

"So…you want me to move in with you based on what, the way you touch me?"

"Elise," he pushes out a breath full of frustration, "what are you getting at, baby?"

"I want to know why you want to be with me. What do I have that Kylie doesn't have? What, I'm better in bed than her?"

"That's not—" he huffs in disbelief, "that's not what this is. You're not hearing me. This chemistry transcends the physical. But we don't need words. We don't need talking. We only need this." His hands plant firmly on my hips and he presses his erection harder against me, eliciting a whimper from somewhere deep in my throat.

Why does he have to be so damn good at that?

"We can't survive off of that alone. It doesn't work that way."

"Of course it does." He blinks, looking at me as if this is a no-brainer. "Think about how many people share a marriage based on other compatibilities, but there's nothing deeper. No passion. There's none of this." He lifts a hand and pinches my nipple between his fingers. I groan. "I would know, Elise. I've been in one of those marriages for five years now. There's no such thing as a perfect relationship, married or not. When you find a connection like we have, you recognize it. You grab hold of it and take it for all its worth. You don't let it slip between your fingers."

"What if that connection's not enough?"

"There's no such thing as enough. It's an illusion."

"What happens when someone else comes along? When this grows dull?"

"It won't," he insists, stunned, like I can't possibly be saying what I'm saying to him right now. "No one can ever replace you."

"You say that now."

His nostrils flare and he tilts his forehead to meet mine, staring me square in the eyes. "You're a keeper. Not a substitute or a flavor of the week, baby."

"Why do you want me? You don't know me."

His eyes burn with determination, but he comes up pitifully short. "Because we fit."

"Simple as that?" It comes out quietly.

"Simple as that."

A lump forms in my throat and a civil war breaks out, wreaking havoc on my mind. He's giving me all he's got. He's not being cold or insincere, or even dishonest. He's 100 percent genuine about his perception of us. What we are, what we've been, and what we will be, if we stay together.

But it's not enough.

And I think he's right. Enough doesn't exist. Even if I want it to, it doesn't, and it probably never will. So where does that leave me? Where does it leave us? Right now, it leaves me against a wall with an Adonis of a man worshiping my body like I'm the shrine of an adored idol. Right now, there's nothing else.

For now, that has to be more than enough.

***

I leave Christian's house thoroughly spent and sated. One afternoon of love making with that man, and my limbs are weak and aching in all kinds of delicious ways. I remove the awareness that I'm oddly restless, even after our tiring romp, from my mind, determined to get home in time to get ready for my evening out.

My brain does somersaults while I shower and change, tossing Christian's words around like laundry in a dryer. They feel perpetually damp, spinning round and round on a broken cycle. But I made a promise to Natalie, and more importantly, to Ryder, and for once, I don't feel like being the town tramp loner girl. I want to be normal, even if only for a night. I'll have to return to my pumpkin carriage before the clock strikes midnight, but I can live with that.

Stella's parking lot is packed when I arrive. It's hard to find a parking space, but I manage to pull into one before a blue sedan cruising for a spot beats me to it. Parking around here is always brutal around this time of year, regardless of the night rush at Stella's. As soon as the annual holiday festival begins, people are out and about, braving the chilly temps in exchange for hot cocoa and the array of eclectic booths that set up shop along the waterfront. There are foods from all over the world, and unique arts and crafts at every turn.

I step out of my car and wave to Jay through the diner window. He's busy, running around like a mad man as usual, but he waves back and gives me one of his signature smiles. I check my watch to make sure I'm on time, and it turns out I'm a few minutes early. I begin to stroll down the diner's front walkway, stopping when I come to the end of the building, where there's a sweeping view of the harbor.

The waterfront is always charming at night, especially with the festival lighting. The evergreen trees lining the sidewalk have been lit, even though we haven't made it to Thanksgiving yet, and caramel and pumpkin aromas are everywhere. This is without a doubt my favorite time of year, and it reminds me of the times Tee and I spent together during high school, tasting our way through the festival, trying new foods and sneaking booze along the way.

"Hey Elise," Natalie's voice sings in the distance. I spin to find her walking toward me from the other end of the sidewalk. Nate is at her side, their hands comfortably linked. Nate is holding a cold beer in his free hand, his eyes traveling up and then down when he sees me.

I smile.

"You look gorgeous!" Natalie hurries up to me and gestures for me to turn, so I oblige and give her a little awkward spin, wobbling to the left. My long blonde hair is down, with soft curls that hit just above my breasts, and I'm wearing a snug-fitting cream turtleneck that shows off my curves. A pair of dark skinny jeans and tall, black suede boots complete the ensemble, leaving me feeling casual, sleek, and elegant.

"Thanks," I say. "You look nice, too."

She shrugs with a grin, looking down at her bright red sweater and black-wash jeans. Her red hair is thrown up into a loose, pretty bun, and her pale skin is fresh and bright. She really is an attractive girl, but I can tell she doesn't seem to think so. "Sorry we're running a few minutes late. Nate couldn't find his car keys. I swear, he loses everything. Then he wanted a beer, so we had to stroll a bit."

Nate looks sheepish for a moment before he speaks up in his defense. "We're also fashionably late, thanks to Natalie."

Natalie rolls her eyes playfully. "Hey, I couldn't decide

on the flats or the heels. Cut a girl a break!"

"She changed her shoes like ten times." Nate gives me a bland look.

"I finally decided on the heels," she laughs, showing off her black, shiny shoes. "Unlike Elise, I don't have legs that go for miles. I need a little height."

"*Hhhmmm*," I respond half-heartedly, looking over her shoulder for my date. I'd love to stand here and continue to listen to Natalie drone on about clothes and hair and make-up—okay, not really—but I'm far more interested in finding Ryder. I have no intention of being a third wheel tonight.

"So, where's your date?" Nate asks. His delivery seems natural enough, but the eagerness in his tone grabs my attention. I quit looking for Ryder and bring my gaze to his. There's something different about him tonight, something I can't pinpoint. But I think it's lurking in his eyes. There's a secretive glint in them, like he's uncovered something about me and is keeping the discovery all to himself. I don't miss the way he can't seem to hold eye contact with me for longer than a few seconds.

"He should be here soon," I reply, the corner of my lips twitching with a ghost of a smile. He really has caught on. My cover is blown.

"Where'd you guys meet?" Natalie pipes up, her eyes alive with curiosity.

"Hate to burst your bubble, but we just met. He's not my boyfriend. He actually works at my apartment building. He does maintenance."

"Ohhh," Natalie gives me a sly look. "A Mr.Fix-It type, huh? I love guys who know how to get their hands dirty."

I glance only briefly at Natalie, quickly pinning my gaze back on Nate's. "So do I," I say, not missing a beat.

Nate chokes on his beer, and Natalie looks completely baffled. I'm not sure who to feel sorrier for: Nate, for trying so hard to appear comfortable, or Natalie, who has to put up with the poor guy.

I'm about to go easy on Nate and change the subject, but warm fingers on my shoulder distract me. "Hey you," a friendly, smooth voice comes from behind me, and Natalie's eyes widen, her mouth gaping slightly.

I glance back and find Ryder standing there, his usually disheveled hair covered by a loose, gray cable-knit beret. A long-sleeve flannel shirt is fitted to his firm build, and a dark blazer gives him just a hint of sophistication. I grin in appreciation, knowing underneath that blazer lies a bold, beautiful canvas of poetic ink…among other delectable things.

His tattoos might be covered up tonight, but his masculine good looks are on full display. He is pure ruggedness but polished, with traditional, boyish charm. His jaw line is tinged by just the right amount of hair—not yet a beard, but darker than a five o'clock shadow. His strong cheekbones and warm, intense eyes give him an earnest yet approachable look, and the scent I've come to recognize as uniquely Ryder's—pine and cinnamon spice—is ever present. He's so close, I discreetly breathe him in.

"Hey," I say, liking the way his hand moves to the small of my back. It's such an easy, natural movement, I almost don't sense it, except for the fact that my body is apparently hyperaware of his hands. "You made it."

"Yeah, I hope I didn't keep you waiting long."

"Not at all. Ryder, these are my friends, Natalie and Nate. Guys, this is Ryder." Saying I have friends is like saying I'm a nun. It's a completely unholy union. But I don't know how else to refer to these people. I step aside to allow them space for introductions. They turn chatty in a matter of minutes, and I'm happy to see the exchange. It helps that Nate is just as much into the outdoors as Ryder. They talk boating, camping, and hiking, and then the subject of kayaking comes up.

"Kayaking's like a religion around here," Nate says as we all walk side by side down the town's main drag. "We should all go some time."

"You've never been kayaking?" Ryder asks with interest.

"Nah, I'm still new to town. I'm from the desert. Well, and the concrete jungle. Phoenix." He shrugs. "I'm dying to get out and try it, though."

"Maybe we can camp one weekend," Natalie says, locking arms with Nate. She eyes me and Ryder, her gaze falling on his left hand. It's still casually resting against my lower back as we stroll down the sidewalk. Little sparks tickle the skin beneath my sweater where his fingers rest.

"I'd be game for that," Ryder says. "What about you,

Elise?"

"Sure, maybe," I shrug, keeping my arms crossed over my chest. I've never been opposed to the great outdoors. It's hard to reside in the Pacific Northwest and not be drawn in to its natural beauty. But being here tonight is already so out of my element, I have no idea how I'd function a whole weekend in such an intimate social situation.

I remind myself I came here strictly to get Natalie off my back, and that Ryder's company is just a plus.

"Oh, I want to try those," Natalie gasps, her eyes widening to the size of golf balls as she hones in on a huge selection of brownies at a nearby food booth. I have to admit the smell of warm, gooey chocolate coming from the tent is divine, and I'm tempted to try some myself.

Ryder seems to notice this, and his hand suddenly finds mine. "You want to try something here?" He looks down at me, all the while gently tugging my fingers to pull me toward the booth. Natalie has already dragged Nate over for a taste.

"Sure," I say, "it smells so good."

Ryder sends me a crooked smile and takes the lead, ordering two salted caramel brownies and two small hot chocolates. "Hope you're in the mood to overdose on chocolate tonight." He hands me a scorching cup of cocoa and grabs some napkins, tilting his chin to gesture to a nearby bench.

"Hey, I'm not complaining. Chocolate is my weakness."

"Oh, yeah?"

"Guilty as charged," I say, taking a seat on the bench next to him. Nate and Natalie have found themselves fascinated with the blown glass art tent next to the chocolate booth. I watch them being all coupley, strolling along together and studying the collections of delicate ornaments and paperweights as they bite into their warm, fresh brownies. I'm immersed in their innocence for a moment, but I'm quickly drawn back to my conversation with Ryder.

He sips his hot cocoa and lazily drapes an arm around the back of the bench. "A woman after my own heart."

"Chocolate is your weakness, too?"

"Oh yeah, big time. That and other things."

"Like?" I challenge him, taking a small bite of my sweet treat. Just as I suspected, it's divine.

"Broken, beautiful things."

I swallow the piece of brownie and flutter my lashes. "Well, that's a loaded response."

"It's true." He lifts a shoulder and his head tilts to the side. "Ever since I was a kid. In elementary school, I found this bird on the playground one day. He couldn't fly. Broken wing. He was this shade of blue that just stopped me in my tracks. I picked him up before any of the other little shitheads found him, and one of the teachers called an animal rehab center down the road. They came and took him, fixed him right up."

"Wow. Ryder, the bird whisperer."

White teeth flash as he laughs, shaking his head. "I'm

telling you, I'm doomed. I'm a sucker for that shit."

"So, you're an animal person?" It wouldn't surprise me, considering his love for nature and the outdoors.

"Yeah, I prefer animals to people half the time, to be honest."

"Should I be worried?"

"You're an exception." His hand moves from the back of the bench and his fingers brush the nape of my neck, massaging lightly. I resist the urge to melt into the touch. He's a fine specimen of male, and any other time, I wouldn't think twice about letting him come on to me, but tonight is different.

I discreetly straighten my back and lean forward, redirecting the conversation. He tells me he's 24 and that he used to live in Portland. He likes to move around a lot and staying in one place too long makes him go crazy.

"The Northwest suits me, though," he says, tossing his cup into the trash bin next to the bench. "Guess that's why I keep coming back."

"You live here, in Gig Harbor? Or do you commute?"

"For now, yeah. I like it here. Good people, good food, good kayaking. Can't complain."

"Where else have you traveled?"

"All over the U.S. Since I was 20, anyway. I wasn't interested in the whole college thing. I just want to live, you know? All I need is my dog, my books, and this." He opens his arms, gesturing to our surroundings.

"Good for you," I say earnestly, with a brisk nod. "You sound like you really have your shit together."

"Ha." He looks out at the harbor. "Tell my parents that."

"They don't approve of the way you live?"

"Hell no. They wanted me to go to an Ivy League school, sell my soul to society, and make them proud so I could give them bragging rights to all of their hoity-toity friends back home."

"Where's back home?"

"Connecticut."

I suddenly have a vision of Ryder, living in the wilderness, eating twigs and berries, and hunting game—while cringing at the thought of hurting an animal. He certainly picked the farthest point on the map from his parents, and I don't blame him. I know firsthand just how toxic your own family can be. It doesn't matter that you share their blood. It doesn't even matter if they love you. They can love you, but not respect you. That's still love, but a different kind. It's not the kind I'm interested in, and Ryder clearly isn't, either.

I follow Ryder's eyes, allowing my gaze to trail out to the open harbor, where the dark water meets the faint silhouette of the mountains. I'm about to ask him something else, but Natalie and Nate step in front of us, their noses and cheeks red from the cold.

"We got sidetracked," Nate said, slipping an arm around his girlfriend. Natalie's holding a plastic bag that wasn't there before.

"Yeah, we saw shiny things and couldn't resist. You guys ready to walk?"

"Sure," Ryder says, blinking like he's returning from a trance. He moves to stand and extends a hand to me as I rise.

The four of us mosey around for the next two hours, listening to live bands and filling up on assorted fair foods. Nate and Ryder try beers from different countries, and Natalie and I indulge in a few glasses of red wine, as well as some early Christmas shopping. Two funnel cakes and a pitcher of hot cider later, and we're all thoroughly stuffed and ready to head home.

I toss my bags into my trunk and begin saying goodnight to Nate and Natalie, thanking them for inviting me out. I didn't buy much, just a Christmas tree ornament for Jay and his family, and a vanilla-scented candle for my bedside, but it's enough to make me feel domestic and like I belong to something for a few hours.

"See you at work?" Natalie asks, wrapping me in a hug. My return hug isn't nearly as enthusiastic as hers, but I make an effort. The girl isn't that bad. She's not Tee—there will never be another Tee—but she doesn't look at me like I'm a leper, and she has good taste when it comes to shopping.

"Yup, bright and early."

"Drive safe."

"You, too."

She and Nate exchange pleasantries with Ryder, and Natalie is gushing about how over the moon she is that he came tonight. Nate looks a bit embarrassed by how thick Natalie's laying it on, but he goes along with it, shaking Ryder's hand and telling him he's holding him to those camping plans. Nate gives me a quick wave and doesn't let his wandering eyes linger.

"They're cool," Ryder says as they disappear down the sidewalk.

"Yeah, they're nice." I lean back on my car door, watching them fade into the night.

"Have you known them long?"

"No, not really. Natalie's somewhat new to the diner I work at, and I just met Nate."

"You're a waitress?"

"Yup." I nod my head to Stella's, and Ryder's grin spreads.

"You work right here?"

"Yes, sir. Practically live here."

"Good to know." His grin turns devious, and I'm instantly smitten with the playful glint in his eyes.

"I don't know if you're a breakfast person, but their French toast is out of this world."

"Ohhhh," his eyes squint into little slits and he grips his stomach. "French toast is my weakness."

I laugh. There's something sexy about a guy with an appetite. "I thought chocolate was. And poor, defenseless animals."

"And other things..." He steps forward, placing himself in front of me. "Like beautiful blondes with tattoos in unmentionable places." He smirks and gently hooks one thumb in the belt loop of my jeans, giving my hip a nudge to push me back against the car door. The motion is super light but full of confidence.

Desire stirs low in my abdomen and my breath falters.

"Ryder..."

"I had a great time tonight."

"Yeah?" My gaze rolls upwards, locking with his, and he stares down with smoky, hooded brown pools.

"You kinda scared me that day when I showed up at your door. I thought you were going to bust out a shot gun or something." A small laugh bubbles up. I really was on a warpath that day. I don't regret that he stumbled into my line of fire, though. "I'm glad you didn't. 'Cause I really wanted to do this." He reaches up and brushes a strand of hair from my cheek, then steps closer, so his legs are flush with mine. "And this." His words are low and rough as he moves in, planting a feather-light kiss on my lips.

Time stops and the lights on the surrounding trees feel brighter, almost blinding against my closed lids.

The warmth is entirely too intimate but he feels so damn good, and the discovery that he not only smells like cinnamon spice and Christmas morning but tastes like it, too, unhinges me. I'm freefalling into his scent, into the soft pleasure of his mouth. This must be what a kiss feels like. I immediately feel like I've been gypped my whole life, because I'm certain right now that I've never had one before.

"Ryder," I say again, breathless, "I have to go." I feel Christian all over me, in my veins, underneath my skin. Just hours ago, my limbs were tangled with his, my lipstick was on his pillow, and his cock was in my mouth. I'm waiting for Ryder to see traces of him any second and call me out for being exactly what I am.

Elise Duchamp—notorious, home wrecking whore.

His head juts back slightly and he freezes. A beat passes and his feet catch up with what his mind has just registered. He steps back and puts his hands into his pockets, allowing me to reclaim my personal space. "Oh, okay. Yeah, it's getting late."

"Ryder, I—"

"Hey," he shrugs with a light laugh, looking down, "don't worry about it. You have to work early, you should go."

I hesitate but push myself off the car door to turn around and let myself in the driver seat. "Thanks for everything. I had…tonight was nice for me, too." I don't say another word. I shut the car door and start the engine, my hands shaky as I buckle the seatbelt.

What the fuck is wrong with me?

I inhale a few deep breaths and get ready to back out, glancing out the window first. I can't look at him. I just can't.

But I don't have to, because he's already gone.

People stroll by in front of Stella's, hand in hand, some with children, some with dogs. The street's festival lighting looks just as beautiful as it did before I got in the car, and the celebratory spirit still permeates the air, but I feel cold, and no amount of heat from the car's heater can warm the chill in my bones.

CHAPTER 6

My worst fears come true the next morning at work, and for a whole week after that. Natalie flaps her gums about Ryder nonstop, asking a million questions. Where does he live? Who is his ex-girlfriend? When will I see him again? Have we hooked up? Am I into him? Have I been avoiding him?

On and on the inquisition goes, and I am sure by now that she should've gotten the hint—I don't want to talk about Ryder.

I change the subject over and over again, and the more she tries to chat, the more withdrawn I become. The girl is nice, but she exhausts me. This is what I get for trying to be social for one night in my life. I get stuck with a bubbly, nosey girl who doesn't know how to take a hint. If I thought she was dense before, I have been living under a rock. Because this girl absolutely believes that somewhere between sharing a funnel cake and a glass of wine at the holiday festival, we've become BFFs.

It's Saturday morning and my arm aches from scrubbing down the table tops. It feels good to pour all of my frustration out into wiping down the counters. I'm thankful Natalie doesn't work this morning, because I'd probably snap.

"You okay over there, hon?" Jay asks, adding rolls of coins to the register. We've just wrapped up our early morning rush and the place is starting to thin out. We won't get another rush until late morning, when the lunch crowd begins to trickle in. I'm serving with Brad this morning, and he's uncharacteristically grumpy today. Usually, he greets me with a big bear hug and does a little jig around the breakfast bar.

"I'm okay," I say to Jay, giving my aching arm a break. "I think it's Brad you have to worry about this morning." I smirk and roll my eyes in Brad's direction, and Jay laughs.

"I can hear you," Brad says from the other end of the diner. He's sweeping up a heap of hash browns some kid spilled all over the booth. "Quit talking about me like I'm not right here."

"What crawled up your butt this morning, brother?" Jay chuckles, and there's a shrill ding from the register. I don't know how he still uses that thing. It's so damn old.

"Let's see," Brad drawls, picking up the dust pan. "Got a speeding ticket on my way to work, lost 300 bucks playing cards last night, and my girlfriend dumped me when I got in late with empty pockets." Brad's gaze jumps to mine for a second and I look away, knowing Jay is watching us. The news doesn't surprise me. Brad and his girlfriend have been having problems for a while now. I should know. I've been sleeping in her bed.

"Serves you right, speeding around here," Jay grumbles, smashing buttons on the piece of junk machine. "Money can be replaced, and there are other fish in the sea and all that jazz. You'll recover, my friend. You're young and tenacious."

"Yeah, thanks for the words of wisdom, Gandalf," Brad grumbles back. He finishes collecting the mess from the floor and disappears to the kitchen. I contemplate following him to pull him aside and get the scoop on his break up with Karen, but the front door jingles and more customers walk in.

I swing around and find Ryder and Nate sauntering up to the hostess stand. I'm hit with a plethora of conflicting feelings when I spot them, because they've both been on my mind, but for very different reasons. Nate called me a few days ago, asking if I'd heard from Ryder about going camping, and his inability to hold a steady conversation with me was becoming more and more of an issue. He became a rambling, stuttering mess. I should probably just fuck him and get it over with, but he and Natalie are the only two in this town who haven't written me off. Well, them and Jay. And now Ryder.

Shit.

As Ryder stands there next to Nate, that strange ball of unease forms in my stomach again, and all I want to do is drag Brad back out here and beg him to take their table. But I can't and I won't, because that would officially make me the biggest bitch on the planet. Granted, I'm already up for that title, so maybe a few more nominations won't hurt.

"Hey guys," I say, reluctantly wandering up to them. "Come to harass me?"

"Pretty much," Nate smiles, all cheeky and fresh. His hair is messy and styled to the side, his eyes twinkling. I force myself to look Ryder directly in the eye. I wish I hadn't.

That dark brown, smoldering gaze is just as inviting as before, and I have to look at it knowing I turned it down. The memory of the feel and taste of his lips on mine has lingered since the festival, and I'm seriously irritated by it. What is the big fucking deal? He is just another guy. Just another handsome guy, looking to get in my panties. Just another guy I'd toy with, just because I can. I itch at the back of my neck, the place he gently rested his fingers while we sat on the bench that night at the festival.

"Here," I say, leading them to a table. "Have a seat and I'll be right back to take your order." Tapping the table top, I don't stick around to watch them slide into the booth. I book it to the kitchen and grab Brad's shirt sleeve, pulling him into one of the pantries.

"Wow," he chuckles, "easy there, babe. No gettin' handsy while we're on the job. Not until Boss Man leaves."

"I love how you're in a shit mood all morning, and the second you think I'm trying to fuck you, you're all sunny with glee," I say, trying but failing to restrain my own smile. "Whatever." I swish my hands in the air, squeezing my eyes shut. "Anyway, what happened with Karen?"

"She's just done. I'm done, too. Nothing for you to worry about, girl." He brushes his thumb over my cheek and peeks around before placing a kiss on my forehead. "You doin' alright? You've been looking rough lately."

"Thanks."

"You still look hot. You know I'd do you." He wiggles his eyebrows and grins, nudging my shoulder.

It's then that I realize Karen positively made the right choice to leave Brad. He feels no remorse for his actions, and he's 100 percent serious, even if he is joking. He is like me. He belongs with people like me, and it's wrong of him to try and fit into Karen's world. That's where Brad and I always differed. He tries to hide what he is. I let it all hang out. Except when it came to Jay. And now Ryder.

Again…what the fuck is wrong with me?

I pinch the bridge of my nose when the two men pop into my mind. "I'm fine," I say to Brad with a sigh. "Just…dealing with some shit right now. Nothing new there, right?"

"Story of my life, babe." He slaps my ass and exits the pantry. "Keep your head up," he calls out as he disappears.

I compose myself and return to Nate and Ryder's table, all business. "What can I get you guys?"

Nate is still scanning the menu, but Ryder looks up. My eyes level with his, and he has me again. Those damn eyes are fucking with my head.

He pushes his flannel sleeves up past his elbows. “Coffee and French toast, please.”

“Good choice.”

“So I hear.”

I nod and scribble down the order, waiting on Nate. I don’t bother to ask Ryder how he’s been or engage in small talk. He doesn’t, either, and that tells me he’s not interested in wasting any more time on me. Good, because I have the distinct feeling that he is not the type of guy to want sloppy seconds. Sure, he might want to get in my panties now. But when he learns who I really am? He’ll be running for the hills.

“I’ll take the same,” Nate decides, handing me the menus. I thank him and start for the kitchen.

“Oh hey, wait,” Ryder calls out before I make it very far.

“Yeah?”

“Do you by any chance have a newspaper?”

“A newspaper?”

“Yeah, you know, that outdated thing that no one our age reads anymore but is filled with useful information?” He straightens in the booth and folds his hands on the table, waiting expectantly like a cute puppy. I don’t mention the fact that he isn’t the only one who is “our age” who reads the paper. And I certainly don’t mention the cheesy column I read almost religiously.

“Sure. I’ll bring it with your breakfast.”

He thanks me and starts tapping his fingers on the

table, turning his attention back to Nate. It seems I'm not the only one who senses tension between the three of us. They're oddly quiet, saying few words to one another, and they don't attempt to make conversation with me, either. Then why the hell did they come in for breakfast?

I dismiss that question as a stupid one. Maybe they want good food. Maybe they thought Natalie was working. Maybe they just didn't have anything better to do and I'm a vain hussy who thinks every man in this town wants a piece.

I set my order pad on the counter and hang my head forward with a weary realization: Maybe that's because most men in this town *have* had a piece.

I rip off the order slip with a little too much vigor and pin it to the cook line, calling out what I need. I'm back at Nate and Ryder's table in no time, serving them our famous French toast with a pot of coffee. I remember to bring Ryder's newspaper and leave him to it, happily busying myself with other customers while he and Nate do their thing.

Thirty minutes later, I'm retrieving their empty plates. "Anything else?"

"Yeah," Ryder says, grabbing a napkin. He pulls a pen from his pocket and starts writing on it. "Go out with me again."

Nate's fork tumbles from his hand and clacks loudly on the table top. He clears his throat, and his cheeks turn red. What the hell? My eyes land on Ryder's.

"Okay…"

"Here." He finishes writing on the napkin, sneaking an amused glance at Nate. "I never did give you my number."

"Oh, thanks," I say, taking the napkin from him. "I really did have a good time the other night." My gaze bounces between the two guys, and all I want is for them to both get up and leave. This is beyond awkward.

"Call me." That's all Ryder says before he stands and tosses some cash down on the table. "See you next weekend, man?" he asks Nate before heading for the door.

"Yeah, sounds good, dude. See you then."

Ryder glances back at me as he exits, a sexy smirk curving his lips, but I don't have long to enjoy that or its complementary dimples, because I'm left there with Nate.

"Hey Elise, I've been meaning to ask you…would you mind coming with me to pick out a birthday present for Natalie? I suck at shopping for presents, and I really want to get her something special, ya know?"

I blink, looking at him like he's sprouted three heads. Sure, maybe he really does suck at buying presents, and maybe he could really use the help. But if he's trying to make a move on me and that's the best he can come up with, then the guy's in even more trouble than I'd originally thought.

I do him a favor and play dumb, letting him think he has me. "Oh, really? I understand. Plenty of guys have trouble shopping for women. Sure, I'll help. When do you want to go?"

"Are you free tomorrow?"

I tilt my head to the side, pretending to consider it. "I think so, yeah. What time?"

His eyes are suddenly on fire, like he's just hit the jackpot. "How about noon? Does that work? I'll come pick you up."

"I can do noon. I'll come to you. You live in Outrigger Apartments, right? I have to work the night shift, though, so I'll only have a few hours."

"That's cool. We can get a lot done in a few hours."

I nod as he pulls out his wallet and leaves a few extra dollars on the table, next to Ryder's cash. He walks out of the diner and I watch him drive away through the wide picture windows. I look at the napkin in my hand, where Ryder's number is sprawled across the center. Edginess teases my insides and I scratch my temple, wanting to extinguish the rush of tension I feel piercing my gut.

I crumple up the napkin and toss it over the counter into the garbage can, then move on to my next table.

***

I've spent the morning gloriously naked, lying in bed with my newspaper and a cup of coffee. I slept in and enjoyed every second of it, but it's time to start getting ready. I have to pick up Nate soon. Tossing the newspaper on my bedside, I stand and stretch with a yawn. The Sorry Secrets column has been pretty lame recently.

Where is all the juice? I snicker under my breath at my desire for sorry, broken-hearted people to experience more misfortune just for the sake of my entertainment. What a cruel world.

A brisk knock at the door demands my attention before I'm able to make it to the shower. I slink into my bathrobe and answer it, internally cursing myself when I'm greeted with his handsome face. "Ryder…hey."

"Hey." He looks cautious. He's wearing his work uniform, and his usual scruff looks cleaner shaven than it did at the diner yesterday. "I don't mean to come by unexpectedly like this, but uh…" He rakes a hand through his hair and his eyes dart from left to right. "There's something I wanted to say yesterday that I didn't get the chance to say, and it's better face to face."

I cross my arms over my chest and wait.

"See, I didn't come to the diner yesterday with Nate."

"Huh? What do you mean?"

"We both kind of showed up at the same time and just…bumped into one another out front, as we were walking in. So, we decided to get a table together."

"Okay…"

"I came to see you. To give you my number and ask you out again. But he was there to see you, too."

"Yeah, I know. He wants me to go shopping with him today for a birthday present for Natalie." I turn to glance back at the clock in the kitchen. "I'm getting ready to meet him now, actually, so…"

Ryder's half smile springs up as he shakes his head

thoughtfully. "Yeah, about that…so uh, I think he's into you."

"What?" I snort, raising my brows. This is not a conversation I want to have with Ryder. This is not a conversation I want to have at all. "Ryder, I don't think—"

"Just hear me out." He casually lifts his hands to stop me. "It's your business, I get it. But as far as I know, he and Natalie are together and I just thought…" His voice trails off and he sounds frustrated, like he either can't get the words out or he isn't sure what to say at all.

I study him with narrowed eyes. "What are you getting at, Ryder?"

He straightens and seems to steel himself, taking a deep breath. With another quick rake of his hair, he just comes out with it. "I want you, Elise."

My fingernails dig into my arms and they cross tighter against my chest.

"I mean, I think I made that pretty clear the other night, and I'm almost positive that every man in this town wants you, because…well fuck, I'm not blind to the way they look at you. But you're not up for it right now, I guess, and that's fine. I'm not here to pressure you or make an idiot out of myself. I'm just here to say that if you're available, and you're interested…don't fuck around with Nate. Come have Thanksgiving dinner with me. Get to know me, not him. He's not right for you."

The world spins. I feel it beneath my feet, and I feel it in the air. The awkwardness between the three of us at the diner yesterday suddenly makes sense. "You're…

you're inviting me to have Thanksgiving dinner with you?"

"I am." He nods seriously, like a man who knows exactly what he wants.

I feel a smile teasing my lips and I avert my gaze from his, trying to figure out how to navigate this thing. It's been years since I've spent a holiday with anyone. Jay always offers for me to eat with his family, but I always decline. Thanksgiving usually consists of me in my PJs and a bag of greasy, processed food in front of the TV. There are no phone calls to family, no knocks on the door. Just me, waiting for the day to pass, so there are no more reminders of how truly alone I am.

"I don't know what to say."

"Say yes."

My eyes find their way back to his, and something passes between us. I want to say thanks, but hell no. I want to tell him to run along and find another beautiful blonde with tattoos in unmentionable places to pester, because surely, all he's looking for is a quick fuck. I'm just an itch he wants to scratch.

But I find myself saying, "Okay."

His dimples come out from hiding, and he struts up to me, all cool and confident. "Good choice. There will be lots of chocolate." He leans down and lowers his mouth to my cheek, slowly planting a kiss there, and the sensation travels straight to my toes. He smiles against my skin, like he knows the effect his touch has on me. "I'll pick you up at two. Dress warmly."

I inhale shakily as he pulls away, his stubble abrasive as it sweeps over my cheek. "See you then."

"Later."

"Hey, Ryder?" My voice recovers some of its strength as I call out to him. He's already halfway down the hall.

"Yeah?"

"You're wrong about Nate." I don't know why I lie. I don't know why I do half of what I do, but the words are there anyway.

"No, I'm not." His tone is flat. He resumes his stride with his back to me. "You'll see."

My body is still at the doorway until he disappears, and I'm stuck wondering what the hell I just got myself into. It seems like just as I finally give Tim the boot and begin to make progress shaking Christian from my system, now I have two other men to worry about.

I haven't seen Christian since the day of the festival. It sours my stomach when I think of that day, and I'm not sure why. But since then, some clarity has settled, dispelling the fog from my brain. I need to pull the plug on the Christian Walker booty call for good, because things with him have gone way past complicated.

As for Tim, his attempts to contact me have finally leveled off, and I rarely see him around town. He shows up at the diner every few days to chat with Jay, but his visits are never long and I never garner more attention from him than a quick scowl before he's off again.

As I stand there staring at the empty hall where Ryder stood just seconds ago, I remember I now have to go deal with Nate. "Shit," I whisper as I close my front door. I hop in the shower and slip into a black sweater dress and my tall suede boots, then rush out the door.

I find I'm not nearly as enthusiastic about meeting up with Nate as before, although I wasn't very gung-ho about it in the first place. There's only one reason I've agreed to see him today, and it has nothing to do with warm, fuzzy feelings for Natalie or my desire to help find the perfect birthday present for her. My motive is much less noble but I know that Nate wants the same thing, and that gives me the fuel to make the drive to his place.

Don't fuck around with Nate, he's not right for you.

Ryder's words prick at my skin, but I shake them off. I'm not looking to be Nate's Mrs. Right. And I'm not looking for a Mr. Right. I'm only looking to go where duty calls, and when it comes to Nate...duty definitely calls. There's only one way to get Natalie to shake this delusional belief that we're friends, and to get this unwelcome, stirring sensation in my gut under control. It popped up somewhere between seeing Christian the day of the festival and hanging out with Ryder, and it needs to be tamed.

If Nate's honest with himself, he'll see that Natalie isn't the girl for him. She's too uptight and far too reserved, and the minute Nate realized his attraction to me, his relationship with Natalie was destined for the express train to hell anyway, because unlike some guys' ability to say no, it's obvious that Nate doesn't possess that willpower. He needs to get me out of his system and move on, because this infatuation of his isn't going anywhere anytime soon, and I have problems of my own. Like preparing for a traditional Thanksgiving dinner date with Ryder.

Shit.

I arrive at Nate's place just five minutes after noon. I apply a dab of lipstick to my lips in the rearview mirror and I'm on my way, giving myself a mental pep talk as I step from the car. Ryder's words haunt me the whole way up to Nate's door.

Get to know me, not him.

I extinguish them immediately and knock.

CHAPTER 7

Nate answers the door in a casual blue oxford shirt, buttoned up tidily to the neck. I want to undo the top button—or two—and ruffle his hair a bit.

"Hey," I say, my tone carrying a sensual lilt. My smile is a serpent's smile, and I don't dare take my eyes from his.

"Wow," he breathes, blinking when he takes in the length of my tight sweater dress. His eyes drop down, then shoot back up. "Uh…hey. You're here."

"Can I come in?"

His mouth slackens slightly and he watches me carefully, like a lion is about to pounce on its prey before his very eyes.

It's his lucky day. He's going to get a front row seat to that spectacle.

My mind goes numb as I step past him, but my body is a live wire. Ryder's words have been thrown to the very back of my skull, where I'm sure they'll wreak havoc later, but for now, I'm safe. There's no going back once I do this. No repairing my friendship—or whatever I have—with Natalie, and no undoing yet another nail in my coffin.

But this is what girls like me do, right? This is my path. Nothing exists beyond this fate. And it has to be done.

"So are you ready to go?" Nate asks, shutting the door quietly behind him. I begin to amble around his living room, checking out his various sports trophies and academic award plaques. I don't see a lick of dust anywhere, and there are coasters on the coffee table. Coasters. With palm trees on them. We're in the fucking Northwest.

I'm feeling more and more edgy as I stroll around the couch, and I decide it's time to get down to business. Natalie is working at the diner until six tonight. I'll see her in passing, when I go in for my shift.

I don't dwell on that thought.

"What's the rush?" I respond, sending him a coquettish smirk over my shoulder. His hands move to his pockets, and I see his Adam's apple bob. His face is pinched with tension as he watches me prowl around his apartment.

"No—no—nothing," he stutters, making a move for the kitchen. "Can I get you something to drink?" His voice is coarse and tight.

"Please."

He opens the fridge and reaches for a bottle of water. "Something with more kick," I say, before he even pulls it from the shelf.

"Oh." He stills. "Okay, sure." I hear him rifle around in the fridge for a few seconds as I study the picture frames on the wall. There are pictures of him with soccer and baseball teams, and shots of him with his family. Portrait-type shots, where they're all fanned out beautifully on a massive lawn, the landscape dripping with elegant oak trees.

He returns with two beers and I thank him, clinking our bottles.

"Thanks for coming with me today," he says, eyeing me as I lean forward to get a better look at his shots of the Grand Canyon.

I go straight for the kill. "Do you want to fuck me before we go shopping, Nate?"

Beer sprays from his lips and he struggles with a cough, but that doesn't deter me. I begin to cruise toward him, taking a slow sip of my drink.

"Wh—what? Elise—"

"It's a simple question," I shrug, my smirk tipping my lips to dangerously challenging levels. "See, because I think you do. I want you to, and I'm not ashamed to admit it. So, I say we just cut through the bullshit and skip the whole dance. Show me to your bedroom."

"Natalie—"

"Is working at the diner," I finish for him. I drop my chin playfully and I reach out for him, placing my hands gently on his chest. He's strung so tightly, the tension bubbling beneath his muscles pierces my fingers. God, has he been getting any at all? "We have plenty of time."

Leaning in, I nudge the edge of his jaw with my nose. My lips skim the space just below his ear and he hisses through clenched teeth.

"Elise," he chokes out, gripping my shoulders. The muscles in his throat flex as I kiss a trail along his earlobe. "Natalie's your friend."

"She's your friend."

"She's my girlfriend."

I don't respond, just back away slightly until I'm walking backwards, teasing him with a sway of my hips. I lock gazes with him and reach back for the zipper on my dress. His jaw is working so hard as he watches me, he's going to chip some teeth. The sound of my zipper permeates the silence around us, and my sweater dress falls to the floor, forming a puddle around my feet.

"Holy shit," Nate whispers, tugging at his collar. His eyes roll up to the ceiling and he begins tapping his fingers on his pant leg. It looks like he's mentally counting to ten. My fingers reach behind my back again, this time locating the hook of my bra. In seconds, it's undone and I'm standing before him in nothing but black lace panties and tall suede boots to match.

His eyes rip from the ceiling and land back on me, wide and desperate. He scans my body and I lean my weight on one hip, brushing my blonde locks over my shoulders so he gets a good look at my rack. "I can't do this," he says quietly. "Goddamn it, do I want to… you're…fuck!" He covers his face and groans. "You're so sexy, it's killing me, Elise."

"Then touch me."

"Tell me not to."

"I don't want to."

"You really want me to do this."

Once again, I exchange words for action. I resume my prowl backwards and hook my thumbs into the sides of my panties, slowly wiggling them down my hips. A strangled sound emanates from Nate's throat but he remains still, watching me feverishly. Just as my panties slide to my knees, I dip my fingers inside myself and then slowly withdraw them, bringing them to my lips. I suck on the tips and moan softly, fastening my eyes on his.

That's all it takes.

He snaps and bolts forward so quickly, the breath is knocked from my lungs. His lips crash down on mine and I'm lifted off my feet and carried backward. My back slams into a wall and Nate's hands are everywhere, groping my breasts, cupping my ass, and tearing my panties from my knees.

In seconds, my boots are off, and I scramble for his belt buckle. His fingers fumble over mine as we both work to get his pants off, followed by his shirt. I weave my fingers into his hair, gripping at the back of his head, and I lower him, guiding his mouth to my breasts. He latches on and sucks, and I reach down and wrap my hand around his cock, squeezing hard.

"You're wicked," he pants against the hollow of my throat as he trails back up to my lips. "So, so wicked."

I bite down on his bottom lip and a little laugh

simmers beneath my words. "You've wanted to be," I whisper. "And now you are."

He lifts me again and my legs fall around his waist as he carries me into his bedroom, where we collapse into a heap of pillows, sweat, and sin. I feel the roller coaster track clicking. Higher. Higher. Higher.

I'm right where I belong.

***

A lone tear sneaks down my cheek as I sit in my car. It's raining and the heater's on, creating splotches of fog on the windows. I stare out the front windshield, watching the droplets of rain hit the glass. They roll and merge, roll and merge, then slide down the car and back into the earth, where they'll be useful again. Rinse and repeat. Beautiful.

I capture the rogue tear with my thumb and stifle a deep-building sob, one that I refuse to let out, because once it escapes, the dam will burst and I'll drown myself right here, in my own car.

In less than five minutes, I have to step inside Stella's. I have to say hello to Natalie and clock in for my shift, then go on for the next four hours pretending like my tryst at Nate's never happened. Like I haven't poisoned another man, another relationship.

My body feels limp as I pull it from the car and out into the rain. I dash inside Stella's and shake out my hair, shivering as I remove my trench coat to hang it on the coat stand.

"Oh good, you're here!" I hear her before I see her. Natalie trots up to me with a small gift box. It's wrapped in red, green, and gold paper, and little golden specks of glitter give it a polished shine. Jay and Brad greet me from behind the counter in between speaking with customers at the bar. I nod to them but fix my eyes on the gift in front of me.

"What's this?" I ask Natalie, wiping wet strands of hair from my face.

"It's just a little Christmas gift," she says modestly, talking it down like it's not a pretty, well-presented present. She obviously went through a lot of trouble to wrap the thing. "I know it's early, but since I'll be out of town visiting family during Thanksgiving and Christmas, I decided I wanted to give it to you now. Besides," her shoulders lift in a shrug, "my family has this geeky tradition. We give at least one person an early gift, right before Thanksgiving. And I'm just so freaking excited to give it to you, so..."

She thrusts the box in my face and all of the air punches from my lungs.

"Well?" She makes an excited clap. "Are you going to open it?"

"Um..." My throat restricts and I fight for breath. "Don't you want me to take it home and open it on Christmas?"

"Where's the fun in that?" She laughs, smoothing her red hair behind her ears. "No, open it now, lady!"

I survey the diner for the first time since I stepped through the door. The place is packed. No surprise there. I swivel around, in search of a place to set the box down. "Okay, here," I say, leading Natalie to the end of the dining bar. My legs are jelly. There are two open seats and we squeeze into them, Natalie leaning forward expectantly while I struggle to keep my hands from shaking.

My fingers work over the elaborate gold bow, and I snatch a tiny gift card message from the corner before unwrapping the paper.

To keeping your dreams alive. Merry Christmas, lovely! xoxo Nat

It takes everything in me right then not to smash the box I'm holding, because my fingers are digging into it with reeling force. I work to loosen my death grip on the edges, taking a deep breath as I begin tearing at the festive paper.

A plain white box is revealed, and I tug at the top flap to peek inside. Two pieces of Styrofoam are smashed together, forming a casing of some sort. I pop out the case and pick at the tape keeping the Styrofoam pressed together. Natalie is barely containing her excited, hopeful squeal. I pull off the tape and the casing falls open, revealing a snow globe. I blink, and when my eyes focus on what's inside the snow globe, my heart plummets to the bottom of my stomach.

The Eiffel Tower. The whole city of Paris, to be exact. A miniature version that is overshadowed by the historic landmark that frequents my dreams.

"Do you like it?" Natalie asks, her voice soft and full of apprehension. "Whenever you talk about visiting France and about how you almost majored in the language… well, you just light up. I saw it at the festival that night and just couldn't resist."

I can't answer her, because my tongue is numb. I'm rooted to the seat, and my whole body feels like it's been hit by a train. I hesitantly lift my hand from my lap to touch the globe. The city inside is carved so intricately, each little detail surprisingly crisp for such a small model, and there are little crystals mixed in with the snow that make the whole piece shine.

It's the single most magical thing I've ever been given.

"Elise?" I hear Natalie's voice again, but it's muffled. Stilted. I have to stand up. I have to move, right now. "Are you okay?"

I'm suddenly on my feet, standing there, looking down at the fragile globe and all it represents. My throat is clogged with unshed tears, and I feel the dam from earlier violently growing. If I don't get out of here right this second, I will break down in front of the whole diner, and no one, I mean no one, has ever seen Elise Duchamp cry. Natalie and Nate saw a glimpse of it, the day I had it out with Tim at the diner, but that was nothing compared to the threat looming right this moment.

"It's amazing," I finally say, my voice cracking. "I can't even…" I don't remove my eyes from the globe. If I look at Natalie right now, I will never ever recover from this. "Excuse me." I dart from the dining bar and walk briskly toward the kitchen, where I pass by Brad.

"Elise," Brad says, but I barrel right past him, toward the back of the building. "Hey!"

I reach the back door and slam it open, stepping outside.

"Hey! Elise!" I feel Brad on my tail, but I don't care. I step out into the rain and let it saturate me, tilting my head back to feel the cold drops hit my forehead. "What the hell are you doing? Is everything okay?"

"Give me a cigarette, please," I say flatly, closing my eyes.

"You…you want a cigarette? In the rain?"

"Yes."

"You don't smoke."

"Please!" I sob, a caving feeling crushing my chest.

"Shit, okay." Brad feels in his pockets and ducks inside for a second, returning with an umbrella. He opens it and lights a smoke for me, pulling me under the umbrella with him. "Do you want to talk about it?"

I shake my head, taking a drag. I cough. "Can you please just tell Natalie that I'm feeling sick? I can't speak to her right now."

"Are you two fighting?"

"No."

"You sure you don't want to talk about it?"

"Brad, please."

"Yeah, okay." He sighs. "Whatever I can do, girl." He kisses my forehead and leaves me with the umbrella, stepping back into the kitchen.

The heavy door slams behind him and I flinch. My nerves are fried, my heart is hollow, and my world is black. The rain continues to beat down on me, and it's so clear, so pure, the sight of it makes me ache. The grass looks especially vibrant amidst this gloom, and glancing down at my feet, I realize even the black asphalt I'm standing on is pristine compared to the filth encasing my skin. I take deep, thorough drags from my cigarette as I'm bombarded with words that scrape at the wounds.

That's all you are, you slut—a replacement. Sloppy seconds and an in-between quickie for every guy in this town who's looking to fill a hole.

You're wicked. So, so wicked.

You're a dirty, filthy girl, and I fucking love you for it, baby.

I don't hate those men for saying these things to me. Because I did this. It's all me. They're only voicing the truth, what they see and what they know to be real. I must have been dreaming to think I could cross over into Natalie's world for a while—hell, even for a night. Or to think that I could fool someone like Ryder, that I could have a meal with a man on Thanksgiving without any lies, without any dirt. That I could be clean.

I can never touch foot on the solid ground enjoyed by people like Natalie, because I destroy everything I touch, and I am sinking—sinking into the quicksand I created.

"Elise," a voice breaks my train of thought, and I'm further shaken to find Jay standing there in the open kitchen doorway. He lifts an umbrella above him and steps out to join me, his face solemn as he studies the cigarette in my hand. "Talk to me, hon."

My lip quivers with my words. Part of that is the dampness sending chills down my spine, and the other part is those dormant sobs, waiting to rupture from my throat. "Did Brad send you out here?"

"Maybe." He exhales and looks at me intently. "Is this about Tim?"

"What?" I'm so startled that I drop my cigarette and curse as I see it hit the wet ground.

"Here," Jay says, handing me another from his pack. He lights one for me and himself. I accept gratefully, unable to look him in the eye. "Let me guess. You think I don't know about Tim."

My heart stalls in my chest.

He gives me a side glance. "Come on, hon. Who do you think I am, a chump?" He reaches out and strokes my cheek, and the touch causes me to wince. Why is he being so kind? Why is he so calm about this?

"Jay, I..." I fix my gaze straight ahead, watching the rain fall in sheets over the harbor. "I don't know what to say."

"You don't have to say anything." He is calm, but there's a snag in his voice as he speaks, like he's struggling to maintain his cool. "I've known for a while now."

"Tim told you."

"Are you kiddin'?" He huffs with a sarcastic laugh. "He doesn't need to say a word. I know his game. I knew it the moment he started coming into the diner.

I remember telling him to stay the hell away from you, that he was skating on thin ice." He shakes his head and takes a drag, watching the harbor with me. "The son of a bitch makes me so mad. You don't know the half of it, hon. Cheryl's always been so good to him—so good to me. What he's been doing with you isn't just an insult to her, it's an insult to our whole damn family."

"Jay—"

"No," he raises his hand with his palm facing me. "Just listen to me, Elise. Tim is a schmuck. He's my brother, but he's always been a schmuck. You weren't the first and you won't be the last. Cheryl knew what she was getting herself in to when she agreed to marry him, believe you me. That's not what matters. That's not my point."

I am still frozen, staring out at the rain. Ashes spill from my cigarette, sending a gray flurry into the wind.

"All I want to say to you is that you're too goddamn beautiful, too goddamn smart, and too goddamn *good* for a life like that, you hear me? Tim's responsible for his own shit. So is Cheryl, for being with a schmuck like Tim. We all do what we do and we live with our choices. Some people do what they do because they don't know any other way. They're tainted. Bruised." He turns to me now, and I'm forced to shift. He waits until I turn completely, so that he can look me straight in the eye. "I know your mother's death wrecked you. I knew your father long before your mother died, and if you think that no one in this town knew what he was about, then you're blind. We knew. We all knew. It's why I gave you this job when you left college, and I don't ever regret that decision."

"Jay, please," I cry, the volcano of hurt tearing through my chest, fighting its way up my throat.

"Nah-ah," he reaches out from underneath his umbrella and places a hand on my wet cheek, like a father would a daughter, "I'm not done. You listen to me. Those other people don't know, Elise. They don't know how to change. They trudge through life just trying to survive, hurting themselves and dragging everyone down with them, because they're sinking ships and that's what sinking ships do—take the weight. But you—" he points to me, holding my gaze with hard, fierce eyes, "you know another way."

"No. No, I don't."

"Yes you do. Your parents might have let you down, you might have lost them, but you never lost yourself, you hear me? You always had something right. You had this." He places his hand over my heart and the sob I've been holding in breaks free. An explosion bursts from my chest and my head rolls forward, my whole body caving in on itself. "You always had heart, kid. And dreams, and ambition, and spirit. You know innocence, Elise. You possessed it once. But the world will crush you if you let it, and kid, you let it. Nothing breaks my heart more."

A tidal wave of anguish washes over me and I succumb to it, feeling it rush over my skin. "I know."

"Just because the world breaks you doesn't mean

it has to win, hon. You remember that." His big hand clasps my cheek once more and then he releases me, quietly closing his umbrella and retreating back into the kitchen. He leaves me with the rain, and I'm left stunned. Somehow, in the span of a few short minutes, my world has been turned upside down, and it has nothing to do with learning that Jay has known about Tim all along.

Jay lumped my name and the word "good" into one sentence.

I'm not a competitive person. I have never aspired for greatness or dreamed of winning an Olympic gold medal. But hearing that sentence makes me want to win.

CHAPTER 8

Tap, tap, tap.

A sound ripples over my thoughts like a stone skipping across a pond, but I focus on my father's face as it appears in my vanity mirror. He steps through my bedroom doorway and our gazes meet. The grey of his hair is dull and tired, like his eyes.

I stop brushing my hair and meet his glare in the mirror. "What is it, Dad?" I ask, shifting in the vanity stool. "Did I do something wrong?"

He sticks his hands in his pockets and continues to glare at me from behind, the hard set of his jaw telling me I indeed did something wrong. Tori Amos's "Spark" plays in the background, but as far as I'm concerned, the room is starkly quiet.

"Yes," he says, his voice even and hard. "You." He moves, keeping his hands tight in his pockets as he walks up behind me, never letting go of my gaze. "You ruined your mother, do you know that?"

The brush is still at my side, suspended next to my

silky blonde hair. I don't blink, don't breathe, don't move. My father has never hit me, but his words sting as much as any backhand. "I don't understand—"

"Don't!" he shouts now, the veins in his neck bulging. He raises a finger sternly and points at me through the mirror. His anger is uncontainable, and for the very first time, I think his verbal rage might spill over into something physical.

For the very first time, I am afraid of my father.

Inhaling quietly, I realize why. He's been drinking. The harshness of the liquor wafts off him and covers me like a blanket. I take another deep breath through my nose and look down.

"Don't you dare look away," he hisses, stepping closer. Suddenly I feel his fingers on mine, covering my brush. He grips the handle and I let go, and he holds the brush there next to my head, still watching me.

I look back up.

"Dad," I whisper, "you're scaring me."

"You should be scared, Elise. Do you know why?"

I barely shake my head, a trace of a movement.

"Because you're going to be just like her. And soon, you'll be alone. I'm leaving you and your mother. Do you know why?"

I know he wants me to nod again or acknowledge what he's saying, but I can't. My body is frozen.

"Answer me!"

"Nnnn—no, no."

"I'm leaving your mother because she gave up. She

gave up on her body, on her life. She doesn't care how her image reflects on me, do you understand?" He crouches down next to me and his whiskey-laden breath hits my forearm. "She's sick, because of *you*. You gave her cancer, Elise."

"How…how could I do that, Dad?" My voice is so small, and he is an ogre, about to devour the sound.

"You worried her sick. Running around with that dyke friend of yours. Out late drinking, doing God knows what. Are you one of them?" His knuckles crack as he balls his fists up.

I flinch.

"Well, are you?"

"One of what?"

"Are you a dyke, like your *dyke* friend?"

"What? No."

He quietly rises back to his feet, and his stare rains down on me. It burns me, singeing my flesh. I hate him for what he's calling Tee. I hate him for accusing me of something that's shameful in his eyes. And I hate him the most for what he's doing to my mother.

My bottom lip begins to tremble and my whole body stiffens under his appraisal. "Why are you saying these things?"

"Because they're true! You're a bad girl, Elise. Do you know your mother gave up her perfect body for you? When you were in her womb, I could barely look at her. But she worked hard, said *'darling, I'm going to be beautiful again soon, just for you.'*" He finally breaks his stare and looks across the room, as if he's searching for something. "And she was, Elise. She was beautiful again. She worked hard, put herself back together again, and then…" his words trail away as he shakes his head.

"She still is beautiful," I say, knowing my words are risky. I swallow down the fear, because the truth is important.

My father's eyes widen a fraction, his chin slowly tilting as he brings his cold stare back to the mirror, where he takes my gaze ransom.

Tap, tap, tap.

The sound invades again, but I push it out, enthralled by his eyes and his words.

"*You* are beautiful," he insists, crouching back down to lean in to me. "You, my dear, are perfection. You can have any man you want, do you know that?" The air goes ice cold. His fingers brush lightly over my cheekbone, slipping into the tips of my loose, blonde curls. "But you're rotten inside. You're your mother's cancer."

"No," I whimper, chills running sharply down my spine as his fingers roll down my locks and land on the back of my neck. "That's not true."

"You're responsible for what you've taken from your mother now, Elise. Don't waste her beauty, do you understand? She passed it on to you, my dear. Harness it," he lets go of my hair and rises, his stance rigid, "and own it."

My entire frame is quivering now, the shaking causing my teeth to chatter. "I don't understand."

A small, mocking smile twists his lips, and I bite down on my lip to restrain the terror coursing through my veins. This man is relishing in my discomfort. He is not my father. I don't know this man. I've always known him to be nasty when he drinks, but this…this is something else.

"You've never been with a man, have you, Elise?"

I blanch at his question, my shoulders caving forward as I work to hold myself upright on the vanity stool. My stuttering is uncontrollable. "Nnnoo—no."

"*Mmm.*" He nods slightly, eyes dropping to my chest, lingering until my skin crawls. They glaze over with something perverse, and I squirm away from his appraisal. "When you're with a man, you will. You'll see." He breaks his stiff stance and turns, his limbs loosening as he staggers away toward my bedroom door. He mumbles incoherently and disappears, and the sound finally breaks through.

Tap, tap, tap.

I gasp and jolt upright in my bed. I'm 23, not 17, and I'm in my own apartment, not my old bedroom back on Blackbird Lane. My skin is drenched with sweat and my chest is heaving with the memories of that night, when my father poisoned me. It was also the night I'd slipped out my bedroom window to sleep over at Tee's house. She'd stayed up with me until 3 a.m., feeding me soup and hot chocolate to calm my nerves.

That weekend I'd lost my virginity to Riley Donovan. He'd told me I was good at giving head—the best he'd ever had—and I believed him. It was like winning a metal. A weight was lifted and I could breathe again, but that didn't last long. Mom grew sicker and I was consumed with graduating. It didn't leave much time for boys. Before I knew it, I'd walked the stage and Tee had moved away, and that's when the real search for redemption began—the quest to expel the same vileness in me that made my mother sick.

College. Beginning with Skyler Marks, from English Composition.

On and on my conquests went, until I dropped out of college and moved on to more local pickings while I worked at Stella's.

Tap, tap, tap.

The sound is still light, but more pronounced now—a knocking, I think. I scramble from bed and brush my matted hair away from my forehead, reaching over the nightstand for the alarm clock. Two o'clock p.m.

"Shit." I tear across the bedroom to my front door. The tapping stops as I open up, and overcast light hits me, causing me to wince.

"Elise," Ryder says breathily, eyeing me up and down in concern. "What the hell…are you okay?" He makes a move for me but I back up, working to cover myself. It's pretty useless. I'm in my usual sleeping attire: tank top and panties.

"Hey," I reply, my voice coarse. "I'm sorry, I…I don't know how I slept so late. I took a nap and…"

"It's okay," he says warily, glancing inside my apartment. "Are you feeling okay? Can I come in?"

"Yeah." I step aside and he hesitantly strides inside, his cautious gaze raking over me. "Jesus, you're sweating." He steps toward me in a flash, his hands reaching for my shoulders.

"I'm fine."

"You're shaking, too. Elise? What's going on?"

I pull away from his grasp, clearing my throat. "I need some water, do you want anything?"

"Huh? No." He watches me as I walk to the kitchen for a bottle of water. I crack the lid and chug it quickly, taking the whole thing down in a few gulps. The empty plastic crackles in my hand, stabbing at the quiet space. "Hey, if you're not feeling well, we don't have to do this today."

"No," I set the empty bottle down and turn to face his direction, unable to fix my gaze on him, "I want to go. Just give me a few minutes to get ready."

"Okay…"

I walk to the bedroom and shut the door, bee lining it for the shower. I emerge fifteen minutes later, feeling fresher and more alert. My wet hair is tied up into a smooth bun and my face is bare, but my clothes are crisp and neat and my mind is less foggy.

"Sorry to keep you waiting like this. I hate to make us late for Thanksgiving dinner. Where are we going? Is what I'm wearing okay?"

Ryder's eyes scan my cranberry red boat-neck sweater and dark jeans with a nod. "You look gorgeous.

Of course, whatever you want to wear is fine."

I nod stiffly and drink in his carefree flannel and jeans, pausing when my eyes land on his boots. "Do you plan on hiking or something?" I laugh lightly, feeling like my sense of humor has finally returned since waking from my nightmare.

"Not exactly," he answers, his features relaxing a bit. "Why, would you like me to take you on a Thanksgiving Day hike?"

"Not exactly," I drawl, lifting my bag from the kitchen counter. "You ready?"

"Sure." He waits for me to join him and we walk down to his Jeep, where he opens the passenger door.

"How gentlemanly of you," I croon with a playful smile. He grins back and that dimple is medicinal, like a syringe drawing the tension from my body.

"Don't be fooled," he winks before shutting the door, "I'm not always a gentleman."

Now that, I don't doubt.

Maybe it's his calloused hands, distressed leather belt, or the fine veil of stubble covering his jaw, but something about Ryder tells me he knows how to get his hands dirty, and his manners aren't always in check.

A fine shiver runs down my spine as I watch his confident stride to the other side of the Jeep. He gets in and his woodsy scent engulfs me as he starts the ignition. We drive for about twenty minutes, making small talk and casually flipping through radio stations when it hits me that we're not approaching a neighborhood, but a campground.

"Uh...so you really are taking me for a Thanksgiving Day hike?" I look at him in surprise, not at all prepared for a romp in the mountains. I'm still recovering from my dream and the fact that I slept straight through my alarm this afternoon, not to mention the fact that my black heeled booties aren't very proper for a hike in the woods.

"Before you panic," he says, parking the Jeep and leaning across me to reach the glove compartment, "shut your eyes."

"Shut my eyes?"

"You heard me."

I do as he says and can't help the smile that's forming on my lips. I can hear the smile in his voice and his closeness is causing all of my muscles to lock up. As I hear him open the glove box, I'm swamped with the realization that I want him to kiss me again, the way he did the night of the festival.

But that was a first kiss and I ruined it, and Nate's fingerprints are still branded on my skin.

I hear the rustling of a bag and a soft snap, and then something is touching my lips, but it's not Ryder's mouth. It's sweet and salty and divine. "Open," Ryder says patiently, his tone smooth like silk. My lips part and my tongue is met with luscious chocolate tinged with sea salt. I purr in satisfaction and his finger slides the piece of heaven further onto my tongue. "Nice?"

"*Mmmm*," I hum, more enthusiastically now. "Oh my

God...so good."

"You can open now."

I allow my eyes to drift open, and I'm greeted with his, dark as the chocolate melting in my mouth. I swallow and feel my eyelashes flutter with his closeness, his face just inches from mine.

"I don't believe you, though," he says. He tilts his head slightly. "I need to taste for myself."

A hot rush of breath hits my lips and his mouth presses down onto mine. I melt into the seat, my muscles relaxing from his touch. This is nothing like the first kiss. I lean into it, let him draw me into his warmth. The driver's seat groans as he shifts, cradling my neck and jaw with his rough hands. Our tongues meet and glide, mixing and exchanging the remnants of chocolate, and I moan into his mouth, absorbing the taste.

"Elise," he whispers against me, deepening the kiss. I fall into him, everything plummeting like there's nothing left to live for and today is the apocalypse. My hand finds and unclicks my seatbelt, then his, and then I'm lifting myself from the passenger seat to slide over the console and onto his lap. He pants as he accepts me, a low groan sounding from deep in his throat. It's like a grenade in the quiet car, fueling my desire.

I slip my thighs over him, straddling him in the driver's seat. My hand slips down his chest and grabs one of his, guiding it to my breast. His head falls back against the headrest as I devour him, and he squeezes, rolling his thumb around and around, moaning in satisfaction.

Things are spiraling out of control fast, but his touch is so gentle, so patient, like he's touching glass. I'm breakable to him, but the pressure is firm and certain.

It makes me want him even more.

My hands glide over his hard abdomen and find their way under his shirt, fumbling with his belt buckle. I'll ride him right here if he'll let me.

"Wait," he breathes, dropping a hand to his belt.

"I got it," I say, undoing the loop. "Keep touching me." I continue undoing his belt while I reach back with my free hand to loosen my hair tie, letting my wet hair fall around my shoulders. I feel naked already, with no powder on my nose or mascara coating my lashes. My hair isn't blown out to perfection, and my lips are natural, but I'm raw and open to him, and it makes me brave.

"Elise, not yet." He smiles against my mouth and brings his head forward, his breathing labored. "I owe you dinner, beautiful."

"I don't want food." I roll my hips to meet his erection and his head snaps back, smacking the headrest.

"Shit, baby, you're killing me here."

"So quit struggling." I lean down and bite his neck, dragging his flesh sharply through my teeth.

He groans. "I don't have anything in here."

"In my bag." I blindly feel my way to the passenger seat for my purse, digging out a condom.

He lets me tear at the wrapper for a second before snatching it from my hand. "Elise, I really want to give you that meal."

I stop kissing him, pulling back to search his eyes for traces of evidence of sarcasm, but I only find sincerity. Our chests rise and fall against each other as our breathing slows, and I slowly shift off of his lap, lazily sliding back into the passenger seat. My head rolls toward him. "You have the restraint of a saint."

"You have a sinful body. There are too many things I want to do to it to qualify as saintly."

"Well, we can't all keep our wings clean."

"My wings are black when I'm near you."

"You're in luck." I straighten my sweater and sit up. "My wings are black all the time."

He huffs in amusement and adjusts himself, securing his belt buckle and tucking the condom in his pocket. His humor fades for a second as he looks out the dash window, then sends me a side glance. "You ready for that meal?"

"Sure, why not?" He helps me out from the Jeep and I register our surroundings, surveying the pitched tent and camping gear, all piled up and arranged at the side of the tent. There's no one else in sight. "Where is everyone? Are you camping all alone out here?"

"I live here."

"You what?" I blink as we stand in front of the large tent, shivering from the harsh whip of the wind.

"I told you not to panic."

"I'm not panicking." Good God, he really is a Boy Scout.

"You're freaked out. It's okay, I understand. But don't

knock it 'til you try it. Come on." He takes my hand and leads me into the tent, zipping up the flap once we're inside. It's a good size tent. We have to duck to stand, but it's not so small that we have to crouch down to our knees.

"Wow," I say, surveying a long horizontal row of paperbacks. The collection is diverse and the spines are so worn, it's hard to make out some of the titles.

"Is that a good wow or a bad wow?"

"It's just so…" I scan the rest of the paperbacks and then the sleeping bag, pillows, and cooler, which is nestled up against a small shelf. "Homey," I decide, eyeing the toothpaste and travel size mouthwash on the shelf. The shelf is handmade and there are all sorts of words carved onto its sides, kind of like Ryder's tree tattoo.

"It gets me by."

"So, when you said you move around a lot…"

"I pitch a tent, yeah. I've lived out of my Jeep, too." He glances at me cautiously, but if he's expecting me to be freaked out, he's going to be disappointed.

"You really are free," I say, moving to sit down on his sleeping bag. I cross my legs and look around, instantly feeling cozy. "I dig it."

"You...you do?"

"Yeah." I shrug, extending my hand to his. "What, did you expect me to run?"

He takes my hand and lets me pull him down to the sleeping bag, where he scoots next to me and mimics my posture. "Maybe a little."

"I'm not your ex."

"No, you're definitely not. Ah, hey, that's not why I brought you here—"

I sway to the left and bump my shoulder into his. "I know," I say. "So, where's this Thanksgiving dinner you promised me? And didn't you say you have a dog?"

"Oh, now you're in a rush to eat?" He smirks and sweeps a lock of hair over my shoulder, brushing it back as he stares at me thoughtfully. "I do. His name's Duke. You'll meet him soon."

"Well, don't tease me."

"Right this way, baby." He rises and offers me a hand, pulling me up. He unzips the tent and we step back out into the cool, damp air. We begin walking down the main dirt path, leading away from the campsite. "Everyone's really excited to meet you."

My steps slow. "Everyone? Everyone who?"

"You'll see." He reaches out and brushes his thumb over my cheekbone. "I love this look on you, by the way."

"What look?"

"No makeup. It's sexy."

"Seriously?" I find myself fidgeting under his appraisal, so I fall back into a stride, keeping our fingers linked.

"Why does that surprise you?" he asks as he resumes the lead. "You're a beautiful woman, Elise. Inside and out, no makeup or hair products necessary."

I want to say, *You don't know my insides. You don't know I just fucked Nate. You don't know the damage I'm capable of.*

But I remain quiet, letting him guide me through the woods.

"You know what I don't understand?" Ryder breaks the silence, with his curiosity.

"What's that?"

"Why you seem confused by my impression of you. You know you're sexy as hell, and you have the confidence to match. You're bold. So, why the confusion?"

"I'm not sure what you mean." My voice is breezy and I look away, pretending to admire the tall, majestic tree trunks surrounding us.

"What are you hiding, Elise Duchamp?" He smiles and watches me for a moment. "You should know I'm pretty persistent when I want to know something."

"Is that a threat?" I retort, sending him my most devious grin.

"Something like that."

The mood lightens, but our banter is interrupted by sounds of music and laughing. "What's that?"

"*That*," Ryder says, dropping my hand to slip an arm around my waist, "is the sound of a good time. Come with me." He squeezes me closer and begins to hustle, his excitement making me giddy as we trail around a cluster of trees toward the source of the noise.

"Ryder, my man!" a voice hits us, salty and cordial. "Is this her?"

"Hey Richard," Ryder replies, looking between me and the man. "Yup, this is her. Elise, this is Richard, a good neighbor of mine." He whistles over Richard's shoulder, calling to something in the distance. A black Labrador retriever trots over to us, and Ryder crouches down to give the dog a good rub on the head. "And this is Duke," he says, looking down at the dog fondly. "Rich watches him for me sometimes."

"Hi," I say, extending a hand to Rich. "Nice to meet you."

"Same to you, gorgeous, same to you. We've been hearing a lot about you around these parts lately."

"Oh?" Heat rushes my cheeks as I turn my attention to Duke. The dog gives me a sloppy kiss and rolls over to let me pet his belly. This guy Richard has long, curly hair, tied back in a ponytail. He's got kind eyes and an even kinder smile, and a bandana wraps around his temples. His clothes are gritty and for all I know, he brews his own beer and sings "Kumbaya" near the fire every night. One glance at the rest of the crowd here, and I'd venture to guess they all do.

Do these people know me the way the rest of Gig Harbor does?

"Oh yeah, Ryder here has told us all about you."

I rise from petting Duke and my surprise intensifies as I look to Ryder, who's grinning slyly at me. "I might have mentioned you a time or two."

"Hey," Richard laughs, leaning in like he's about to tell me a secret, "don't let this boy fool you. He's a smart son of a bitch and knows the hand he's playing."

"Okay, Rich, time for me to get my girl some food,"

Ryder chides. He rustles up a stray stick from the ground and tosses it, giving Duke a signal. Duke runs off to play and Ryder's arm resumes its position around my waist. I'm swept away from Richard and led toward a smoking charcoal grill and an old wooden picnic table. The way Ryder calls me his girl doesn't escape me, but I don't bother correcting him.

"Take your pick," Ryder says proudly, waving to the array of food scattered on the table.

"Classy," I laugh, nodding to the plates of hot dogs and hamburgers, tubs of coleslaw, and bags of potato chips.

"Hey, I never promised fancy." He hands me a paper plate and a beer, then studies me for a moment, chewing his lip as he does. "Are you freaking out again?"

"None of this freaks me out, Ryder."

"Good, because these are the best damn burgers you'll ever taste." He holds my gaze for a second more and then breaks away, filling his plate with the Thanksgiving cookout fare.

I join him in loading my plate with a little bit of everything, and then Ryder guides me around the campsite, introducing me to a handful of people I know I'll forget the names of in a matter of minutes. I am never good at names, and this entire situation is beyond overwhelming. Instead of judgmental stares, I get hearty hugs and handshakes. Instead of snide comments, I get laughter and grins all around. The people don't know the dirt I'm carrying around, right here, on their front lawn.

We sit on tree stumps around a campfire, feasting on grilled meat with all the fixings and chatting about all of the things we're thankful for. Ryder is thankful for freedom, as are many of his friends, while others ponder the luxury of warm food and the company of good friends. When all eyes are turned on me, I say I'm grateful for today's invite. A woman named Cindy squeezes my shoulder good naturedly, and Richard cracks me open another beer.

"Sun's going down soon, man," Richard says, lighting up a blunt. He passes it around the fire and we all share. "You going to take Elise to see Stevie?"

"Stevie?" I ask, taking a sip of my beer. Duke settles down at Ryder's feet, content with a bone Rich gave him.

"I don't know," Ryder says to Richard, "do you think she would approve?"

"I think she would," Richard nods solemnly, then bursts out laughing. "Go on, man, what are you waiting for? Scat! Duke's staying with me tonight in the RV. It's too cold for him in that tent of yours." He waves us off and Ryder grabs a flashlight from one of the picnic benches. Saying goodnight to everyone, Ryder gives Duke a pat on the head, then takes my hand to lead me away from the party, toward another path that branches off into the nearby woods.

"Are you going to tell me who Stevie is? Please don't say your ex." I give him a pout, jutting my bottom lip out.

"You have your secrets, I have mine," Ryder says, his warm eyes twinkling like the twilight that's quickly descending upon us.

I don't say another word, letting him guide me along the dim path. Branches snap and twigs crack at our feet, and the wind picks up, lashing at my neck and shoulders like a harsh whip.

Ryder switches on the flashlight and comes to a dead stop, leaning down to lift me off my feet. "Let me warm you up," he says, sweeping me up into his arms. He cradles me against his chest and I nuzzle into his neck, feeling him shiver from my cold lips pressing into his skin. "We're almost there."

"You still haven't told me where we're going."

"To meet Stevie."

"Ryder," I groan, kissing his neck.

"Patience, baby." A few seconds later, I'm placed onto my feet and I'm met with a large, black telescope. "Elise, meet Stevie."

I glance at the telescope and then back at Ryder. "You named a telescope."

"I did."

"Care to share what compelled you to do such a thing?"

"Fleetwood Mac," Ryder says nonchalantly, shrugging his shoulders. "Speaking of," he raises a finger and pulls out his iPod, thumbing through a playlist. "Richard, the crew, and I all chipped in and bought Stevie. Tonight's the perfect night for star gazing. Come here." He slides his iPod in his jacket pocket and walks me up to the telescope, placing one earbud in my ear and the other in his, stationing me in front of him. His arms wrap around me from behind, and he leans down to brush his lips against my earlobe, triggering a wave of pleasure down my spine.

"The sky's so clear," I say, tilting my head back to look up. The day's gloomy cloud cover has dissipated and is now replaced with a stark black canvas of sparkling stars. The night is crisp and fresh, and Ryder's right. It's the perfect night for star gazing.

"It's something, huh? And to think it's all for free." He presses up against me from behind, aligning his legs with mine, and burrows into me, holding me snugly in his arms. "Nature's always the best entertainment. You can't see much with this thing. It's a piece of crap, actually. But it's better than nothing." He bends slightly and adjusts something on the telescope, gesturing for me to take a peek. "Give it a try, baby."

I accept the invitation and reach up to hold the telescope, squinting to get a good look through the lens. Fleetwood Mac croons dreamily as we speak. "I haven't done this in…well, ever, I think."

"You've never looked at the sky like this?"

"Never."

"You've been missing out," he says, dropping a hand to my hip. "My dad used to teach me all about the stars and shit. He loved telling me about the planets and different galaxies. That was before."

"Before?"

He shakes his head against the back of mine. "Yeah,

when he was cool. Before all the college bullshit."

I hum in realization, recalling the way his parents had pressured him to go to an Ivy League school. "So you guys had good times…before."

"Yeah. Yeah, we did."

I release my grip on the telescope and crane my neck to the side, letting him have a turn. I study him as he looks up, wanting to run my fingers through his hair and taste his lips on mine again.

I don't move.

"What about you?" he asks, focusing hard. "You and your parents get along?"

My throat goes dry but I fight for words. "Nah, not really."

"Sorry to hear. Do they live here, in Gig Harbor?"

"Did."

"Oh, what, did they move away?"

"My mom died, and my dad moved to L.A."

"Shit," he pulls his head back from the telescope, looking down at me. "Sorry, Elise."

"Thanks."

"So, your dad moved to L.A.? Did he get remarried or something?"

"Yeah. She looks like me, actually. Close to my age, too."

"Damn."

"Fucked up, right?"

He nods, watching me carefully as I lift my gaze back up to the sky. "How did your mom…"

“Cancer.” My skin turns icy, prompting me to break out into a fit of uncontrollable shivers. As I say the dreaded word, my father’s voice haunts the air, reaching into the deepest part of me. “You wanna head back to the tent?”

When I return my gaze to Ryder, he blinks. “Uh... sure, yeah.” He tilts his head for a second, scanning something over my shoulder. “Sorry, you’re probably freezing.”

I am freezing. On the inside and out. But I don’t want to think about that. All I want is to go back to Ryder’s tent and pick up where we left off in his Jeep. The stars aren’t lonely up there, hanging with such bright, spotless company. As for me, I am drowning in a sea of longing. I need to be seen, to be touched, to be heard. And Ryder’s affection is the remedy.

CHAPTER 9

The air in the tent is warmer and stuffy. I slip off my jacket and crawl onto Ryder's lap, stationing my knees on each side of him. He welcomes me, drinking me in. His eyes rake down, then back up, and his arms move to encase me against him. I look down into his soulful gaze, running my fingers through his hair just as I've been wanting to. The soft crackle of the fire outside seeps into the tent, mixing with the music Ryder's turned on. I recognize it: "Born to Die" by Lana Del Rey.

"Touch me," I whisper against his mouth, pulling lightly on his bottom lip with my teeth. I bring my arms up and rest my elbows on top of his shoulders, tangling his hair tighter between my fingers.

"This position feels familiar," he laughs under his breath, smiling into my kiss. He cups my head, skimming my cheek lightly. I feel as if I'll shatter in his hands. "How do you want it, baby?"

"Like this."

"Is this your favorite?" He subtly rolls his hips up,

meeting me with a soft thrust.

"Yes." With him, it will be. I couldn't hold back the truth if I tried. I'm rarely on top, and when I am, it's with a man who doesn't know how to touch me. And one who certainly doesn't look at me the way Ryder does.

His hands find the hem of my sweater and slip underneath, slowly creeping up. They explore the sides of my torso, then glide down my rib cage before climbing back up to the bottom curves of my breasts. I whimper and dip my hips, prompting a sharp hiss from his lips. He pulls back from my mouth and gasps slightly, grazing his fingers along my curves, running them from side to side. He plays with each swell, taking his time feeling their weight.

Another whimper breaks free from my throat and his control slips.

His hands become more desperate, cupping and kneading my breasts, groping hard at my nipples. He stops abruptly, reaching down to snatch the hem of my sweater up and over my head. My bra goes right with it, and I hear the fine sound of a zipper beneath me, feel him tugging at the button of my jeans. I don't wait for him to undo it, instead reaching for his jacket. I shrug it down his shoulders and work fast over the buttons of his flannel shirt.

"I can't wait to feel you," he breathes, glancing down as I work to undress him. His mouth doesn't wander far from mine, nipping and sucking at my lips as I go. "Can I taste you first?" he asks when I reach the bottom button.

My throat locks up and I forget how to speak.

No one's ever asked me like that before.

I nod softly and let his shirt slide down his arms. It gathers at his wrists and he discards it to the side, then shifts to lower me down on my back in front of him. I'm waiting for him to sense Nate all over me, to freeze and turn disgusted, to cast me out of his home. Instead, he slides my jeans down my legs and trails one finger along my panty line. The sensation makes my skin burn and I wiggle against his fingertip.

"There it is." He continues teasing my panty line, his eyes falling on my tattoo. It's just below my right hip bone. "What does it say?" He grazes his thumb over the birdcage and then skims the bird flying from the open door. The bird carries a heart with an inscription. "Quand on veut, on peut," I say. "When one wants, one can. The French equivalent for *where there's a will, there's a way.* "

His gaze lifts and burns me for a moment. "I love it. Just like I love this," he says, kneeling in front of me. He sits back on his heels and appraises me. I can feel his gaze make a lazy trail from my eyes to my lips, then down the slope of my neck. It lingers on my breasts and slithers down to my navel, finally landing on the panty line he's been playing with. "Seeing you bare, wet, and mine." He lowers himself to my thighs.

I have to look away.

"Elise," he breathes against my inner thigh. "Don't take your eyes off me."

I don't speak, just hook my thumbs into the sides of my panties and start to peel them down my hips.

His hands reach out and stop me. "Let me." He maintains his stare, but I can't give him what he wants. I can't hold the contact. He finishes peeling my panties off and his head floats back down, his mouth just inches from my clit. "Delicious," he whispers, sliding two fingers inside of me just as he leans in to lick slowly. My back arches and I bow off the sleeping bag at the feel of his tongue.

"Shit," I pant, my hands drifting down to his head.

"Elise, your eyes." His fingers glide deeper inside as his tongue flicks my clit. The pleasure is so deep, so razor sharp, I can't focus on anything else but his touch. "Stay with me, baby."

He pumps his fingers back and forth and my lids flitter open. I roll my head slightly so I'm able to look down at him. His penetrating chocolate eyes hammer into me and he rewards me with another luscious lick. He pumps his fingers harder as he works me with his tongue and I begin to grind against him, the rhythm he's setting sending me coasting into a tumultuous storm. It's brewing inside and out, rattling my bones, and everything about it makes me squirm.

"Ryder, oh my God." The pressure of his tongue is too much, sending me to the edge too fast, too soon, but I can't pull away. I wriggle beneath him as I feel the build, but his hands clamp down on my hips and he holds me still, pressing me into the sleeping bag. "Ryder, fuck!"

He groans against me, his tongue thrashing harder and harder. I'm going to explode. His neighbors, nearby park rangers, and all of Snow White's little animal friends are going to find pieces of me strewn across this tent, because he's turning me inside out and I can't fucking hold myself together.

I resort to begging. "Please," I cry, shamelessly guiding his head against me, "oh please, please, please." I feel the thrum of a laugh deep in his throat—a smug, really fucking sexy laugh that reverberates sublimely against me, causing a desperate gasp to rise from my chest. A beat passes before he increases the friction of his tongue while thrusting a third finger inside of me.

An explosion of light sails over me and I free fall into a blanket of clouds and stars and pale moonlight. The universe wraps its arms around me and wrings me dry, until it has taken every last drop from my veins. I shout Ryder's name and jerk beneath him. His hands turn iron-clad on my hips, the pressure of his mouth unyielding as I seek relief. I twitch and twist from left to right, and the warmth of his mouth finally lets up. I hear the tear of a wrapper and another zipper, and his coarse hands slip underneath the small of my back. He tenderly lifts me up and guides me back onto his lap, his hand grasping the nape of my neck.

Our eyes meet.

"You're dangerous," Ryder says. "Bad fucking news, baby." He draws me up and then sinks me slowly down, until he's buried deep, stretching me completely. We both release an unrestrained breath, adjusting to the sensation. He grasps tighter at my neck, bringing his forehead to mine. I'm able to hold his gaze longer this time, relishing in the way he prompts me to ride him. His fingers dig into my hips and urge them on, rocking them back and forth. Moaning, he tilts his head to suck at my neck.

My rhythmic waves are fast, the soft graze of Ryder's teeth on my flesh drawing a long, feral moan from my throat. "Damn it," I hiss against his shoulder, taking him deeper and deeper with each new wave. It's then that my eyes begin to drift shut, and I begin to grant myself the luxury of allowing my head to fall back. He doesn't seem to mind. He's too preoccupied with his tongue and his teeth, and his hands are frantically gripping at my back, grasping at me like I'm the air he needs to breathe.

"Slow down, baby," he works to ease the roll of my hips, "let me watch you. I like to watch."

I'm burning from head to toe, and my body has taken the reins, but I focus on slowing my pace. It's worth it to watch him watching me. If that's what he wants, it's his.

My waist rolls and I rise, then glide back down in descent. His chin drops slightly, his eyes crawling up and down my silhouette as I move, his jaw slightly agape. With blazing eyes, he leans forward every few seconds to steal a taste, drawing my skin into his mouth and sucking hard. He especially likes my breasts. He can't keep his eyes or mouth off of them, and I have no problem with his obsession, except for the fact that it's speeding up the simmering pool building low in my stomach. My inner thighs are buzzing, my clit throbbing painfully with the impending release.

"Let me hear you again," he says gruffly, running his nose up the length of my exposed throat. "Come for me." His words are a siren, and I surrender to them, holding nothing back. I let go, allowing sensation to slowly unravel me. I'm just about there.

Flashes of Nate pinning me to his apartment wall pierce my thoughts, followed by visions of the few times Christian let me ride him. His hands were strong, his words powerful, but no matter how careful he was with me, I was never fragile in his arms. Not like this. Not like I could shatter into a million pieces.

My mind quickly expels the images so intent on steamrolling me. They rush forward at a hundred miles an hour, relentless and showing no mercy, but I hit them like a dam and they crash. I focus on the delicious sounds Ryder's making beneath me: pained moans and tight, low growls as he pumps deep, mouthwatering thrusts into me, over and over again. The gentle determination of his hands distracts me further, and I realize I'm in trouble. He has it all wrong.

He's the dangerous one.

We both come on loud, stilted shouts, and it takes a few seconds for me to roll to a complete stop before I can manage to catch my breath. I teeter to the side and fall off his lap. He sighs and flops onto his back, letting his legs go slack against the sleeping bag. He lifts his head and slides his arm underneath, propping himself up. I move to lie next to him and snuggle up to his chest. His arm drifts down and lands perfectly around my waist, like a puzzle piece that's been missing. Our breathing begins to even out and Lana Del Rey's soft, sensual vocals continue to play as we lie there quietly, listening. The music begins to lull me into a deep rest. Sleep finally takes me, and I gladly give in.

Snip, snip, snip.

A slicing sound shreds my thoughts, cutting deeply.

"Darling, please," my mom's voice splinters through, claiming my full attention. "Don't make her do this. It's cruel."

"She has to learn, Elena," my dad says sternly. His face appears and I realize I'm sitting at the vanity table again, facing the mirror like I always am. My mother stands to my left, her arms crossed nervously across her chest. She's biting her nail, her brow and lips pinched in concern. My father is directly behind me, his reflection forming a halo over my golden blonde hair. "Get rid of it, Elise."

"But Dad," I cry, feeling my body shake on a sob, "you always tell me my hair is perfect. Don't you want me to be beautiful, like Mom?"

"You've forgotten what a gift you have," he replies, his hand hovering over my shoulder, handing me something sharp and shiny. "You want to spend time with dykes? Then it's time you look like one."

"Please," I choke, unable to rip my eyes from the large

pair of scissors he's forcing into my hands.

"Darling," my mom says with urgency, "this has gone far enough. You've made your point."

"Keep quiet, Elena. Don't tell me how to parent my daughter. She will do this." His cold, clammy fingers hit mine, shoving the scissors into my hands. He closes my fist, forcing me to grip them and I squirm, trying desperately to pull my hands away. "Elise," he barks harshly, "that's enough. Either you do it, or I will."

His words are so callous, I try appealing to his paternal side. I drop the scissors and swivel around to reach for him, grabbing and pleading for him to hug me. If he'll just touch me, just hold me. "Dad, I love you. Please, don't do this to me. I'm sorry you're upset with me—please!" I manage to wrap my arms around his waist, but he peels them off and pushes them away, bending down to snatch the scissors up from the floor. His fingers dig into my hair, grasping at the roots, then clamp down hard as he turns me back around to face the mirror.

"Darling, no!" my mom cries, jolting forward to intervene.

"Elena, get out." My father blocks her and gathers up another fistful of my hair. "Get out *now*, before I do something I'll regret."

"I'm begging you, darling, stop. Please, please God, stop!"

Snip.

I cry out at the first cut. My mother covers her mouth, tears streaming down her cheeks. "Why are you doing this?" she sobs, her hands trembling.

"I said get out, you stupid, hideous whore. Out!"

My mother finally breaks, her entire frame caving in on itself. She flees from the bedroom, leaving me at the mercy of my father. He grabs another fistful of hair, then another, each slice more frantic than the first. His movements are rough and erratic, my head being yanked every which way as he hacks at my long locks. My hysterical cries have been replaced with deep, internal wails, sobs that can only be heard on the inside, beating their heavy drum at my soul. My heart is thrashing against my rib cage and I pray for it to be quick.

Someone or something must hear me, because my father's hands let go.

The scissors drop to the vanity table with a loud clatter, and a cloud of blonde hair hovers all around me, strands floating down to my shoulders. Chunks tumble off my chest and arms, plummeting to the carpet. My father looks at me once through the mirror and then stalks away, shutting the bedroom door quietly behind him, as if he didn't just manhandle me and massacre my perfect blonde hair.

In less than a minute, his and my mother's screams commence.

I drown them out, rocking on the stool, my gaze frozen on the reflection staring back at me. My hair is slaughtered—choppy and uneven, misplaced and abused.

Snip, snip, snip.

The sounds still puncture my thoughts, but I'm coming around, feeling balmy, compassionate hands rubbing up and down the sides of my arms. "Elise?" Ryder's voice slips through the cracks. "Wake up, Elise."

I begin to stir, shifting in Ryder's arms. My eyes flutter open and I stare up at him. I freeze and blink, then bolt upright in the sleeping bag, grasping my hair. I tug on the long blonde waves, rolling the ends between my fingertips. My cheeks are damp and my chest is heaving.

"Hey," Ryder says soothingly, "are you okay? You were crying in your sleep."

I drop my hair and bring my knees forward, pulling them tightly to my chest. "Yeah," I sigh, "just a bad dream."

"You wanna talk about it?"

"No," I answer quickly. "What time is it?"

"Just past seven." His concerned expression softens when he sees me begin to calm down.

"Wow." My voice is groggy as I process the time. We'd slept the whole night straight through. I hadn't woken once.

"I was beat. You wore me out last night." He chuckles deeply, and the smooth, sexy sound ignites a tingle deep in the pit of my stomach. Thankful for the distraction, I push out a tired breath and crawl on top of him, straddling him and brushing myself over his cock. He's hard and ready. "Damn," he groans, letting his head fall back onto the sleeping bag pillow.

"I'm not done with you yet." I smirk and lower myself

down his body, bending to tease him with a lick straight up his shaft. Feeling him twitch against my lips wakes me right up. "*Mmmm*, can I have more?" My eyes roll up and lock on his, and he's enraptured, staring at me, dropping his gaze from my eyes to my lips, then down to his cock, willing me to make the connection.

Damn, he's beautiful.

He answers by lifting his hips, bringing the tip to my bottom lip, slowly thrusting himself into my mouth. He watches the action and gives his cock a slight roll, rotating himself around with indulgent exploration. His smile is lopsided and he has absolutely no shame in using my mouth for his pleasure.

I twirl my tongue around the tip and then dip to take him all the way, sucking hard as I pull back, drawing a deep groan from his chest. His eyes drift shut and his jaw clenches. "Oh, fuck yes. Damn, baby." I repeat the motion and a surge of wet warmth swells my inner thighs.

He is singlehandedly the most sexy, gentle man I have ever laid hands on, and he is completely oblivious to who and what I am.

That thought should be a buzz kill, but instead, it only heightens the urgency of the moment. Who knows how long I'll get to be with a man like Ryder. This could be the last time I ever feel this way in someone's presence. I feel utterly spoiled and wrapped in luxury, and any second, it's going to be ripped from my grasp.

I suck and take him deeper.

He exhales harshly through clenched teeth, and his

fingers are pressing into my scalp now, urging me on. At the feel of his climbing desperation, I flatten my tongue for a few strokes, and then roll and suck, roll and suck, creating a pattern designed to drive him to the brink.

It's working.

"Elise," he chokes, "shit, if you keep that up..."

I increase my speed, humming against him. The vibrations resonate from my throat to his hot, sensitive skin. His waist jerks at the sensation and he bucks his hips, trying to pull free from my mouth, but I give him a taste of his own medicine and latch onto him, pinning him to the sleeping bag while closing my lips harder around his cock.

No way in hell is he going anywhere.

My hands glide up his strong torso and dig into his skin, my pace unyielding. His frame stiffens beneath my fingertips and a garbled moan spills its way from his throat, riding a wave all the way down his body. His hips continue to jerk and he convulses, coming hard in my mouth. I make most guys wear a condom—even repeats, like Christian and Tim. Especially Brad. The thought doesn't even cross my mind until Ryder is coating my throat.

My inner thighs are drenched now, and I've never wanted anything more than I want him inside me right that moment. I swallow and moan in pure gratification, reveling in the feel of him hitting the back of my throat as he pumps hard.

"Damn it, Elise!" he sighs, lifting his head to peer

down at me.

"Is there a problem?" I ask coyly as I pull my mouth away and rise to sit up on my knees. I stare down at him triumphantly and totally brazen, still completely naked from the night before as I drag my wrist across my mouth. My tongue darts out and sweeps across my bottom lip, licking the last remnants of him away. I savor those last few drops.

"Every time I go to kiss you now, all I'm ever going to be able to think about is what you just did to me with that lush mouth of yours." His breathing is still heavy, his brown eyes glazing over with satisfaction and something else, something I don't think I've ever seen before. It jars me for a moment, but I quickly brush it away when I'm reminded of the ache between my legs.

"Are you saying there will be future kisses?"

"Do you want there to be future kisses?"

My playful smile droops a bit. I clear my throat and roll off of him, sprawling out onto my back. I run my hands down my neck and breasts, lingering at my nipples for a beat before letting one hand wander down to the junction of my thighs. I rub my fingers over the moisture and I look over to find him doing exactly what I want him to. What he likes to do.

Watch.

"Just what do you think you're doing?" he asks quietly, with that husky lilt. He turns onto his side, leaning up on his elbow. His hand snakes out to touch me where I'm touching myself, but I bat him away and grin deviously.

"Showing you what you do to me." And giving him what he wants. I'm compelled to now that I know what he likes.

"Elise," he warns teasingly, "I'm a weak, weak man." He makes another reach for me, but I bump his hand away again, quickly covering and cupping myself.

"Just watch," I whisper, closing my eyes and purposely arching my back. He swallows hard, the sound filling the quiet tent. Even though my eyes are closed, I can feel his gaze crawling all over me. I press down and then give myself a stroke, rubbing up, back, and forth. My legs fall open and my other hand lands on my breast, exploring and groping. "Do you see?" I ask, letting my eyes drift open into narrow slits.

"Oh, yeah," he breathes, "I see." His lids are hooded, eyes smoky, flaming with desire. His whole body is tense as he restrains himself from pouncing on me.

My fingers increase their friction, gliding with more precise, intense strokes. Quiet whimpers fight their way from my throat and the buzzing between my thighs is becoming unbearable. I won't last long. Going down on him was my foreplay, and I'm ready to rupture. I call on the memories from just seconds ago: taking him in my mouth, watching him grin wickedly at me as I tasted and sucked, feeling him swell at the back of my throat.

I'm so turned on, so close to tipping the edge that I don't register the light brush of more fingers grazing my inner thigh until my hips lift in anticipation. The sneaky bastard.

I smile.

"You're so damn beautiful," Ryder murmurs at my ear. He's moved closer, still sitting up on his elbow as he looks down, enjoying the show. He's rapt with attention, grazing his fingers along the insides of my thighs, his knuckle bumping mine as I work myself. His words smack into me and then bounce off, ricocheting to some unknown, lost place.

There's a lag in my building orgasm and I flinch, wiggling away from his touch.

Ryder's mouth meets my shoulder, kissing me like I'm golden. The touch is so sacred, so benevolent, I can't concentrate. "Shit," I breathe, squeezing my eyes shut as tightly as I can. His fingers touch my forehead and delicately brush my hair back, and once again, I'm afflicted.

I wiggle again, opening my eyes and scrunching up my forehead to escape his fingertips. I stop touching myself and release an exasperated sigh, dropping my arms to my sides. I wait a second before looking at him.

His brow is furrowed in confusion and his expression is a baffled one.

"I don't think I can do this right now," I say, moving to sit up. I immediately start scrambling for my clothes. I need air, and I need it now.

"Wait, what?" Ryder sits up, too, bringing his body up on the sleeping bag in a half crouch. His dazed eyes are darting everywhere, looking back and forth, between me, my clothes, and something in the distance, as if it can offer him an explanation.

"Sorry, I just…I can't right now. I gotta go. I have to work this afternoon." I throw my clothes on and grab my bag, checking to make sure I have everything I need.

"Elise, did I…did I do something? What's the rush? Hey." He reaches for me, but I yank my arm away coldly, not missing the hurt that flashes across his face. He backs up and drops his head, his jaw flexing.

"You didn't do anything wrong. You are… you were amazing. Thank you."

"You're thanking me?"

"Yeah, I had a great time. I'll see you later, okay?" I start for the zipper on the tent door but Ryder speaks again, causing me to fumble with the flap.

"Let me drive you home. You can't walk all that way. It's cold out there."

"I'll be fine."

"You don't know the way."

"There are signs. I'll figure it out."

He's quiet for a beat. I have him there. I vaguely remember seeing signs along the main path that direct you around the campground.

"Hey, I don't know what's wrong, but please don't take off like this. Talk to me."

"I can't, Ryder, I'm sorry." I step out of the tent and inhale a deep breath of cool air. "I need to get home and get ready for work. I'll see you later." I haul ass away from his campsite and toward the main path. I don't look back until I'm halfway to the cluster of trees leading into the woods. One quick glance over my shoulder makes my insides churn.

Ryder's standing there in the tent doorway, holding a blanket loosely around his waist. His gaze follows me, eyes hard, jaw clenched, and I look away.

It's time to go back to the real world. No more rolling around in sleeping bags in the woods with men like Ryder. No more cookouts or hanging with kind hippies near the fire. No more basking in fantasy because fantasy is what fairytales are made of, and my world is no fairytale.

***

The rain's light mist kisses me as I hurry up to my apartment door. I'm tired and desperate for a cup of hot chocolate and a warm shower. I managed to find my way off the campsite and then called for a taxi when I made it to the main road. Thankfully my phone had some juice left, and the sweater I wore for my date with Ryder yesterday was just enough to keep me from freezing.

I step into my apartment to find it just as I'd left it the day before. The Gig Harbor Weekly is open on the kitchen counter and my bathrobe is strewn across the edge of the bed. The pile of bills I've been avoiding is on the coffee table, and the little scrap of paper with notes about the materials I'll need for my French lessons is pinned to the refrigerator. A sigh of relief escapes me. Home.

I toss my keys on the counter and start for the kitchen,

but there's a knock on the door. I freeze.

"Elise?" a voice comes from outside, uncertain and urgent. It's not Ryder's, so I relax a little, but wince when another knock sounds. This voice isn't any better. In fact, it's the very last one I want to hear right now.

I unlock the bolt and answer. "Nate, now isn't a good time."

"I'm sorry, but I need to talk to you. Can we talk?"

"No, no we can't."

I go to shut the door, but he thrusts out his palm and stops it with a smack. "*Please.*"

"Two minutes," I say, delivering my best glare.

"That's all I need." His expression turns cautious as I step aside and let him in.

"So, what's so important?" My tone is flat, completely devoid of emotion. I lead him further into the apartment.

"I think I'm going to break up with Natalie."

My eyes bulge and I swing around to face him. "*What*?"

"I know how it sounds, okay? But being with you..."

"No. Nate, don't even go there." I fucked Nate hoping Natalie would find out and realize she shouldn't treat me like a charity case. I wasn't her friend, and I wasn't trustworthy. She wanted to save me from the town's gossip, wanted to tell everyone who ever spoke ill about my reputation to go screw themselves. But she must've missed the memo that I wasn't looking to be saved.

"I'm serious, Elise." He starts pacing, shaking his head. "Being with you changed something for me."

"Oh, yeah? Like what?" I fold my arms across my chest and look at him blandly.

"I'm different, I don't know how to explain it."

"Well, let me enlighten you, then. You're different because now you're a lying, cheating scumbag. That's what's changed."

He stops pacing. "You seduced me."

"Right, I made you trip and fall into bed with me."

"You did, Elise. You wouldn't let up."

My nostrils flare and I stalk up to him with a heated gaze. "I took what I wanted, when I wanted it. I'm not responsible for what you chose to do with your dick. If you honestly came here to pedal that bullshit, you can turn right back around and pedal it somewhere else." I scoff and whirl toward the door, thoroughly disgusted. He used to be too-sweet-for-his-own-good Nate, all innocent and endearing. Now he's just like me, and I want no part of that mutation.

"I didn't come here to argue or insult you," he speaks softer now, not bothering to make a move for the front door. "You're not listening. I came here because I want to know how you feel about me breaking up with Natalie. I want…"

Oh God, don't say it.

"I can't stop thinking about you. I want to be with you again. I mean, do you think…" He looks at me with puppy dog eyes, the ones that I recognize. They're the only thing giving away traces of Nate's lost naiveté.

I sigh and rub at my forehead. This is Christian

Walker all over again. I can't handle this shit. "Nate, first you come over here blaming me for your decision to cheat on Natalie, and now you're telling me you want to be with me again? You want to know how I feel about you dumping her?" I narrow my eyes and suddenly I can't contain the rage that's building inside of me. Nate steps back a hair, looking frightened. Good. He should be frightened.

"That's not what I meant." He's putting his hands up in the air, slowly stepping backward. "I know how that sounded, but I swear that's not what I meant. I'm just… confused."

"Confused about what?" I snap, cocking my head to the side. "Confused about wanting to fuck me again? I don't think there's anything confusing about that, do you?"

"Elise. Listen to me. Being with you just made me realize I shouldn't be with Natalie. I've been blind or something. I don't know how I didn't see it before. We don't fit."

"Nate," I say evenly, closing my eyes to count to ten, "you need to get out. You need to go home and understand that what happened with us is never going to happen again. Whether you do or don't end things with Natalie is not my problem. Is that clear enough for you?"

My eyes open and I expect to find Nate's puppy dog eyes again, but I find something new: Anger.

There's a gleam there, and a bout of silence stretches between us. His mouth opens slightly and he pauses before choosing his words, a veil of thoughtfulness dropping over his features. "You really don't give a shit, do you?"

"Nate."

"Wow. I see that now. I mean, I thought I saw it before. But I wanted to give you the benefit of the doubt. That's why Natalie wants to be your friend, you know that? Because she likes to see the good in people. She likes to judge someone's character for herself, not base her opinion on what everyone else says." He laughs dryly, scrubbing his hands over his face. "Oh my God, I'm such an idiot."

"You should go." I open the door and create a path for him.

"Can I ask you something?" He smiles at me in complete, dumbfounded wonder. "Why do you do it, huh?"

"I said you should go."

"Come on, Elise. I want to know. Why do you screw half the town and make fools of us, huh?" His eyes squint into thin slivers and they study me. "Why do you ruin people?"

The breath in my lungs stabs at me, forcing words up my throat, but I can't get a grip on them.

"Tell me, damn it," he insists.

Tears brim my eyes and I look away, opening the door wider.

Nate huffs and finally makes his move, barreling toward the doorway. "Forget it," he mumbles. "It's a good thing you're alone, Elise. It's a good thing you keep everyone out. The world's a lot safer when you lock yourself in a cage." He shoulders past me and the cool air drifts into the apartment. His words are hanging there, weighing down like a heavy quilt. I quietly shut the door.

My need for hot chocolate and a shower are sidelined by my need to crawl into bed. The clock on the wall tells me I have at least four hours before I'm due at the diner for my shift. Dragging my feet into the bedroom, I let my body sink into the mattress. I fall flat on my back and look up at the ceiling. There are no answers there, no remedies for the hollowness that I feel. I shift my head and look to the right, at my dream jar. It seems to sparkle. I lift a limp hand and lazily unscrew the lid. Pulling out a wad of bills, I place the money on the nightstand and screw the lid back on. I stare at the bills for what feels like hours before I begin to doze off. Sleep has never felt so good.

CHAPTER 10

It's been a week since I left Ryder naked in his tent. I've been pouring myself into my French audio lessons and focusing on picking up as many extra hours at the diner as possible. Extra Christmas money would be nice, not that I have anyone to shop for, but buying a few extra things for Jay and his family makes me feel good.

Crazy as it may be, I also want to get a gift for Natalie, especially after the snow globe incident.

Since I ran out on her at the diner that day, she has backed off. She has been her kind, polite self, but she has given me space. I don't know whether to be relieved about that or to feel worse about...everything.

Things haven't gone as I expected.

Nate hasn't told her about what happened between us, but he did break up with her. Natalie was a wreck for a few days, having to excuse herself at work a few times in the middle of waiting on tables. I didn't say a word, just cut her a break here and there by taking over the tables when she needed to step out.

Now here I am, entertaining the idea of buying her a Christmas gift. I'm telling myself it's only the courteous thing to do, but when do I ever care about being courteous? And didn't I throw the whole courteous thing out the window when I decided to sleep with Nate?

That isn't the only thing getting underneath my skin this week. My nightmares are getting worse. I blame Ryder, which is completely irrational and probably unfair of course, but since I met him, a ball of discomfort has roiled deep in my stomach and shows no sign of relenting any time soon.

The diner is bustling on Friday morning as I clock in. The regulars have taken over their usual section, and Jay is wiping down the counters as he greets me. "Morning, hon."

"Hey, Jay."

"Hey, Brad's in the kitchen. Said something about needing to speak with you when you got here."

"Okay, thanks. I'll go find him now." I wrap my apron around my waist and tighten my ponytail, swinging over to the kitchen.

"Hey Princess, you're here." He's lifting two plates when he spots me, his smile lighting up.

"Yes sir, I am. What's up? Jay said you needed to talk to me?"

"Yeah, I do—uh hey, Natalie?" He nods over my shoulder when he sees her, giving her an impish grin. "Sorry to ask, but ah, could you run these out to table five?"

"What do I look like to you, huh?" Natalie's eyes sparkle and she grins back.

"You know you love me." He winks, and her cheeks flame as she takes the plates from him. "I owe ya, babe. Thanks." She says hi to me and rolls her eyes, then hustles out of the kitchen.

"*Babe*?" I arch a brow at Brad.

"Hey, don't start on me. It's too damn early in the morning. I've just been helping her work through some stuff since that Nate dude dumped her."

"Uh huh…"

"Elise, don't give me that look."

I raise my hands and lean on one hip. "Just don't hurt her. She's a good girl." My insides cringe as the words come out. What the hell am I saying? "Anyway, what do you need?"

"Come here." Brad pulls at my elbow and gives the cooks a cheeky smile as he tugs us into the pantry. He scoots up into the far corner, along the wall. "I was just wondering if you were up for getting together this weekend. It's been a while. I miss ya."

"You had to pull me in here for that? You have my number, Brad. You're like…my brother, or something. You can call any time."

"You did not just call me your brother."

"God," I drop my head in my hands with a laugh, "that's so not what I meant and you know it."

"Uh huh…"

"I mean, you always call when you wanna hook up.

We've never had to do this—" I swish my hand between the both of us, "you know, because it's just understood."

"I guess you have a point." He puts his hands on his hips and pretends to be deep in thought.

I sigh. "Is that all you needed? Seriously?" I give him a playful jab in the shoulder, turning on my heel to leave the pantry.

"Nope," he grins wide, grabbing my wrist. "I needed this, too." He abruptly pushes me up against the wall and kisses me, tilting my chin up to meet his mouth.

I squirm and push him away. "Brad, come on."

"What's this?" He waves his hands in the air as he beams. "You're my number one girl, Elise. Work with me, here."

I smile with him but quickly stifle it, not wanting to encourage him anymore. "Look, I'm very flattered, Romeo. But I think this has run its course, ya know?"

Brad's smile fades a little as he realizes I'm serious. "You're for real right now?"

"Yeah," I shrug, tucking a rebellious strand of hair behind my ear, "I'm just not feeling it anymore. Nothing personal."

"I can't believe you don't want any of this," he gestures to his body, his eyes wide and ego out of control. He's just playing around, but I know that deep down, even if it's only a shred, there is a part of him that's kind of disappointed. "Elise, you're killin' me here, girl. Why the change of heart?"

"It's just time, Brad. I mean, I was there for you for a

while during all the drama with Karen, but you two are over now, and...ya know, this is just over, too, that's all." I reach up and give him an exaggerated pat on the cheek. "I'm sure you'll get on without me just fine." Pushing off the wall, I saunter off and make my way out of the kitchen.

My mind chews over what I've just decided. I've been thinking about cutting things off with Brad for a while, but never really got around to actually doing it. Brad was always fun, carefree, and easy. Simple.

A certain outdoorsy type with smoky brown eyes and intriguing tattoos crosses my mind. I sweep those thoughts away.

"Hey, Elise?" Natalie asks as I step back out to pick up my first table of the morning. She's still holding back, even coming across a bit timid. I wonder if I should say something about the snow globe. Maybe tell her it's sitting on my bedside, next to my dream jar. Maybe I should ask her how she's been. Damn, I suck at making conversation.

Especially when I've fucked the person's boyfriend. Or ex-boyfriend.

"Hey," I say.

"How's your week going?"

"Okay, thanks. Yours?"

"Okay." She starts fidgeting with her fingers, her gaze bouncing between me and the booths to our left, which are all waiting on service. "I was just wondering if you wanna grab a coffee later. Or maybe lunch? I just checked the schedule. It looks like you don't work a double today, so…"

"Oh." I glance over at the busy cluster of customers waiting to be seated at the front door. There are at least four tables I need to wait on, and Brad is running around as fast as he can, serving plates. I start moving for the hostess stand. "Sure, maybe. Let me uh…let me seat these people and we can chat later, okay?"

"Okay, yeah. Sounds good." She nods quickly and scurries off, and I stride toward the entrance, thankful to have delayed that conversation. "Hey, how are ya? How many?"

"Three, please." I seat the first party and let them know Natalie will be right with them. As I return to the hostess station, I decide to fill up Natalie's section as much as possible between now and the end of our shift. Maybe if I keep her busy enough, she won't have time to ask me about lunch again. I might feel compelled to buy her a Christmas gift in reciprocation, but my feelings are still the same. I cannot be friends with the girl.

My shoulders tense when I greet Tim and his fiancée Cheryl, but I play it cool, giving them a tight smile as I lead them to a booth. I make sure to sit them in Brad's section. Tim plays it cool, too, acting as if he's never seen me in his life, and Cheryl eyes me curiously but remains polite when Tim and I exchange glances. I make my way back to the hostess station for round three, scribbling some notes on the seating chart. I exhale and raise my head to greet the next customer.

My lungs seize up.

"Just one, please," Ryder says, all cool and calm, with a rolled-up newspaper tucked beneath one arm. "Oh, and ah, I'd like your section, please." His expression remains neutral as he holds eye contact, and I begin to stutter in response.

When the hell did I begin stuttering?

"Okay—sure—here…this way." I start to lead him to a far booth on the left side of my section and hand him a menu. "I'll be back to take your order in just a few minutes."

"I already know what I want," he says, before I can slip away. His words root me still, and I find him watching me with a steady gaze. One look at those eyes, and it's abundantly clear that he refuses to be ignored. "I'll make my order now, if that's okay with you."

I swallow down his loaded statement and click my pen. "That's fine. What'll it be?"

"French toast and a coffee, please."

"That's it?"

"For now."

"No problem. I'll have that right out for you." I turn, feeling my stomach roll with the movement, but he stops me again. This time, when I face him, I absolutely cannot escape the intensity in his eyes and the fact that he's ridiculously handsome. It's goddamn unfair.

"You ever read the Weekly's Sorry Secrets column?" he asks nonchalantly, flipping open the paper he's brought with him. "I just started reading it a few weeks ago. There's some crazy shit in there."

"Um…yeah, yeah I do, actually. I didn't think anyone paid attention to that column but me. It's kind of—"

"Cheesy?"

"I was going to say it's a guilty pleasure, but…"

"Why, do you find pleasure in other people's hurt?"

My heart hammers against my chest and then plummets, cracking a few ribs along the way. "No. Yeah, maybe. It's not that, really. It's just—"

"Entertaining?"

"Will you stop putting words in my mouth?" I shift my weight, crossing my arms over my chest. I tear my gaze from his and look down.

"Sorry, am I not giving you a chance to speak? I know that's frustrating, especially when you have something to say, right?"

"Ryder. That's enough."

He sets the paper down and drills holes into me. I force myself to meet his stare, and I see it, now—that indifferent expression he walked in with moments ago is replaced with hurt, and a tinge of anger. "There was so much I wanted to say to you that morning. You just walked out."

I grind my teeth. "I know."

"I'm so confused, Elise. I mean, right in the middle of that—" he lowers his voice and glances discreetly from left to right, "I thought things were going great."

"They were."

"Then what was the problem?"

"Ryder, this really isn't the place or the time."

"I know." He returns his gaze to the newspaper and flips the page. "Which is why I want to take you out when you're done with your shift."

"I don't get off for another four hours."

"I'll wait."

"Ryder—"

"Elise, I'll wait."

"Fine," I sigh, sliding my pen behind my ear. "I'll be back with your breakfast."

He thanks me and busies himself with the paper. I don't make it ten feet before Brad pulls me aside. "Hey girl, homeboy's lady over there keeps eyeing you like she wants to dig her claws into you. She's kinda freaking me out. Is there something I should know?" Brad's eyebrows rise as he gestures over his shoulder to Tim and Cheryl. I scratch at my temple and lower my head, carefully glancing behind me at Ryder. His eyes lift from the paper for a moment and meet mine, but he quickly averts them and resumes reading.

"Cheryl?" I ask quietly.

"Please don't tell me you banged baldy over there."

I smack his shoulder. "Don't call him that."

"Oh damn, you did, didn't you? When was this?" He laughs but his eyes look worried as he glances in Tim and Cheryl's direction. "Jay's brother? Really, Elise?"

"Jay knows," I whisper harshly. "So just leave it alone, Brad. Please?"

"Whatever, Princess." He zips around me for the

kitchen, shaking his head. "Just steer clear of them. He's a prick, anyway."

"You're not telling me anything I don't know." I follow him to put Ryder's breakfast order in, even more on edge now than when I seated Tim and Cheryl. Ryder and Tim are under the same roof, just tables away from one another, and it is making my nerves jump.

Thankfully, I manage to keep busy the rest of the morning, effectively dodging Natalie's lunch invitation. Until it's time to clock out, anyway.

"So, what do you think?" Natalie asks as she removes her apron, all chirpy and smiley. I can tell she's still a little uncomfortable, but she's hiding her timidity well. "You still up for lunch?"

"Actually, I might have to take a rain check." I nod to Ryder, who's still sitting and reading in the same booth he's been sitting in since I waited on him this morning. He's read the whole paper—or most of it, anyway—and then moved on to McCarthy's "No Country for Old Men."

"Oh, okay," Natalie winks, "I understand. I can't believe he's still here. It's getting serious, huh?"

"No," I shake my head, "not at all. I just feel bad blowing him off after waiting for me all morning, you know?"

"It's totally fine." She gently touches my shoulder and adjusts her purse strap. "He's hot. You're crazy if you pass that up for boring ol' me." Laughing, she waves and starts for the door. "Maybe some other time. See ya."

"Um, hey…" I take a step forward and stop, unsure of what to do with my hands. I smooth them over my hair and tighten my ponytail. "I never told you thank you. For the snow globe, I mean. I was going through some shit that day and my head was a mess. I didn't mean to… yeah, anyway, it was a great gift. Really. So, thanks."

"Oh, no," she quickly raises a hand to stop me, "you don't have to…just don't worry about it, okay? I never meant to upset you, and I'm sorry that I did."

"But you didn't." I press my lips together. I want to just come out with it, I want to burst and tell her the truth. But instead, I lie some more. "I was sick that day and I just wasn't myself."

"Yeah, Brad mentioned you had to run out back because you were nauseated or something. I just thought, I don't know." She giggles and looks down. "Maybe I misread things. I thought we were friends, you know? But maybe…maybe that wasn't mutual or something."

My mind is swimming, searching and struggling for the words, but it comes up short. I can't tell this girl we're friends, because we're not. I'm not her friend, anyway. What she's saying is actually an accurate guess, only she's missing the part about me screwing her boyfriend. Despite all of this, I open my mouth to lie some more, to spare her feelings and save my ass, but Ryder appears at my side.

"Hey Natalie," he replies, giving her a small wave. "How've you been?"

"Hey Ryder, good thanks." Her eyes quickly flick

away from mine and land on Ryder. "How about you? You and Elise have plans this afternoon, I see."

"Something like that." Ryder unleashes his sexy dimple and his hand touches the small of my back. I feel his warmth spread to my toes.

"Cool, you guys have fun. I'm off to run some errands. See you guys later?"

"Sure, see ya," I say, giving Ryder a side glance. He's watching me, even as Natalie says her goodbyes.

"Can I steal you away now?" he asks as soon as she's gone.

"I think that can be arranged." Despite my unease, a grin splits my lips and I hurry off to say goodbye to Jay and Brad. Brad smiles cheekily, making sure to let me know he's well aware I ditched hooking up with him for Ryder, but I don't acknowledge the gesture.

As Ryder walks me to his Jeep, I'm beginning to sweat, but I do my best to maintain a composed façade. This has the potential to turn fifty shades of awkward any second. "So, where to?" I ask when I click my seatbelt.

"It's a surprise."

"Uh oh."

He snickers and starts the engine, making conversation about the past week and how his parents want him to fly out to Connecticut for Christmas. He's not thrilled by the invitation, but he's considering it.

"So, what are you doing for Christmas?" he asks as we make our way out of downtown Gig Harbor. "You going out of town or anything?"

"Nope. Just staying home, nothing exciting."

"Wait, by yourself?"

"Yeah."

Ryder glances at me with narrowed eyes and his hands grip the steering wheel. "You're telling me you're going to be alone on Christmas?"

"It's not a big deal." I shrug and look out the passenger window, catching glimpses of the harbor through the winter-worn trees.

"Elise, there's no way you're spending Christmas by yourself. Not happening, sorry."

"I really don't think that's any of your concern."

"Seriously?"

Before I can respond, the Jeep jolts to the right and the tires screech as Ryder rolls us to a hard stop on the side of the road. My seatbelt digs into my chest and my head smacks the headrest as I look around. "What the hell are you doing?" There's nothing around but trees and more trees, and the steep road ahead of us, leading further into the woods.

Ryder unclicks his seatbelt and turns the car off, yanking the keys from the ignition. I glance over at him and he's breathing heavily as he stares straight ahead. "You are my concern," he says evenly. "Whatever we started, whatever we have going here…I fucking *like* it, okay? And I'm pretty sure you were liking it too, until—" he gives the steering wheel a frustrated jab, "until you took off. Now you're treating me like just another customer back at the diner, and saying shit like that? Just tell me what the hell is going on, will you? Can you help me out here?"

I suddenly feel too close to him. The air is suffocating and the silence stretches between us.

"That's the problem," I answer quietly, my voice breathy. "I wish I could tell you, but I can't."

"I think you can."

"I can't," I insist, unbuckling my seatbelt, too. I finger my collar, desperate for some cool air. "I have no excuse, Ryder. All I can say is…I'm not…I'm not who you think I am. I don't do this."

"You don't do what?"

"This." My left hand flails between us as I search for the words. I can't find them.

"What do you want, Elise? Just tell me what you want. Just be real with me. If you're not interested, I'll leave you the hell alone, but you have to tell me."

Before I know what I'm doing, I'm cupping his face. "No. It's not that, okay? I want you. I do."

His gaze travels down to my mouth and a ghost of a smile traces his lips before he hesitantly leans in. He stares for another beat before he kisses me, and the second I feel his warmth, I sink into him, breathing deeply. "You're still a little piece of heaven, baby," he pants against my mouth, "even if your halo's broken."

I suck on his bottom lip and open my eyes to find him staring back at me. Our tongues dance and teeth clash, but our gazes are rock steady. A surge of guilt, gratitude, and something stronger swells tight in my chest, and I know in that moment I have to tell him.

Maybe not everything, but something.

I can't go on like this. I've hurt a lot of men, but I'll lose sleep at night if I damage this one. "Ryder," I whisper, slowly pulling back. His arms snake out and grasp my hips, lifting me up and over the console. He sets me down on his lap and cups the back of my head, silencing my words by kissing the life out of me.

"Don't," he says, trailing a hand down my neck. It drops to trace along the undersides of my breasts, triggering chills on my arms and legs. "You don't have to talk about it if you're not ready. Just don't leave me like that again, okay?" His hands slide down underneath my ass and cup me, and his head tilts back against the headrest as he presses hot kisses beneath my ear. My fingers begin fumbling with his belt buckle but he stops me, his laughter tickling my neck. "You have no idea how much I'd love to take you right here."

"What's stopping you?" I try for his belt again but he pulls away from my neck and collects my wrists behind my back.

He grins up at me, his eyes hazy with desire. "The fact that your surprise is waiting, just up the road."

I whimper playfully, like a sad puppy, and even pout for good measure, tossing in my sexiest smile. "Please? Just a quickie?"

He groans as I wiggle my hips, but he stands his ground. "You're bad news. You're going to slay me, have I told you that?"

"Maybe." I bat my eyelashes.

He shakes his head and lifts me off him, leaning over for one last kiss as he buckles my seatbelt. His fingers linger on the ends of my hair as he pulls back, and once again, I feel pampered—entirely spoiled by his attention and gentleness. My mind squirms, but my body and heart seem to warm to it like a stray kitten warms to a new owner. The discomfort in my stomach is tamed by the fascination.

Ryder restarts the car and we turn back onto the road, arriving at a small grocery store a few minutes later. "This will be real quick," he says, jumping out to help me from the Jeep. "I just have to grab a few things."

"This isn't the surprise?" I take his hand and let him lead me into the store.

"How lame do you think I am?"

"Well, you did turn down a hot quickie in the Jeep back there. That was pretty lame."

"You're never going to let me live that one down, are you?"

"Are you regretting it yet?"

Ryder groans deeply and discreetly adjusts his groin as we step under the shopping plaza overhang. "Immensely." He gives my hand a squeeze and we enter the store, heading straight for the freezer aisle.

"Ice cream in the winter?" Amused, I watch him load up a basket with four cartons of ice cream, all different flavors.

"Winter is the best time for ice cream."

"I beg to differ."

"You haven't eaten ice cream with me yet."

"You have me there."

Ryder strolls down a few more aisles, choosing wine, marshmallows, and caramel syrup. We get in line at the first open check-out counter and Ryder begins unloading the basket's contents. A hushed chorus of snickering calls my attention to the two guys in front of us, who are waiting to be rung up behind another customer. They're flipping through magazines as they wait, their eyes glinting with laughter as they watch the customer reach for her wallet.

"Leslie Mann always did look like a *man,*" one of the guys taunts, a little louder this time. My gaze darts to the woman checking out in front of them, and my blood boils. I recognize her. I know Leslie Mann.

Not only was she Tee's first girlfriend in high school, she was there for me when my mom's cancer worsened. When Tee had to work, when I'd have a bad night at home and she wasn't there for me to turn to, Leslie was there. Like my best friend, Leslie was loyal that way. I remember being completely shocked when they'd broken up, because they always seemed to be on the same wavelength, even at such a young age.

More laughter brings a wave of goose bumps springing up on the back of my neck. These assholes are taking cracks at her right there, standing right next to her. Unbelievable.

One of them finally speaks directly to her. "Hey

Leslie, long time no see. What happened to your rack, baby? How do you strap those things down, huh? With duct tape?" Asshole Number One jabs Asshole Number Two in the side, cackling like a damn hyena, and my fists tighten at my sides. The cashier glares at the guys, looking nervously at Leslie, but Leslie doesn't blink, doesn't flinch. Just hands the cashier her credit card and keeps her gaze trained straight ahead, on the register.

"Too bad you're such a dyke," one of the guys sneers, not deterred in the least by her silence. "My friend here would bang you, wouldn't you, Mike?" He chuckles and claps hands with his friend Mike, when the cashier decides to speak up.

"I think that's enough," she snaps, ripping Leslie's receipt from the register. The guys start reaming into the cashier for spoiling their fun, but their retaliation is cut short, because I am suddenly in front of them, weaseling my way in between the tight space that separates them and the checkout counter. I glance at Leslie, who's stopped short, her hand suspended mid-air, taking the receipt from the cashier. When she regards me cautiously, I don't see her. I don't see the woman being verbally stoned to death by these bigoted douchebags. I see Tee.

"What the fuck is your problem?" I spit, glaring at them both. "Are you enjoying yourselves? Is this making you feel better about the size of your dicks or something?"

"Holy shit," I hear Ryder whisper under his breath.

He is next to me in an instant, his hand wrapped around my forearm. "Elise."

The guy named Mike lights up with delight, the same mean-spirited kind that he'd been taunting Leslie with. "Sorry, honey, how is this any of your business?"

"Yeah," his friend laughs, stepping forward, bringing his face level with mine. His eyes drop down my body and back up, a slimy grin crawling onto his lips. "And as for the size of our dicks, we'd be happy to show you we're not lacking in that department."

I don't think, just spring forward, like a feral, rabid animal in need of a cage. "Apologize to the woman, you piece of shit." I dig my fingers into Mike's chest and shove him backward. He slams into the candy shelf, and chewing gum and chocolates go flying everywhere, skittering around our feet.

"Elise!" Ryder grabs me again, but I am on a mission.

My hand closes around Mike's throat, and his dumbass friend jumps back, keeling over in laughter. My senses are on overdrive, adrenaline searing hot in my veins. The cashier's voice hits me from behind. She's on the phone, calling for security, and Leslie has backed up to the very end of the checkout line, her eyes wide in shock.

"Who do you think you are, treating people like shit, huh?" I give Mike's friend a shove, slipping out of Ryder's grasp. "What kind of *sick person* hurts people for his own amusement? Have you seen the news lately?" My hand clamps over the guy's throat and he grapples with me, pushing forward to reverse our positions. "The world's asshole quota has been met, so find something more productive to do with your goddamn time!"

Ryder throws his body in between me and the guys, yelling at them to keep their hands off me, but his shouts are muffled. The blood is still pounding in my ears, each nerve ending firing away. All I hear is the fury fueling the flow.

"This, from *Elise Duchamp*?" Mike jeers, his eyes flicking all over my body in disgust. "Are we the only two guys in this town you haven't banged? What a dumb slut, throwing your weight around, like you're so much fucking better. What about this dude, huh?" He eyes up Ryder and Ryder glares at him in warning. He looks like he's two seconds away from pummeling these guys, and I wouldn't lift a finger to stop him if he tried. "Is he paying you for your services? Or are you still giving that shit away for free?"

And that does it.

Ryder surges forward, leading with his fists, but I sideline the hit, bulldozing my way into the line of fire. Mike and his dipshit sidekick are waving their hands, telling Ryder to bring it, but I talk Ryder down, dragging him by the shirt out of the aisle. Security shows up as I pull him away, and Leslie grabs her bags and takes off, insisting to the cashier that she wants no part of what just went down.

"Elise, my stuff!" Ryder shouts as I guide him to the store exit, his nostrils flaring. He yanks his way out of my grip and storms back toward the check-out counter. Security is escorting Asshole Number One and Two out of the store, while the cashier wipes down her counter and mumbles under her breath.

"Ryder, let's just go somewhere else."

"No. I'm not leaving until I get what I came in here to get." He shrugs past me and silently pays the cashier, offering a quick apology for the scuffle before he rejoins me. I'm standing there with my arms crossed, feeling every eye in the store on us.

"What?" I say, loud enough so everyone can hear me. "You've never heard an argument before? Carry on." My hands wave from side to side and I work to regain my composure, smoothing down the front of my shirt and meeting the gazes of the customers in the next check-out line. They quickly look away, their whispers sinking into me from every direction.

Ryder and I finally exit the store and walk quietly to his Jeep.

Not a word passes between us as he drives us to wherever the hell he's driving us. Only the sound of The Animals' "House of the Rising Sun" fills the car, carrying my mind to a former time, to a wistful place, where youth was pure and time hadn't tainted the blood of the old. Every cell in me craves that untouched place.

I look out the window and watch the trees pass. I think of Tee and of Leslie. I think about the man sitting next to me, and how that little scene at the grocery store gave me a sad dose of reality. I can't keep Ryder, and I'm a fool to think I ever even had him.

CHAPTER 11

Ryder doesn't say much as we pull up to a small cabin near South Bend, buried deep in the woods.

"What's this?" I ask softly as he turns off the engine.

"My place for the winter." He gets out and jogs around the Jeep to open my door, and I let him guide me out and up the front porch.

"Your place? But I thought..."

"The campground shuts down in November. Won't reopen until March. Richard is letting me rent this place until then."

"This is Richard's?"

"Yup."

"So, where does he live, then?"

"His RV. Shares it with a few of his friends—some of the people you met on Thanksgiving. They drive to California for the winter."

"Where does everyone else go?"

"All over." He shrugs. "Some crash with friends, some stay with family for a while. Others couch surf or head south, like Richard. Here." He unlocks the door and flips a light on as he steps inside. Wafts of evergreen and remnants from burnt embers hit me as I follow him inside and I inhale deeply, surveying the quaint living space. Native American art lines the walls and coarse, time-worn rugs cover the bare floors, hugging the corners of the red plaid couch and rustic coffee table. There's an old stove and fireplace near the far window and no TV or telephone in sight. Duke trots happily over to Ryder and Ryder greets him, filling a bowl with some dog food.

"This is amazing," I say, moving toward the fireplace mantel. I trail my fingers along the top, rubbing the dust between my fingers. Pictures line the mantel, painting a vivid portrait of Richard and his travels.

The guy's lived a colorful life.

Ryder finishes feeding Duke and then unloads the bags from the grocery store. I hear him sift around in the kitchen cupboard for dishes. When I turn around, he's regarding me closely, spooning ice cream into two bowls.

I remove my jacket and rub my hands up and down my arms. "This is a nice place."

"I think so, too."

My fingers itch at my sides and my gaze turns to the plaid couch. "Mind if I use this?" I point to a folded up blanket, beneath a stack of pillows.

He nods and places the ice cream cartons into the freezer, keeping his eyes on me the whole time.

I wrap myself in the blanket and take a seat on the

couch, directing my stare ahead at the fireplace, which is the focal point of the cabin. Duke finishes up the last of his food and makes himself comfortable on a big floppy pillow near the window. "So, you get to crash here all winter? Nice."

Ryder doesn't respond, just walks over to hand me a bowl of ice cream, then walks to the fireplace and crouches down to start a fire.

"How about some of that wine?"

"Sure," he says, retreating quietly back to the kitchen once the fire's lit. He returns with a deep red, one glass for each of us. I thank him and pull my legs up, folding them beneath me so I'm cocooned in the blanket's warm wool. The couch dips next to me as Ryder sits, taking a long, slow sip of his wine. I place the bowl of ice cream on the cushion between us and we both stare straight ahead at the fire.

A bout of solemn silence stretches between us before he finally speaks.

"What happened back there?"

I raise my wine glass to my lips, keeping my gaze fixed on the fire. The sound of my tight gulp punctuates his question and I don't move. "What do you mean?"

"Elise."

I chance a peek at him, and he's watching me now, his expression curious but guarded. I glance down and reach for the spoon in the bowl. I toy with it for a second, rolling it over the colorful scoops of ice cream. "I know that girl. Leslie."

"That much I gathered."

"She was my best friend's girlfriend in high school. We were close for a while. People teased her all the time, like those dicks at the store. I just…lost it, I'm sorry."

The weight of my explanation hangs between us, but I know it's about to get heavier. "And those guys? What about them?"

I stop twirling the spoon.

"What about them?"

Ryder releases a frustrated sigh. "Come on," he says with an affronted laugh.

"What do you want me to say?"

"I wanted to pound the living shit out of them." His knuckles crack as his fists tighten. "I'm not a violent person."

"Look, I get it if…" I swallow, my fingers gripping the edges of the blanket, "I told you I don't do this, okay? There are reasons I don't…I have my reasons."

"Yeah, you've said that. Elaborate, please."

My gaze darts to his, and his brown eyes ensnare me. There's no looking away now. "I don't get involved. I'm not in to relationships, and you seem to be interested in something like that, so…I get it if you just want to drive me home right now and let this thing go."

Ryder lets out a deflated sigh and he leans forward, resting his arms on his knees. He stares at the fire, watching it acutely. "My ex, Lauren, hounded me for two years to get a real job. I grew up with her, ya know, we were high school sweethearts and all that."

He quiets for a moment and I remain still, just listening intently to the sudden change in subject.

"Anyway, one day she came home from work and looked straight at me. We were standing across the kitchen counter from one another. I'll never forget it. And she says to me, *You're never going to settle down, are you?* I ask her what she means, and she proceeds to lay it all on me, how she hates when I travel because I'm gone for so long, and how she wishes I'd take my parents up on their offer to go to college.

"I tell her she should come with me, that she might actually enjoy it, and how traveling gives me perspective. How it's something I'd never give up, not for anyone or anything. This look came over her, like the veil had finally lifted—hell, I guess it probably did—and she finally realized I would never change for her. I'd never change for anyone. She tried to argue that she'd only hold me back and that I'd probably rather be on the road with my friends or go solo, so I could hook up with whomever I wanted and be young and free and all that shit."

"That's when things ended?" My voice comes out weakly.

Ryder wipes at his jaw, closing his eyes. When he opens them, he stares hard at the carpet, folding his hands in front of him. "She never let me finish. She was so hell bent on hearing what she wanted to hear, she never heard me out."

"What did you want to say?"

"That she was wrong. I knew exactly what I wanted,

and it wasn't to screw other girls or be rid of her. I wanted her by my side. I wanted to be young and stupid *with* her. I wasn't afraid of that commitment, she was. She wanted a way out."

"Why didn't you ever tell her that? I mean, after... everything?"

His head lifts and his gaze holds steady on the crackling flames. "I gave her what she wanted. It turns out that was the right choice."

I follow his line of sight, watching the flames as they dance over the logs, chewing on the off-beaten path our conversation has taken. I take another sip of wine and wait.

"We all have a past, Elise. Sometimes we don't like where the road takes us; sometimes it leads us exactly where we need to be. I don't regret my past, and I don't give a damn about yours. All I care about is this." He flicks his brown eyes to mine, and they smolder with the heat of the fire. "Where I'm sitting right now, and where you're sitting right now. That's all I give a shit about. You're not up for any sort of relationship? I can accept that, but it doesn't mean you won't change your mind. And when you do, I'll be sitting right here, saying I told you so."

A short huff escapes me. "What makes you so confident?"

He slowly shifts and turns his body toward me, lifting the ice cream bowl. "Once you eat this with me, you won't be able to resist my charm." His sullen expression disintegrates and a sheepish grin takes its place.

My eyes drop to the bowl of dense, glistening mounds. "That life changing, huh?"

He tilts his head and lifts a shoulder, digging a scoop of chocolate ice cream from the bowl. He moves the spoon to feed me, but swings it away at the last second and shoves it between his lips instead.

"Hey!" I nudge him and watch him laugh.

"What'd I say?" He mumbles with his mouth full. "I'm not always a gentleman."

"Tease."

His chest continues to shake with light laughter as he spoons another scoop to my lips, this time letting the confection hit my mouth. Just as I'm about to open for the remainder, he moves in and kisses me, slipping me his tongue instead. Pleasure shoots straight down my spine and I accept him, the thick layer of cold cream making me shiver as it glides between our lips.

"You're rich like chocolate, baby," he replies, tracing the tip of his tongue along my bottom lip. "Bold and beautiful, and so fucking delicious." He nips softly at the corner and goes for a scoop of strawberry next. He feeds me some and dips his finger into the remainder on the spoon, sucking at it before trailing it along my jaw bone. "Now, strawberry's different. It's loyal. You always know what you're getting with strawberry—sweet and tangy every time. Unlike chocolate and vanilla, which can vary depending on the type. You're strawberry, too."

"I am?" I ask, my voice breathy. Loyal would be the

last adjective I'd use to describe myself.

"Yup." He tilts his head and blows softly along my collarbone, running his chilled finger downward, tugging the blanket away as he goes. "That move at the grocery store back there? That was strawberry." The blanket rests at my waist and his mouth grazes the neckline of my shirt, eliciting a delicate moan from my lips.

"I like strawberry."

"Yeah?" He thumbs my collar aside and brings his mouth down on my breast, rolling his tongue over my nipple. My breath hitches at the contact. It's cold and warm at the same time. "I can give you more strawberry. All you have to do is ask."

"More, please."

The delectable sensation eases up as he disappears to retrieve another spoon of pink cream, but it's back again the second he places a drop on his tongue. He blows over my nipple and watches it harden, smiling as he licks at the pink swirl he's created. "I like strawberry, too."

"Oh?"

"It's my new favorite." He tugs at the other side of my collar and pulls my bra cups farther down, giving the other breast the same treatment. He's right. This is divine enough to have me second guessing my strict code against relationships. Well, it's more like a necessity, not a code, but whatever it is, my mind is frazzled enough to question it. In a flash, he's discarded my shirt and bra and has pulled me down to the floor with him, placing his back against the edge of the couch. Positioning me in front of him, he props up his legs and wedges me between them, pulling my back flush to his chest so we're both facing the fire. "Lean your head back, baby."

I do as he says and exhale, letting my head roll back against his chest. "Whatever your game is here, you're winning."

"So soon?" His hands wrap around my waist and move upward, cupping my breasts. My nipples are still cool and hardened from his tongue, and all I can think about is his hands warming them up.

"I'm easy."

Ryder presses his erection against my back and lets one hand drift beneath my skirt. He rubs softly over my panties as he nibbles on my ear. "I'd say you're pretty challenging. Speaking of a challenge, I want to play a game."

"A game?" I give him a little wiggle, hoping to affect him just as much as he's affecting me. I hear a soft intake of breath over my shoulder, but his voice is steady as ever.

"*Mmhhmm*. It's called Truth and Bare."

"I'm intrigued."

"I ask you something, you tell me the truth. Each time you answer honestly, the reward is one less article of clothing."

My hand glides down to meet his, but he nudges me away, continuing the slow torment over my lace panties. "I only have two things on."

"Three."

"Two."

"Three. Your shoes."

"They don't count."

"Do you want to play or not?"

"Will I get more strawberry?"

"You'll get a whole fucking banana split if you just play the game, Elise."

"And if I don't?" I swivel in his arms, just enough so I can see him over my shoulder. "What if I just take what I want?"

"Nothing's stopping you. But don't you want the crème de la crème?"

"I want more strawberry."

Ryder bites my earlobe and turns me back around, nudging my head so I'm looking back at the fire. His fingers continue to stroke me, so lightly I could cry. "What's your favorite childhood memory?"

"Pass. Next question." His stroking ceases and his fingers lift from my skin, sending me into immediate withdrawal. "Ryder," I groan, arching my back and lifting my hips in protest.

"Answer the question."

A frustrated breath explodes from my lips and my head falls back onto his chest. "Favorite memory? I don't know, watching *I Love Lucy* with my mom, I guess."

"*I Love Lucy*?"

"Yeah, you know, the classic TV show?"

"Why is it your favorite memory?"

"I don't know." I shrug, lifting my left shoulder, then the right. What kind of question is that, anyway? And when can he finish this game so I can feel him inside of me? "My mom was always into those old TV shows. Movies, too. She loved James Dean and Marilyn Monroe."

"*Rebel Without a Cause*?"

"Especially *Rebel Without a Cause*. I don't know, she was always fascinated with the old Hollywood glamour and all that. When my dad was out working, we'd watch that stuff together and I liked it. It made me feel…safe, or something."

"What about it made you feel safe?"

"Hey, that's a lot more than three questions. We both should be naked by now."

Ryder's soft laughter rocks my back. "You're not getting off that easy."

"Gah! You're so stubborn. I've never worked so hard for an orgasm."

His head glides forward and his mouth hovers over my ear. "It'll be worth it," he whispers. "Come on, tell me."

I cross my arms and squirm. "I don't know…maybe because those times were simpler or something? It was comforting getting to live in that world for a while. Especially with my mom. When my dad was gone, things were—" I stop and bite down on my lip, but Ryder doesn't let up.

"When he was gone, things were what?"

"More peaceful."

"How so?"

"It was like…my mom and I could live in those

simpler times together, back before things became so messed up. Like we were right there, in the movies we were watching."

"You mean before the cancer?"

"No." I think, and for a second, I'm actually distracted from the heat of Ryder's fingers. My gaze settles on the fire's flames and Ryder is silent. "Before I knew who my father really was."

"Who was he?"

"A bastard." I bite down on the inside of my lip until I taste blood.

"I'm sorry," Ryder says, his voice dry.

"Whatever." I roll a shoulder. "Typical daddy issues. Nothing you want to hear about, I assure you."

"And your least favorite childhood memory?"

"Damn, Jacobson. Just go straight for the jugular, why don't you?" I release a dry laugh but swallow back the discomfort, wanting to play his game. Maybe because this means I'll get to ask him some questions.

"I wanna know." He nuzzles his nose into my hair.

"Watching my dad drive away," I say flatly. "When he moved out." I don't mention my hair being brutally chopped off against my will or the names he called my mother. I don't speak of the insults he hurled at my best friend or the fact that he left me and Mom when she was dying of cancer. All I can think of is that final image—that last glimpse of him as he backed out of the driveway. How there was no goodbye hug or kiss. No explanation or assurance that everything was going to be okay.

Only a slam of the front door and the soft purr of an engine, followed by my mother's heavy sobs down the hall.

"He left her when she was dying," I say, bitterness in my voice. "Left me to take care of her. He just...drove away."

Ryder's fingers slide out from underneath my skirt and I'm swiftly turned around in his lap, my bare breasts brushing up against his chest. My face is blank and my limbs are numb, the blood slowing in my veins. I don't like this game.

I want more strawberry.

"That's shitty, Elise. Really shitty. I'm sorry."

"Can I have a turn?" I am more than ready to ditch the direction of this conversation.

"Okay. Shoot."

"If you had a million dollars and could do anything in the world, what would you do?"

He furrows his brow, shaking his head as he scans the room. "Damn, I don't know. That's a tough question. I hate that question." He keeps one hand firmly around my waist and runs the other over his head, rumpling his dark brown hair. "Donate a shit ton of money to causes I care about, read all day, live out in the middle of the woods and become a recluse...I don't know, go to Europe, I guess."

I study him as I digest his response, and instantly want to know more. "What's your favorite book?" He huffs and lets his head fall back on the edge of the couch.

I take advantage of his position and lean in to kiss his exposed throat. His Adam's apple bobs beneath my lips.

"These are not valid questions for Truth and Bare," he groans playfully.

"Says who?"

"Says me, that's who."

"How are your questions any more valid than mine?"

"*What's your favorite book?*" he mocks, lifting his head back up. "Asking a bibliophile that question is pure evil. There's no way I can choose only one, and if you make me choose one, you're forcing me to betray the hundreds of other books that have knocked me on my ass and shaped my soul. If you ask me that, you're the devil."

"Okay, then. I'm the devil. Get over it. Answer the question."

His eyes narrow and his lips swish to the side with a smile. He plants a hand on his chest like I've just shot him. "How can you be so cold hearted?"

"It just comes naturally, I guess." I look down and begin playing with the hem of his shirt. An unwelcome cloud of gloom drifts over me.

His fingers find my chin and he pulls my gaze back to his. "Hey." Smoothing a thumb along my jawline, he pauses then lets his hand fall back to my hip. "I'll answer the question."

"Forget it." I smile and square my shoulders, lifting my chin. "I have another one."

"Okay…" he regards me curiously, a trace of mirth

still glimmering in his gaze.

"Have you ever hurt someone?"

The fleck of humor disintegrates and the muscles in his neck flex. His light is gone, but he works hard to keep his gaze on mine. "I'm sure I have."

"Intentionally?"

"Not intentionally. No."

"Has anyone ever hurt you?"

"Of course." A quiet sigh escapes him and he sits back and removes his hands from my hips, letting his elbows rest behind on the sofa. His gaze drops for a few seconds to admire my half-naked state. That ghost of a smile of his appears, and I want to crawl inside his mind and know exactly what he's thinking as he's ogling me. Ten bucks says I have a good guess, though.

"Wait." He seems to shake his thoughts, shifting beneath me. We're both struggling to maintain focus, but he seems just as intent as I am to finish the game. "Are we talking like bodily harm, here? Or relationships. Or hurt in general?"

"Yeah, any kind of hurt."

"What if I tell you I've killed someone?"

"Not funny."

"Not for you, it isn't. You're the one locked in a cabin in the woods with me." He grins cheekily and reaches to give my hip a squeeze. I buckle to the side and an uncontrollable giggle slips out. "Oh damn, you're ticklish, too? You just keep getting sexier and sexier, Elise Duchamp."

"Stop!" I shriek, thrashing on his lap like a fish out of

water. "Ryder, stop!"

He digs at my hip again, sending me tumbling into an endless fit of laughter. My lungs burn because I can't breathe and my sides ache from the exertion. I topple over and land on my side, and Ryder comes with me, sliding on top of me in one smooth, swift movement. "I think we've played enough games for today," he says, running the palms of his hands up the sides of my thighs. His thumbs roll slow, soothing circles into my skin before hooking into the sides of my panties to peel them down my legs. My laughter subsides and I look up at him, my chest heaving as I regain my breath. We lie there on the floor in a tangled heap of limbs, while the fire's warmth gives Ryder's face a soft glow.

Small pops crackle from the fire and gravitate toward us, saturating the silence.

Lowering his forehead to my shoulder, Ryder kisses the skin there. "Do you feel it yet?"

"Feel what?" Desolation? Helplessness? Excitement? I feel all of those things.

"This." Ryder's hand slides down my chest and torso like silk, slipping beneath my skirt, easy as breathing. I gasp as his fingers slip inside of me. "Desire. The same kind I feel for you."

"You know I do."

He strokes me for a moment then stops, leaving me panting while he reaches back to the couch to pick up the bowl of ice cream. It's melted now, each color swirling together like mixed paint. "Feed me," he whispers, lifting the bowl to me.

My dazed gaze drifts to the bowl. I hesitantly sit up on my elbows and cradle it, watching him curiously as I begin to spoon him the milky leftovers. He accepts a spoonful, then another, groaning in appreciation. He pushes the spoon away when he's satisfied and I set the bowl down, watching as he brings my hand to his lips. Sucking one finger then the next, he moves slowly from tip to tip, drawing me farther and farther away from our question-and-answer session.

"Ryder," I breathe.

He closes his lips over my right index finger and sucks, drawing it slowly from his mouth. The mixture of cool and warm coats my skin, and I wonder how I'll ever enjoy ice cream without Ryder after tonight. "I really want this," he says. "Us."

I shut my eyes and he moves in, brushing his lips against mine. "You have us. Right here."

"Do I?"

My eyes drift open.

He deepens the kiss, murmuring against my mouth. "I'll never just drive away, Elise Duchamp."

The words zap me like a stun gun. My voice comes out in a light rasp. Small and breathless. "I've hurt people, Ryder."

He studies me for a moment but doesn't respond, only deepens his kiss. I cave into him, letting him devour me whole. I don't know what I can give him. I don't know if I have anything at all. But I do know that Ryder Jacobson

is trouble.
The good kind.

CHAPTER 12

My tattoo seems to tingle on my hip, as if the bird's feathers are itching at my skin, reminding me it's there. *When one wants, one can.*

I scratch at my hipbone as I drive to work, lost in memories of the night before. Ryder and I hadn't moved from the cabin's living room floor, except to cook a late dinner and to roast marshmallows over the fire. We'd indulged our bodies, spoiling ourselves rotten in pleasure until I insisted he drive me home so I could have a hot shower and get some sleep before work today. My stomach is in knots, twisting and turning with the realization that Ryder isn't planning on going anywhere any time soon. Even more pressing is the reality that I don't want him to.

My hair is quickly thrown up and my apron is tied around my waist as I rush to the kitchen to find Natalie. A relentless feeling drives into me, urging me forward. "Um…hey, Nat?"

She's fumbling with order slips on the line-up, looking

flustered, as usual. When she hears me, she turns in surprise. "Hey, Elise. What's up?"

My wrists float behind my back, my fingers toying with the apron strings even though they're already secured. "Hey, before I start waiting tables, I just wanted to let you know that I'm…I'm free tonight. After my shift, I mean. Thought maybe I could take you up on that meal. If you're still up for it, that is." Natalie's expression reveals genuine surprise, her brows lifting and eyes widening in what I think is shock. She's in shock, but I'm just speechless once the words come out of my mouth.

This is one fucked-up move on my part.

"Oh! Sure, of course. You want to do dinner, maybe?"

"Yeah." I tug at the hem of my skirt. "Sounds good. I'm done at five, so…"

"How about I pick you up at your place around six? I'm getting ready to clock out. I just need to finish up these orders."

"Okay, how about I meet you somewhere instead?"

"No problem. Just pick a place and call me when you're ready to go out."

"That works."

"Yay!" She pins the last of the order slips to the line-up and gives me a smile before shouting out orders to the cooks. I take that as my opportunity to escape from the kitchen and dash back out into the restaurant. My heart's pounding.

There's no way I can ever take back what I've done to Natalie, and I don't expect to. I don't expect anything, really. All I want is to try to move on, no matter how much of a bitch that makes me.

I already know what I am. No use in groveling over the truth.

Nate hasn't been around since he and Natalie broke up, and I haven't heard a word from him since the day he left my apartment. Things are settling down, and spending time with Ryder flipped a switch in my mind. Things look different, even taste different. Like Stella's famous French toast.

Even though it is a town favorite, I was never actually a fan. It tasted soggy to me. And far too bland. Now the syrup swirls on my tongue like irresistible nectar, and the cinnamon awakens my taste buds, heightening all of my senses. Including my curiosity.

I haven't been a friend to anyone in…well, since Tee was in town. I don't even know where to begin. It probably doesn't help matters that I'm choosing Natalie of all the girls in Gig Harbor as my guinea pig, but it's not like I have a line of girls looking to make friends, rolling up to my doorstep saying, *sign me up*. I have to start somewhere, and if Nate is out of the picture, it's worth trying to salvage. I can't hurt Natalie any more than I already have. The damage is done. It's me who has to suffer. Every time I speak to her—even look at her—I'm reminded of what I've done. This could be possibly the stupidest idea or the smartest idea, depending on how I look at it.

Today I choose to look on the bright side.

I saunter up to my first table of the afternoon, a good-looking guy in his thirties checking me out as I flip open my notepad to take his order. He smiles at me, all charming and debonair, but I'm all business.

Only one charming smile affects me lately, and it is nowhere to be found in this restaurant.

"Is that all?" I ask after I take his order, clicking my pen.

"Actually, no. Can I interest you in dinner tonight? I'd love to take you out." The guy's blue eyes sparkle and I take in his spiffy suit jacket, which is black and crisp to perfection. He's sharp. A businessman. Like Christian. I think I've seen him here before.

As if he can read my mind, he clears his throat and his smile widens. "I'm Chase. You've waited on me before. I've just been trying to work up the nerve to ask you out."

"*Ah*," I tap my pen on the notepad, "I thought I had seen you before."

"Well, I've most definitely seen you." He pulls at his tie and locks me with a confident gaze. This guy is all white teeth, fitness model body, and money. I've been with a handful of men like him. Beautiful, but not Ryder.

Habit suddenly takes over and I playfully run the tip of my pen over my bottom lip, unleashing a small smile as I drop my chin and peer down at him. "That's sweet, but I'm kind of seeing someone." Those words have never left my mouth before. I lean in and place my hand over his, giving him a light squeeze. He looks down at the contact, laughing under his breath.

"That's a damn shame," he says, lifting his gaze back to mine. With a knowing smile, he retrieves his wallet from his back pocket and hands me a business card. "If things don't work out, give me a call. The offer stands."

I make sure to let him see me give the card a good, thorough scan, and then slip it in my back pocket as I move to step away. "I'll keep that in mind," I say, grinning over my shoulder as I turn for the kitchen. Jay's voice distracts me before I disappear through the doorway. He's laughing.

Not that Jay laughing is strange. He's a friendly guy, probably one of the happiest people I know, actually. But this laugh is different. It's sincere and hearty to the core, and it's not alone. Ryder's laugh is mingling with it, natural and breezy, as if they've known each other for years.

I glance at the entrance, where Jay and Ryder are strolling in with bags in their hands. My feet take a cue from my curiosity and begin to carry me over to them. "Hey, you two," I say, waving gingerly. This is just all sorts of weird. "So…what's going on?"

"Hey there, hon," Jay grins, his cheeks rosy with warm merriment. "Ryder was just telling me all about the trouble his pup gets into. Reminds me of our labs at home. They can be quite rambunctious, you know."

"Okay…"

"Hey," Ryder says, moving to kiss me on the cheek. He and Jay are holding paper bags, loaded up with books. Old paperbacks, from the looks of it.

"What are you doing here?"

"I'm here to steal you away for the afternoon."

"I work until five."

Jay chuckles and sets his paper bags down on the counter near the register, then reaches for Ryder's bags. "Go on," he says, shooing Ryder away. "We're good here."

"You're what?" I pipe up, confusion wrinkling my forehead.

"Ryder bought me off today," Jay explains, waving his hands nonchalantly. "Bribed me with books I've never read—that he swears are life-changing, or something—and a damn good breakfast."

"Books?" My brows lift. "And *breakfast*?"

"Yeah," Jay claps Ryder's back, "over at his cabin. Really great place. Anyway, I'm here just in time to take over for you. Give me that notepad and scat."

I don't move. "You had breakfast…at Ryder's cabin?"

"Sure did, hon. You look confused."

"I am confused. You're going to wait tables? My tables?"

Jay scoffs and shakes his head. "*Like I've never waited a table before*. Yes, hon, I'm going to wait tables. Now you two get out of here before I change my mind. Go on, get!"

Ryder smiles and grabs my hand, quickly pulling me away. Stunned, I forget to hand Jay my order pad, but Ryder snatches it for me just in time and tosses it to Jay before he whisks me out the front door.

"What—where are we going?" I ask, shivering the

second the cold air hits me. "I need my coat!"

"Here," Ryder says, opening the Jeep passenger door. He hands me a leather jacket that's draped on the seat and helps me inside, quickly jogging to the driver's side. He cranks the heat up the second he starts the engine. "We have to get moving if we want to get there on time."

"Get where? What's going on? Since when are you all chummy with my boss?" I slip on the leather jacket and zip it up, thankful for the cozy warmth.

"I told you I have a weakness for beautiful blondes with tattoos in unmentionable places." He shrugs coolly and pulls out in reverse. "They make me do crazy things." He turns up the radio until Eddie Vedder's version of "Society" blares loudly, drowning everything else out. He guns the engine and we're off, leaving Stella's in the dust.

***

Hot chocolate warms my frigid fingers as we step off the ferry from Seattle to Bainbridge Island.

Ryder is right. He has indeed gone crazy.

After corralling me into his Jeep and leaving Gig Harbor, he headed for downtown Seattle, where we caught the ferry over to Bainbridge. Ryder hails a taxi the minute we step off of the landing, and the next thing I know, I'm strolling up to a tattoo shop on Madison Avenue.

"You can't be serious," I say, beaming at him despite

my disbelief.

"I thought you loved ink."

"I do, I just..." Eyeing the shop sign above us, I drag in a deep breath. Maybe it's the fact that I'm still getting used to spending time with a man outside of a bedroom, or maybe it's because I'm still surprised to be whisked off to Bainbridge Island for the afternoon, but adrenaline is pulsing in my blood and I'm completely floored by the fact that Ryder thought to bring me here. Some girls find flowers and chocolate romantic, but this? This is my kind of romance. Art and ink and blood. It's damn sexy, and the gesture has rendered me speechless.

"Come in and meet Tracy," Ryder says, taking my hand. "We have all afternoon, so get whatever you want, baby. It's on me."

"Holy shit," I whisper as he leads me inside. It's a small, clean shop, nestled into a line of stores that seem to be off the beaten path from the rest of downtown Bainbridge. Everything about it feels removed from the more upscale businesses that grace the main street. It breathes, natural and open, its walls sprawled with heart, edge, and argument—a modest display of the artist's work. I'm enthralled, and the second I meet her, I'm ready for the needle.

"Hey, how's it goin'?" Tracy asks, shaking my hand. "Ryder tells me you guys want to get some work done today? Do you have an idea of what you're looking for?" She smiles and sets a sketch pad down, motioning for me to have a seat on one of the stools. Her feet are in dark brown boots, her hair is back in a loose bun, and The Smiths play in the background. Her voice matches her laidback persona, and I'm instantly at ease.

"Not really, no. This is sort of a surprise, so..."

She laughs and pulls out some books with various font styles. "That's Ryder. Always full of surprises." She eyes him for a second, handing me the books to flip through. "Just take a look at these and if you get an idea of what you might want, we can toss some ideas back and forth and see what we come up with. Sound good?"

"Definitely." I settle onto the stool and begin flipping pages, sneaking a peek at Ryder. He's admiring the art on the wall, chatting with Tracy while she begins setting up the equipment. Her voice suddenly turns low and they both glance over their shoulders toward me. I avert my eyes.

I thumb through a few more pages until I settle on a concept I like. There's no need to pick out a font style, because I won't be needing one this time. I close the books and stand from the stool.

"Any ideas?" Tracy asks, rummaging through supplies.

"I think so, yeah." I lift up my shirt and shimmy my skirt waistband down to bare my hipbone. "I want to continue what I have going on here, on the other hip."

"Oh yeah? Come here, let me get a better look." She squints and waves me over, studying the art with an approving smile. "Alright, we can do that. Let me sketch something up and see what you think."

"Sounds good." Excitement unfurls deep in my gut as I watch her reach for her sketch paper. Ryder joins us, moseying up behind me to slip his arms around my waist. He rests his chin on my shoulder and watches Tracy flesh out some ideas while I describe what I want.

Two hours later, my other hip is glistening with fresh black ink. My bird has a home—a nest in a lush tree, which holds a pile of hearts similar to one the bird is carrying from the cage. A trail of smaller hearts trickles over my lower abdomen, just along my panty line, leading to the tree's nest, creating a path from one hip to the other. I'm completely smitten and even more thrilled that I get to watch Ryder get inked next.

He removes his shirt and takes a seat, falling into easy conversation with Tracy. The needle starts buzzing away and I settle into the small sofa up against the wall, where I get a perfect glimpse of the show. Tracy makes jokes about Charles Bukowski and starts telling Ryder all about the sailboat she and her husband built together from scratch. She says it's right there on the harbor and invites us to check it out after she's done, but Ryder politely declines. He smirks at me from the chair, unleashing that damn dimple as he explains that we have to catch the ferry to make it back to Gig Harbor on time for me to meet my friend. I'm already going to be late meeting Natalie, but I'm hoping she'll understand. I'm sure Jay filled her in on Ryder's surprise.

The hard planes of Ryder's chest and abdomen flinch and flex as the needle works over him. He's so at ease as

Tracy works, but I'm anything but comfortable. I have to press my knees together to keep from squirming, and my mouth waters as I watch him. He's casually sprawled out in the chair, one arm behind his head propping him up, his legs splayed wide and loose as he leans back. He's chatting away—talking books, of course—completely oblivious to the fact that I'm so turned on I can barely think straight. All I want to do is jump him.

One agonizing hour later, when we board the ferry home, I finally get the chance.

The ferry bathroom door slams behind us and Ryder reaches to click the lock, but I stop him. "Leave it open," I whisper, as I drag him inside by the collar of his shirt, gripping him hard. I feel a mischievous glint in my eye as I lead him into the closest stall. My back hits the side of the stall and he swings the door shut, fumbling with the lock as he hoists and pins me up. I don't want to know how filthy the stall is, I only want to make it dirtier.

Ryder's hands wildly grope my thighs, shoving my skirt up and tearing my panties right down the middle. I cry out and bite down hard on his lip. I'm going to combust at any second, and the hiss of approval that sizzles through his teeth speeds up my impending release. It's on its way. It just might kill me. But if Ryder keeps manhandling me like this, I'll die one happy girl.

I focus on grasping at his shoulders, working the sleeves of his blazer down his elbows. I mess with the top buttons of his shirt next, but he's too impatient. His hand glides up my neck to the back of my scalp and threads into my hair, yanking my head to the side. He spins me around and slams me forward, pressing my chest into the stall wall.

"Like this," is all he says, angling my head to the side so my cheek is smashed against the wall. The sound of his zipper echoes off the tile floor and he thrusts into me in one swift, sharp movement. He doesn't bother with slow build up. There is no steady pace, no chivalry. Just fast, hard abandon, as if he knows it's exactly what I need. His palm slaps the wall next to my face while the other grips the side of my hip. He's careful not to touch the bandage covering my new tat. This is the roughest Ryder's ever been with me, but his touch still feels attentive, like he's handling a precious artifact.

A squeak and heavy creak sounds from the bathroom entrance as someone strolls through the door. Shoes shuffle along the tile into the stall next to us, and Ryder stills inside of me. I freeze against the wall, working to quiet my breathing as one of his hands glides around to cover my mouth. His body trembles against mine from behind. A sheen layer of sweat on his chest touches the back of my neck, sticking to my skin. His fingers clamp down harder over my mouth and he begins to move inside of me again, careful and even, slow and measured. The thrill races through me, the adrenaline heady and dangerous.

Tameless need ignites my bones.

I bite down on his finger and push against him, hearing him grunt, working to muffle the sound against my ear. I grin against his hand, my eyes rolling up to meet his over my shoulder. He shoots me an equally devious look, but it's full of warning as the toilet flushes next to us. The stall door swings open and water runs at the sink for a moment before the bathroom door creaks again. The second we're alone, Ryder drops his hand from my mouth and resumes his brisk strokes.

My breaths come out in labored, harsh gasps as I accept him, letting him ram me against the bathroom stall wall. Our moans echo throughout the large space, mingling with the slapping of skin and sweat. Each time his groin hammers hard against my ass, I shudder with a deeper need, one I can't compare to any other I've ever known. Ryder's taking what he wants, giving me what I want. It's wholly physical and entirely carnal, but a deep seed, rooted somewhere in the rich soil of my soul, tells me this transcends the physical.

Ryder is more than perfectly imperfect, sexy, strong male. He's gesture and heart, soul and honesty. His actions actually back up his words and he always says what he means. There hasn't been any question of his intentions or motives, because he wears those desires on his sleeve like a bleeding heart. *When you find a connection like we have, you recognize it. You grab hold of it and take it for all its worth. You don't let it slip between your fingers.* Christian's words zing toward me and I grapple to push them away. Christian is the very last person I want to be thinking about right now.

But what if he's right?

Not only about that, but about the idea of enough being only an illusion? What if Ryder discovers who I truly am and realizes I'm not enough? That he needs more? Something better? Expectations have always scared the shit out of me. Many don't show the people closest to them every part of their true selves. They can't. Even to those they love. They're too close. Too close to the person they want you to be. The truth might carve their heart out. Then what will they do when they're left bleeding? What will you do when their blood is on your hands? I'll tell you what.

Clean up.

A clean-up crew has to swing by and clean up the mess for you both, because one of you is reeling over the realization that he's been in love with an ideal of you—not the real you—and you're too busy trying to hold him together while you deal with the fact that you've been lying to yourself. You're both too shell shocked by the grimness of it all to take care of the mess on your own. And that clean-up crew? The little minions in charge of your hazardous waste? They get the worst end of the deal. Your mom, your kid, your career, whatever. Whatever saves you takes a beating. And it's not fair. None of it is.

"Elise," Ryder groans into my ear, sliding a hand around my torso and down between my legs. He thumbs my clit as he fucks me, picking up the pace. "Where are you, baby?"

"I'm here," I murmur, dropping a hand over his knuckle as he works me. "Right here."

A loud gasp is punched from my lungs when his hips stop rocking and he grabs my shoulders, spinning me back around to face him. He peers down at me, hazy eyes dancing for a second as they study my face, and then his hot mouth covers mine, bearing down like angry lava. He suddenly drops to his knees and shoves his head between my legs, his hands clamping down hard on my hips. A strangled cry breaks me open when I feel his tongue, determined and sharp. I shout, my head slamming back against the wall.

"Are you with me?" He exhales against my pussy, nipping roughly. "Give it to me, Elise." He resumes his persistent strokes, sending me soaring into the sun. Bursts of light rain down all around me, bright and sweet, and my legs tremble with the explosion. I'm gasping for breath, my fingers curling in Ryder's hair, convulsing against his tongue. As his strokes slow and I slide back down from the bliss, I'm ready to be wrung out to dry, but he's not done with me yet.

Standing to his feet, he lifts me by the waist and sinks me back down onto his cock, sliding deep inside with one decadent, firm stroke. I'm still catching my breath, panting and begging him, mumbling incoherent things, but he powers forward, his lips dropping to the crook of my neck. Pleasure radiates from my core and swells, pouring outward and dousing my inner thighs with waves of warmth. He smashes into me, again and again, until he's shouting my name and gripping my hair tightly between his knuckles.

A long, strenuous sigh shuttles through him and our bodies slump against one another, his broad shoulders holding me to the wall. His chest heaves against mine and I suddenly wince, wiggling against him to put some space between us. He looks dumbfounded and a bit slighted as I push him back, but I placate him with a quick-witted smile.

"Our ink," I breathe in explanation, trailing my fingers along the bandage over his chest. It's peeking out from underneath his shirt, just below the top buttons I'd managed to loosen.

"Oh, damn," he laughs, out of breath. "Sorry. Let me see." He rests his hot hands on my waist and crouches down to study the bandage on my hip. Lifting it, he studies it and grins when he's satisfied. "Perfect."

"Like yours," I reply coyly, pulling him up to full height. My fingers slide beneath his shirt, over his exposed chest, and I perform the same check, carefully lifting his bandage. The words *ad astra per aspera* are splayed across the firm skin, across his collarbone, with falling stars on the edges of the phrase. "Through hardships to the stars," I whisper, admiring the new art. I can feel his gaze, penetrating and roasting me from the inside out. "So optimistic."

"You think?" His tone's gritty and dry.

My eyes roam up to meet his. "Not everyone makes it to the stars."

"When one wants, one can," he replies, feeding me the mantra on my own hip.

My lids narrow, and a spark slithers down my spine. "I hope you're right." A sad smile teases my lips and I shift to move. I want out of this stall and off this ferry. I need to get home, need to see Natalie, but most of all, I need to distance myself from whatever being with Ryder stirs in me, so I can think clearly and focus. Today has been art and ink and blood, but it's also been emotion and confusion and sweaty, lecherous sex. It's been a rush of things that I don't know how to define other than danger.

This is the danger zone. The Ryder zone.

"Hey." His arm snakes out and reaches for me, his fingers closing around my wrist before I can open the bathroom stall door. A pause fills the air, pulsing between us like erratic energy seeking an out. "Is there something you want to talk about, Elise?" His voice is even, though I detect a hint of uncertainty there. "You know you can tell me anything, right?"

I swallow, freezing at his touch. "I'm fine." Leaning up on my tiptoes, I kiss his cheek softly. "Thank you." He remains still, his eyes following me the whole way out of the bathroom. I don't have to turn around to see them, because I feel them.

The second I'm out of the bathroom, I head past the rows of seating and bypass the magazine stands for the side exits. Stepping outside, I let the cold blast of Pacific Northwest wind hit me like a glacier and wander around the outer deck to the railing, where I let my weight fall. My cold hands grip the metal and I shut my eyes on a deep inhale.

Just as I begin to let the cold fill my lungs, my phone vibrates in my back pocket and I pull it out, wrapping Ryder's leather jacket tighter around the flimsy material of my waitress uniform. The screen lights up with a new text. My heart smacks the bottom of my stomach like a paperweight. It's from Christian.

Hey, baby. I miss you. Be my date to the masked Christmas ball next weekend. It's at 2424 Rosen Drive. You know the place. Where we spent that incredible night… our favorite suite. Please come. There's so much I need to say to you. I don't need you to move in. I just want to see you again. Call me when you have a minute.

He's still calling me baby. He's still trying to reach me. Will he ever give up?

I quickly exit the text and slide the phone away, bunching my fingers tightly inside my jacket pockets.

"Can I get you some more hot chocolate?" Ryder's voice breezes behind me and I turn to find him looking at me intently. He approaches slowly, eyes surveying the view. Seattle is glimmering on the horizon as darkness falls, blanketing the sky. December days are cold and dark, the sunsets beginning early. "You're going to freeze to death out here."

"Sure, I'll have some," I say quietly. "I'm coming inside."

His arms encase me from behind and he shivers, his lips like ice as they kiss beneath my ear. "So you and Natalie are hanging out tonight, huh? How's she doing?

Since the break-up with Nate, I mean."

Tension blisters at my shoulders. "Okay, I think. I wouldn't know, I don't really talk to her much, actually. But I think she's managing. They weren't dating very long, but she was definitely into him."

"No? I thought you guys were good friends or something."

I clear my throat and try to work the pressure from my neck. "We're friendly."

"Bummer things didn't work out for her and Nate. They seemed good together."

"I guess it just wasn't meant to be." I shift and Ryder's arms loosen around me. "How about that hot chocolate?"

"Sounds good to me."

My eyes flick to his with a halfhearted smile and I take his hand to lead him back inside. My cell phone burns a hole in my back pocket and my nerves rattle wildly from head to toe. Soon I'll be hanging out with Natalie, and it will be time for more lies. Having relationships is a risky, exhausting business. Especially when you are Elise Duchamp.

CHAPTER 13

The next few days are surreal. At least, in my world they are. Natalie and I have been hanging out after work. I've been learning a lot about her, more than I ever anticipated, given the circumstances. She wants to be a nurse, and it turns out she went to the same elementary school as me, only she was two years behind me. Her parents sent her to private school for high school, and she loathed every second of it. I joke that I would've had her back in public school had she gone where Tee and I were, and her opinionated rant about some new romance series she's reading has me cracking up.

The girl is passionate about her books, I'll give her that.

It occurs to me that I now have two new book nerds in my life, and that she and Ryder might actually have a lot to chat about. I love to read too, but Natalie...well, she takes the term *fangirl* to a whole new level.

Tide's Tavern has become our meeting place of choice. I'm just happy to be eating anywhere other than Stella's.

We chat over beer and clam chowder, bitch about crappy tips, and swap high school horror stories. Occasionally Nate comes up and her spirits fall, but she sweeps that subject away just as quickly as she mentions it, and I silently give thanks.

Both Natalie and I are off today and I've spent the whole morning cleaning my apartment. She'll be here soon to pick me up to drive us to Seattle. We have plans to go to Pike Place Market, and possibly a movie. I can't even think about those plans, though, because my head is swimming with the fact that for the first time, Natalie will see my place. Other than Ryder, I can't remember the last time I've had company. The only other action my front door has seen is from desperate men tracking me down after one-night stands, and even that has been rare. My place is usually off-limits.

I trip over the vacuum cord and curse as I stumble and stub my toe on the end of the coffee table. A knock stirs me from the pain and my eyes dart everywhere, sizing up the stack of newspapers on the end table and the sofa cushions, which I hope are fluffed enough. I hobble to the front door, glancing at my watch. Natalie must be early.

"Someone reported a dishwasher problem?" Ryder looks at me, all straight faced and rugged in his scuffed-up boots and maintenance uniform. His fingers are smudged with black and his utility belt hangs low on his hips, drawing my attention to my second favorite part of his body. His shoulders are my first.

As if he knows exactly what I'm thinking, he stretches those shoulders and takes an easy step forward, raising one arm to lean lazily against the doorway. A faint smirk creeps up and he bites his bottom lip to suppress it, his glimmering eyes betraying his mock seriousness. "Mr. Fix-It, at your service, Miss Duchamp."

I grin, wanting to slap some sense into him. He knows I have plans with Natalie today and he's supposed to be working, not pestering me, but he's so goddamn adorable, I can't resist him. My hands land on his shoulders and I don't say a word, just pull him inside and shove him against the back of the door. It falls shut with a loud slam and the apartment is filled with clattering and clinking as I tug at his utility belt. I rip it from his waist and let it drop to the floor with a thud.

"How long do we have?" he breathes hard against my mouth, his fingers fumbling frantically with my jeans button.

"Fifteen minutes."

"Bedroom?"

"Kitchen counter." I stumble backwards and he follows, our mouths never leaving one another. In seconds, he's bending me over the counter, and his cock is nudging at my entrance. The hot, slick ridge slides against my wetness and I shudder, pushing against him, wanting him to fill me to the hilt.

"This is my favorite part," he pants against my earlobe. "Right here." He teases me gently, slipping in just enough to let me feel every hard inch of him, then withdraws to the tip.

"Ryder," I whisper impatiently. His frame caves against my back and we both exhale on a ragged breath. I reach back to guide him inside of me, but his firm arms slide down my shoulders and collect my wrists, planting my hands on the counter.

"How's my girl doing?" he says, covering my fists with his palms. "I missed you."

"I want you."

"I know."

"Stay over tonight," I pant, betraying my own apartment rule. I arch my back and he responds, gliding his cock between my legs.

"Yeah?"

"Yeah."

"I want to give you your Christmas present."

"It's early."

"Don't care." One of his hands leaves mine and drifts over my navel, slipping up beneath my sweater. He cups my breasts hard, biting down on my neck. "I'll give it to you tonight."

"Give it to me now."

"I have something else for you now." He suddenly slams inside of me and my body jolts forward, my fingers scrambling for traction on the counter. A soft whimper slips from my lips and Ryder's flat palm comes down on the back of my shoulder blade, easing me down until my upper body is smashing onto the cold granite. He pulls my ass tightly against him and begins thrusting in and out in measured, slow strokes. "We need to talk tonight, baby."

I moan in response, unable to concentrate on anything but the fullness.

He snickers behind me, rocking his hips. "Is that so?"

"I want to see you," I say suddenly, needing to look straight into his eyes. I need to see the lust there, his desire, need to see whatever it is that he says he feels for me. Need to see if it's real.

His body's pressure eases up at my back and I rise from the countertop. He quickly spins me around and lifts me up, setting my ass on the edge, connecting us at the waist. He slides back inside of me with a grunt, bringing his forehead to mine. His eyes are eager, on fire, swelling with ferocious heat. My eyes drift shut from the pleasure of the reconnection but snap back open as quickly as they close, just so I can see him.

"There she is," he murmurs against my lips. He begins to move, cupping the back of my head as he resumes his command of my body.

"Why me?" I whisper, tilting my hips to match the delicious rhythm he's setting.

He slows for a second and his dark brows lower in confusion. "Why you?"

"What are we doing?"

His jaw goes slack. "You tell me."

I squeeze my eyes shut and roll my hips, capturing the blunt force of another thrust, and we both groan at the friction. Now's not the time to ask him these questions. Now's not the time for any of this. He wants to talk tonight, not now. Not while he's impaling me on the kitchen counter. But I'm suddenly filled with a new kind of desire—a desire to know the truth. Am I really his girl? Does he really mean what he says about not caring about my past? Can I be his…can I be anyone's?

"Elise." His thumb rolls over my cheek.

"Ryder, I—"A timid knock cuts me off, my mouth agape with the intrusion.

"Shit, is that Natalie?" Ryder shifts and carefully pulls out of me, buckling up his pants. I scramble off the counter, hopping to my feet. I quickly button my jeans and straighten my sweater out, wrestling with my bra cups. Ryder works to adjust his hard-on, but there's no concealing it. "Just give me a second." He blows a harsh breath through his teeth and leans on the counter to get a grip.

I feel his pain.

I'm still aching with need, can still feel him inside of me. I groan in frustration and fluff my hair, turning to the sink to splash a touch of cold water on my face. I dab beneath my eyelids with a napkin to capture any mascara smudges and take a deep breath.

"We'll finish this tonight," I say evenly, making a move for the door. Ryder nods firmly, his head hanging between his arms as he continues to grip the counter.

When I answer the door, Natalie's standing there, her hands nervously fidgeting at her sides. Her face is scrunched with unease and it scratches over me like sandpaper. "Hey, come on in," I say hesitantly.

She smiles halfheartedly, her eyes flicking to mine and then over my shoulder. "Oh, hey Ryder," she replies, her expression perking up. "I'm a few minutes early, I hope I'm not interrupting anything."

Ryder's cheeks reveal a light brush of crimson and he straightens up and clears his throat. His dimpled smile appears. "Hey Natalie, good to see you. No, not at all. I was just fixing Elise's dishwasher. I'm on the clock, so uh, I better get going."

I move aside and Natalie takes a step forward, her gaze landing near her feet, on Ryder's utility belt. She raises a brow and Ryder laughs uncomfortably as he hurries across the living room to retrieve it from the floor.

"I'll catch you ladies later," Ryder says, giving me a quick kiss on the cheek. "Have fun."

"See ya." I lean in to the kiss and bite back a grin as he hurries out the door. He's clumsily wrapping his belt around him and cursing under his breath as he tries to secure it, and I can't take my eyes off his backside as he strolls down the hall. What is a guy like that doing with a girl like me?

"He's good to you." Natalie's voice pries my eyes away from Ryder and I finally shut the front door. She's standing there politely, looking around at the apartment, but that strange expression has crept back onto her face, and tension bubbles around me.

"He's a good guy."

"Do you love him?"

I blanch at her question, quickly smothering it with a carefree laugh.

"I'm serious," she insists as she begins to stroll around the living room. "You've been awfully tight-lipped about him. What's the deal?"

I wet my lips and tuck my hair behind my ears. "There's nothing to tell, really. He's just…a good guy. I'm really into him."

"*Hhhmm.*" Natalie continues to meander around, inspecting my place like it's a museum. She stops in front of my bedroom door. It's wide open, and I inwardly curse, wishing I would've shut it before she showed up. It's neat and tidy now that I've spent time cleaning up, but I'm still getting used to letting Ryder anywhere near my bedroom, let alone Natalie. It feels entirely too intimate and the silence that has filled the space is killing me.

"Oh, the snow globe," she says absentmindedly, wandering into the bedroom. My heart rate flutters as she waltzes right over to my bedside table, where the globe sits next to my dream jar.

"I love it," I say dumbly, unsure of what to do as she proceeds to pick it up.

"I thought you would." Cradling it in her hands, she studies it for a moment and laughs fondly, as if a pleasant memory has come to mind. "That night of the festival was really something, wasn't it?"

"Yeah, it was fun." My hands smooth over my sweater sleeves and land inside my pockets.

"Me and you, and Ryder and Nate. We were all so chummy, don't you think?" Carrying the globe with her, she begins to trail back out into the living room. "It's a shame we couldn't have more double dates like that."

"Someone else will come along, you'll see."

"You think?" She glances down at the globe and then lifts her eyes to mine.

The stare lances me.

I gulp and start searching for my purse and keys. We should get out of here, get moving. "I guess that's easy for you to say," she adds, tilting her head with a smirk. "I mean, look at you. You're a goddess. Long legs, celebrity hair, perfect tits...you just have it all, don't you, Elise?"

Ice drenches my bones. My throat goes dry. The room is closing in, and every cell in me shrivels up in panic. She can't be doing this. Not here. Not like this. Not now. "Natalie—"

"You know what I really don't get, though? All these guys you screw—ya know, half the town, Nate included—don't seem to see the ugliness in you." She laughs and shakes her head, rolling the snow globe between her hands. "They don't see your heart, all charred and black. Don't see that you're a liar, a manipulator...a thief."

My hackles raise and despite the fact that she's clearly giving me exactly what I deserve—humiliation on a silver platter—I immediately feel the need to defend myself from at least one of those accusations. The only one that isn't entirely true.

I grapple and cling to it tightly.

"I don't steal," I demand, voice tight and hard.

"Oh, no? So, taking something—someone—who clearly belongs to someone else isn't stealing? Wow, you really are deluded. And here I thought you were just a stupid, selfish slut, just like everyone tried to tell me you are. Silly me, I didn't want to listen."

Her voice is cold, piercing my heart. My black, charred heart. "I understand you're upset. I wanted to tell you—so many times, I wanted to tell you the truth."

"You're such a damn liar!" Natalie suddenly explodes. Her chest is heaving in anger, her eyes flaring with contempt. "The fact that you even *attempted* to be my friend after…after you screwed him, is just a testament to the fact that you're a conceited, selfish bitch. Don't you see that? Who does something like that? Seriously!"

I go to speak but she glares at me, daring me to interrupt her.

"You know what the most infuriating thing is? I think those guys *do* see how ugly you are on the inside. They're just willing to overlook it for a piece of ass. They're bottom feeders, just like you. I just never pegged Nate to be one of them. Do you know what he told me, Elise?" Her eyes narrow and I don't just see disgust, I see the damage.

I finally see the hurt I've inflicted upon this girl, and in that one single glimpse, I see every woman I've ever hurt—every woman who ever belonged to a man I decided to claim as my own personal conquest.

"He told me you *begged* him." She laughs dryly. I'm

stunned to see such smugness radiate from this girl. I guess all things are possible when you're bursting with animosity. I don't bother correcting her. There wasn't much begging involved on my end the day I screwed Nate, but of course he wouldn't tell her that. "And what about Ryder? My God, is he really that blind?"

All of the air leaves me at the mention of his name. My hackles were raised before, but now I feel like a hunted doe, ready to spring into motion at the slightest hint of danger. I look her straight in the eyes. "Don't bring him into this. You don't know him."

"Is he just another Nate?" She lifts her chin, egging me on. "A good guy who's willing to pick up any scraps that might be left for him? Does he even realize he deserves so much better?"

A laugh bursts out of my throat, and I can't control the darkness that creates the sound. "Are you seriously comparing Nate and Ryder right now? Did you really just call Nate a good guy? What kind of *good guy* tells his ex-girlfriend that? He knew telling you about what happened between us would hurt you, Natalie. Don't paint him as something he isn't. He isn't innocent, and he knew exactly what he was doing."

A flash of disbelief flickers in her gaze, and she steps toward me, raising an index finger to jab at me in the air, like a disappointed parent to a misbehaving child. "You're disgusting. If Ryder knows what's good for him, he'll run fast in the other fucking direction and never look back."

My hand acts on its own accord and shoots out, smacking her hard across the cheek. I suck in a breath and stumble back, watching her expression shift from disbelief to pure rage in less than a second. "I'm sorry," I whisper, feeling the tears well up behind my lids. Holy fuck, where did that come from? "I'm so sorry."

Natalie's shoulders spring up and she hoists the snow globe back, sending it sailing over my shoulder and across the room. I shout as I hear the crack, hear it explode as it shatters against the wall. Spinning on my heel, I turn to look down at the broken glass.

"I trusted you," she says flatly, her arms hanging limply at her sides. She looks deflated, like all of the anger she'd been bottling up has leaked from her system. "I liked you. All I wanted was to be your friend. You don't want friends. I see that now." Her eyes glaze over with tears and she levels me with her glare. She shrugs lightly, her voice trembling. "You just want to hurt people, because you've been hurt."

My limbs are numb but I step forward before she can move. "I'm broken," I say, trembling. "Like the globe." I limply gesture to the glass shards. "You can try putting it back together, but it'll never be the same. It's not an excuse, Natalie. It's just reality. I was wrong. I knew what I was doing with Nate would hurt you and I went ahead and did it anyway. I know you will never forgive me. I know there's no going back. I'm not asking for your forgiveness, but it won't change the fact that I'm sorry. Just please...*please*, leave Ryder out of this. He's good, noble, honest…all of the things I'm not. Don't hurt him because you want to hurt me for what I've done." The tears are spilling onto my cheeks, and I let her see them. Every last one.

"Don't worry, Elise." She begins to wander lifelessly to the front door. "I won't say anything to him. Nate only told me today because I went to his place, asking him to give us another chance. Pathetic, huh? Ryder won't hear it from me because I'm not like you. I consider other people's feeling before I act. I'd never stoop so low." Her hand closes over the doorknob and she pauses, her back to me. "For the record, I knew you were broken. Not like it was a secret. I wanted to know you anyway."

The door opens and closes with a quiet click, and all of my hopes for being someone's something follow Natalie out, reminding me of my true identity. I am a substitute. A misfit. A liar, a thief, and a whore. I exist to be used, not to belong.

I steel myself and straighten my shoulders, and my father's haunting voice wraps its icy fingers around my throat.

"You're responsible for what you've taken from your mother now, Elise. Don't waste her beauty, do you understand? She passed it on to you, my dear. Harness it, and own it."

My mother was an accessory, just like me. She knew it, no matter how much she might have concealed the hurt. She found ways to be useful and never once complained about her fate. Maybe it is time to start taking my father's words more seriously. Maybe it is time to own it.

***

Splash, splash, splash.

My feet slap the surface as I float and lean back against the pool wall. It's a warm summer day and the sun is raining down on me as I swim in the hotel's turquoise L-shaped pool, humming softly to myself. My mother is beautifully poised in a lounge chair, her floppy hat and big, round sunglasses shadowing her classic features as she flips through a magazine. Her long, red nails are perfectly manicured and her sleek, white one-piece swimsuit complements her smooth, silky skin. A pair of gold chandelier earrings glint in the sunlight. She is the shining image of old Hollywood glamour, right down to her ruby red lips and romantic, pressed golden waves. One day I want to look like her.

"You'll burn, darling," she says, her eyes glued to the magazine, "you should come in the shade for a while. You know your father won't be happy if you burn."

I don't see what she's so worried about. My dad hasn't been around all weekend. He's brought my mom and me to L.A. for a weekend business trip, setting us up in a gorgeous—and no doubt pricey—chateau, but he hasn't spent any time with us so far. I can see my mother's disappointment. Every now and then, she glances at her diamond-studded watch, her eyes scanning the patio grounds, hoping to catch a glimpse of my father. He never shows.

"Mom," I ask, pulling my wet hair over my shoulders, running it through my fingers, "can I ask you something?"

"Of course, darling, what is it?"

"Do you love Dad?"

She places her magazine on her lap and lifts her sunglasses. "What a silly question, Elise. Of course I do. Why would you even ask that?"

"I'm just curious…how you know, I mean."

"How I know what?"

"That you love him."

She laughs lightly, but it's a fake laugh. A guarded one. "Well I did marry the man, darling."

"People get married all the time. It doesn't mean they love one another."

She slowly slides her sunglasses from the bridge of her nose, pulling them off completely. "Where on Earth is this coming from? You're 16 years old."

"Doesn't mean I don't know anything about love."

"Obviously you don't, if you're asking me that question." She looks defensive, as though my curiosity is an affront. It strikes a nerve in me.

"It's just a question, Mom. No need to get upset about it. I'm curious, that's all. How do you know he loves you back?"

Her pretty, long legs slide to the left, off the lounge chair, so her feet are planted firmly on the patio. "Elise, when two people love one another, they don't always have to label it, do you understand? When you love someone, you just know. You just…fit. You see certain qualities in each other, you dance until the sun comes up and get lost in one another until you forget your name and where you were born. Everything is hazy. You're dazed." She stands in one fluid motion and begins pacing slowly, dreamily, back and forth as she looks fondly in the distance.

"You do crazy, treacherous things," she continues, "and the next thing you know, you're so wrapped up in that person's presence, you can't seem to think about anything else. Those thoughts consume your every waking moment. They become your world. Without them, you cease to exist. Naturally, when you experience something like that, you simply…merge. You're no longer your own."

"That sounds like obsession, not love."

"Oh darling, love is obsession. There is a fine line between the two. One does not exist without the other. One day, you'll understand."

"But obsession is biased," I say quietly, thoughtfully. I swim up to the edge of the pool to look up at her, resting my head over my arms. "If that's all true, then… you're only seeing the good, the exciting, the romance. What about the bad? Are you just as enamored with one another when things are ugly?"

"Elise," she smiles, bending down to gently swipe a rebellious blonde strand from my forehead, "my beautiful girl. So wise beyond your years. When did you become so old?"

"I hope I fall in love some day," I say wistfully, smiling back at her. "I want love and obsession. It sounds exciting."

"You'll experience it for yourself, soon enough." She slides her sunglasses back on, rising to full height. With a delicate hand on her hip, she peers down at me and I can see the warmth in her eyes, even though they're covered. I might not believe my father really loves her, and I might question if what she says she feels for him is truly love, but I know without a shadow of a doubt, she loves me. I don't care how dysfunctional her mind may be, or how life has polluted her thoughts. I don't have to agree with the abuse she endures from my father. Her hurt is my hurt. She's my mother, and I'll always be her biggest fan.

Splash, splash, splash.

The pool water hits the wall as I sink my head beneath the surface. I can hear the soft lapping above me as I descend. When I reemerge, I'm no longer 16 years old. I'm not in L.A., and my mother isn't sitting poolside, sipping on champagne. She's six feet underground, and I'm collapsed on my sofa, wrapped in a throw blanket while the faint laughter from an episode of *I Love Lucy* echoes in the background. A bag of peanut butter cups is spilled open on my lap.

I groan as I recall Natalie's visit earlier this afternoon.

Tossing the bag of chocolates onto the coffee table and peeling the throw blanket from my lap, I pull my stiff body upright, wincing when a pang strikes my forehead. My eyes roll to the near-empty bottle of wine on the table, and I sigh, knowing a headache is just around the corner. It's not even 7 p.m. and I've already drowned myself in a chocolate-and-wine deluge. I didn't even get to sleep through the night. At least that would have delayed the consequences by a few more hours. Flicking the television off, I drop the remote and move to stand, knowing I made other plans tonight, before things with Natalie blew up in my face.

Ryder.

He'll be here soon, and I haven't showered. I need to brush my teeth, hydrate, and clear my foggy brain before he shows up. I don't want to process my confrontation with Natalie, much less even think about how I'll face her at Stella's tomorrow, but I know when Ryder walks through that door, I need to have my shit together, or he'll want to talk. He already wants to talk, but I don't want to add this to the list of things to discuss.

The hot water feels good on my back. I take extra time shaving and primping, making sure to wear my sexiest stilettos. My black thigh-high fishnet stockings hug my lean legs and my lace corset top brings my boobs sky-high. I eye myself over in the mirror.

Good. Nice and distracting.

It doesn't matter that Ryder likes me simple—bare faced and wearing nothing but his t-shirt. I go all out tonight, complete with a touch of my favorite perfume and dramatic lashes. No man can resist this, and he's full of shit if he says he doesn't like the effort. Tonight,

Ryder is mine. All mine, every delicious inch of him, and he's going to love every second of it. Tonight I will prove something to myself. Tonight I will prove Natalie wrong.

Ryder shows around 9 p.m., complete with a bouquet of blood-red roses, a bottle of wine—good, because I'm out now—and a bag full of DVDs. "Take your pick," he says, setting the bag down on the coffee table. He notices my heels as he does, and lets out a low whistle. "Damn, baby." His eyes travel upward, over my stockings and silk robe, and I begin to prowl toward him, setting the wine glasses down.

"The movies will have to wait."

"You have something else in mind?" His brown eyes glint with mischief and he pulls me against him, one of his hands snaking out to tug on the belt of my robe.

"Of course. How lame do you think I am?"

"Ouch," he laughs. "You stole my line."

I peer down to watch him loosen the robe belt. As soon as it's undone, I lift my chin and grin wickedly, flicking the silk down my shoulders, letting the robe slip to the floor. It flutters to my feet and Ryder's eyes flare. I knew it. He likes what he sees.

"There's no way we're making it to the bedroom with you looking like that," he says, tugging at his collar.

"Who said anything about the bedroom?" I take a step forward and give his chest a nudge, shoving him back so he falls to the couch. I bring my legs over his and straddle him, feeling him grow hard as I slowly grind against his lap.

“I want to give you your Christmas present.” He gets the words out, but there isn’t much conviction behind them. He’s too busy skimming his fingers along my thighs, watching as I give my hips another roll. “Baby,” he whispers, “please, I need to—” he groans and glances at my cleavage, spilling in front of his face, “I need to talk to you about something.”

“Talk later.” I nip on his bottom lip and slip my tongue into his mouth, needing him to get lost in me. When he was here earlier, I had questions. Lots of them. Now I have a different mission.

“This can’t wait.” He grips at my hips and eases me off his lap, placing me next to him on the sofa. The rejection crawls beneath my skin, and I can’t sit still. I cross my legs and fold my arms, then let my hands drop to my sides, where I pull at the top of my stockings.

“Okay, what is it?” I ask impatiently. What’s the point in having beauty as a superpower if it won’t let you seduce a man?

Ryder rises to his feet, and as he does, I hear a crunch beneath his boot. He lifts his foot and I spot a tiny Eiffel Tower, now in three pieces, embedded between the fibers of the carpet. I must have missed it in my hasty clean up.

“What the hell?” he asks, his eyes filled with confusion. “Isn’t this from the snow globe Natalie gave you?”

“I knocked into it when I was vacuuming and it broke.” I grind my teeth as I follow his puzzled gaze to the little, delicate tower pieces on the floor.

He regards me suspiciously for a moment but doesn’t

comment. "Did you and Natalie have a good time today? What movie did you see?"

"Nothing. We didn't..." I squirm and uncross my legs. "We didn't have time to see a movie."

"No? What about Pike's Market? Did you have fun?"

"Ryder, what do you want to talk about?" I sound snippier than I intended and decide to make a move for the trash can. Ryder is silent, watching me snatch the can from under the sink with a little too much force.

"Here," he says quietly as I walk over to him, "let me take care of it." I eye him for a moment, but hand him the trash can, waiting for him to discard the evidence. He lifts the pieces of glass from the carpet, dropping them into the garbage can with a small *clink*. He looks up, keeping his eyes straight ahead. "This used to be on your nightstand."

"I moved it."

He quietly rises to his feet and slips his jacket off, tossing it on the sofa. He begins to roll up his sleeves. A muscle clenches in his jaw. "I need to know what we're doing here," he says, meeting my gaze. "I need to know...other things about you, besides the fact that you're a waitress or that you're learning to speak French. I need to know more than your favorite TV show or your favorite wine. I need you to let me in, not lock me out all the time. I need you to not lie to me about something as stupid as how this snow globe broke or where you were all afternoon."

"You do know other things about me."

"Like what?"

"That night we played that game at your cabin, in front of the fire. I answered your questions. We've been spending time together; you've been screwing me. What more do you want to know?"

His shoulders tense and his eyes glaze over with something dark, as if I've surprised him with a punch to the gut. "You shut me out, and I don't know where to go from here, don't know what you want from me. All I know is I can't stop thinking about you. I want to be with you all the time, and when I'm not with you, I'm thinking about when I can show up on your doorstep again, or when you'll show up on mine. I know I don't want anyone else and that I'm jealous as fuck. I want you all to myself, and I want to hear that you're mine and mine alone, straight from your lips. I've wanted to hear that since the beginning and you've known that but I haven't pushed it because I didn't want to scare you away. But this—" he waves a hand in the air, "not knowing where you've been or who you've been with or what you're thinking…I don't know if I can handle it anymore."

My fists open and close at my sides. My mouth goes dry, and it takes every effort to swallow as I stare back at his intense, wholly sincere gaze. I'm rendered speechless.

"I wanted to talk to you tonight about other shit. About this." He reaches in his back pocket and retrieves a folded up envelope. It's red and has a candy cane label on it, addressed to me. He doesn't hand it to me, just holds it and stares down at it, like he's chewing over his decision to say any more. "I wanted to give you your Christmas present and ask you to be mine—not just someone I screw, Elise. *Mine*. My girl."

I swallow audibly, my heart clenching in my chest. He really does want me to be his girl. It's not just an endearment. He wants me to be something. To be somebody's something.

To be his something.

I haven't been imagining this or just hoping for it to be a reality. It's real and it's here, right now, right this second, and now that he's confirmed it all for me, there's no way out. There's no back door, and there's no going back. I know what's next: the mutual exchange. He's made his avowal and it's time for me to make mine. But I can't do that and sleep easy at night. I can't give him that and live with myself.

Not when he doesn't know the truth.

A shaky breath rattles from my lips and I step forward, planting my hands on his chest. "I can't make you any promises, Ryder." My voice is gentle and quiet, as if I'm approaching a scared animal. "I can only do this." I lean up and press my lips to his, lightly and cautiously, one of my hands gliding down over his abdomen. It drifts lower and lower. I reach my target and begin to stroke him, deepening the kiss. "Can you let this be enough?" I murmur against his mouth. "The knowledge that I want you? That I think about you all the time, too?"

His resolve falters as I touch him. He hardens beneath my hand and his mouth is desperate, but his words are stubborn, just like his mind. "I wish it were," he replies glumly, pulling away from my kiss. The envelope he's holding crumples between us, our mouths inches apart.

"I thought you wanted me."

"Don't play that game with me, Elise. Play it with all those other assholes chasing you around, but not with me. You know damn well I want you." He breathes roughly against my cheek, his eyes turning hard as they search mine. "You know you make it excruciating for me. You make it difficult for all men like me, don't you?"

"I'm not making this difficult for you." I take his hand and press it against my breast, begging him to cup me, to respond, but all I'm met with is a clenched jaw and a gaze that aches so strongly I can reach out and touch the pain.

"I'm not talking about all men," he closes his eyes tightly and his fingers twitch against my breast, "I said men like *me*." He grinds that last word out, struggling. This could be a whole hell of a lot less complicated if he just accepts things the way they are, takes them for face value. No explanations, no promises, no nothing. Just this, just the way we are.

"What are you talking about?" I snap, reaching up to bring my lips to his again. If I can just get him to taste me again, he'll drop this. He needs to drop this.

His eyes open. "Men who actually give a shit about you. Who want you for more than just this." He emphasizes *this* by squeezing my breast, his breath catching in the process.

"You're the one making this complicated," I hiss through my teeth, arching my back to press myself farther into him. "Just fuck me, already, Ryder."

His lips part slightly and he tries to reign himself in, as if he isn't drunk on lust, but his uneven breaths and stern jaw still give it all away. Well, that and his raging hard-on wedged in between my legs.

"No."

"What do you mean, *no*?" The words roll off my tongue like they're dirty. "Why not?"

"Because I can't have all of you."

"What does that even mean?" My head drops back in frustration. I know exactly what it means, but I need him inside me, like, yesterday, if I want to save this before it crashes and burns.

"It means exactly that, Elise." He drops his hand from my chest and pushes away from me, shoving his fingers through his hair. "I don't just want a quick lay with you, don't you get that? When I fuck you, I want all of you. Your mind, your heart—I want *you*. How many times do I have to say it?"

"Oh, Jesus," I scoff, rolling my eyes and straightening my corset. He's opting for crashing and burning. He's rejecting what I'm offering. He's going to make me say it.

A switch flips, and my eyes flare with heat.

"Seriously? You're either the dumbest man I've ever met or you've been in the closet so fucking long, you don't know which way is up."

His whole body goes rigid, and he stares at me steadily

when I can't even maintain the simplest eye contact. My gaze darts everywhere, and I begin to pace. Edginess begins to boil in me, hot and dangerous, and I don't think I've ever felt this helpless. Everything—anything good we have going between us—is about to be ruined, all because what I'm offering to give him isn't enough. Just as I'd feared, I'm not enough. Christian was right. Enough doesn't exist.

"You don't get to do that," he grinds out.

"Get to do what?"

"Hurt me, hurl insults like I'm one of your piece-of-shit hook-ups. You don't get to just push me away because you're not in control, here. Relationships don't work like that."

"Oh my God," I laugh, throwing my head back in disbelief, "where the hell have you been? There is no relationship! This *is* a piece-of-shit hook-up, or it would have been if you would've thought more with your dick and less with your head, for Christ's sake! And I'm very much in control, if you haven't noticed. Get out, Ryder." I storm toward the door and pull it open wide, working to keep my arm steady as I hold the knob. He knows about me. All this time, he's known, and now he's using it as ammo. I can't handle the humiliation. I can't let him see me cry. "Please," I repeat. "Get *out*."

He follows me to the door, and the heat from his anger is scorching my face. "Hate to break it to you, but this—" he points between us, "is called a relationship. What we've been doing? It's called being friends, being lovers. It's something adults do when they like each other's company. Damn it, Elise, look at me!"

I take a step back to create some distance between us and he reaches for my elbow. His touch is so soft, so gentle, the way it clashes with his hard tone causes me to bring my eyes to his. I struggle, but I manage to look at him dead on.

He exhales, cupping my face. "I *know*. I know exactly who you are. People talk, you know that."

"Congratulations." I blink, looking away.

"I'm not telling you this to embarrass you, to put you on the spot. I'm telling you this because I've invested enough time in getting to know you that I think I deserve a little respect, a little more than how you're treating me right now. You feel something for me and you can't tame it. I can't tell you how to deal with that because it's foreign to you, and you're foreign to me. But I'm standing here and I'm telling you I fucking feel the same way and I want you. But I won't settle for bread crumbs. I'm an all-or-nothing guy and I'm fully convinced you never do anything half-assed, so just face this, no matter how hard it is for you. Please." He chances reaching for my hand and for a second, I let him hold it. "Don't run from this. Stay. Let me fuck you and adore you at the same time. 'Cause I can do that. I can give you both. I've never wanted anything more."

The brush of his fingertips over mine brings those dreaded tears to my eyes but I push them back, fueled by an ungodly amount of rage surging over my bones. It feels violent and fraught, a strange and entirely volatile combination. I don't know what to do with the anger, so I give it to him.

I pull my hand from his and step back.

"You apparently haven't been paying attention," I say dryly. "I do *everything* half-assed. I'm never all in or all out. I'm whatever suits me at the moment, and on the fence is usually the safest place to be. Whatever you're looking for, I don't have it to give to you. If you can't handle what I'm offering, it's not my problem. I'm hollow, Ryder. There's nothing for you here. Don't try to mold me into something you want to see."

"I know exactly what I see, and I know it's real."

"Why are you so goddamn blind?" I shout. "I'm a whore! I'm rotten to the fucking core, and if you shake this crazy fantasy you have—of me and you frolicking in the fucking woods together, stargazing and listening to Fleetwood Mac—you'd fucking see that! You'd run in the other direction if you have even a shred of sense."

"I told you I don't care about your past, Elise! I care about who you are right now. I don't believe you're that girl anymore. Call me naïve, but even if you are, I think you can fucking change, and I think you *want* to. I think this whole town has been labeling you for so long, you started believing it yourself. Don't let them tell you what you are."

"They're right! Don't you understand that?"

"You haven't been sleeping with anyone else while you've been with me, have you? *Have you*?" He grips my shoulders and shakes me. “Tell me if you have.”

“I fucked Nate,” I whisper, a shudder rolling through my chest.

Boom.

Just like that, it’s over. Ryder will never look at me the same. He made me say it, and while getting it off my chest should give me some sort of relief, it only makes my anger more potent. Natalie was right. Mission failed.

Ryder blinks, and his entire body goes still. “You and Nate? While you were with me.”

“Yes. I mean, before we ever—not since we’ve been sleeping together, no.”

A veil of hurt lowers over him, his gaze glassy. He doesn’t move. If the look on his face doesn’t kill me, the silence surrounding us will. “I know,” he finally says. His voice is quiet, the pounding in my chest drowning out the sound.

My limbs are deadweight. “What?”

“I know about Nate. I’ve known.”

“What are you…you what?”

“I just needed to hear it from you.”

A trickle of wetness teases the tops of my cheeks, and I can’t hold it back anymore. I cave right there, right in front of him. I can’t even bring myself to care that he’s witnessing it, because the weight’s too heavy and it feels too good to let it drop. “How long? How long have you known?”

“A while.”

“Did he tell you? Did someone tell you?”

"No one needed to tell me."

"Why would you..." I press my hand to my throat, feeling it constrict beneath my fingers. "Keep seeing me...all this time."

His face is still full of hurt but it reveals an edge of determination. He steps forward. "It's like I've been trying to tell you. I want you." He reaches out to smooth his thumb over my tears and I flinch, unsure if I'm more horrified by the fact that he's known about Nate or that he's still standing here instead of running out the door. "You never promised me exclusivity. But I'm telling you tonight. I don't want to share you. If you're going to see Nate—or anyone else while you're seeing me, then this is the end of the road for me."

My voice quivers and my knees shake. He can't be serious. "You...you still want me?"

"Elise," he breathes, moving with no hesitation. His arms swoop around me and enfold me against him. I'm numb. I'm safe, encased in his cocoon, but I can't feel the warmth. He swallows hard, the pressure pressing against my forehead as he tucks my head into the crook of his neck. "I'm in love with you. Does that answer your question?"

I stiffen in his arms. Pressing back against his chest, I remove myself from his protective cage. Raising my gaze to his, I level him with lifeless eyes. "Please leave."

"Elise—"

"I said *leave*."

"What? No, wait. Listen—"

"Leave!" I shout, the sound barreling out of me like a siren. My body is stone, rooted to the floor, but my voice…my voice is an ocean of uproar. Ryder might want to give me this—this love I don't deserve—but I refuse to accept the gift. To accept it would be the ultimate act of hurt, and I've already doled out more than I can live with. "Please," I say softer, closing my eyes, "save those words for someone else. Leave and don't ever come back, Ryder. I mean it."

When I feel like I can look at him, I open my eyes.

"Just because I haven't been with other guys while I've been seeing you doesn't mean that I'll be faithful. I've already hurt you. I will hurt you again. It's only a matter of time."

"I don't accept that; I won't buy it, do you hear me? You're afraid."

Damn right, I'm afraid.

I fix cold eyes on his and muster as much strength as I can to keep my tone stern. I have to deliver another hard blow. It's the only way I'll protect him. "I'm not a bird with a broken wing you can fix, do you understand? I'm not a dishwasher or a fucking garbage disposal. I'm Elise Duchamp, and I destroy relationships. I destroy people. Wives, girlfriends, good people. People like you. I fuck their husbands, their boyfriends, eat their food, sleep in their beds. Is that clear enough for you? And don't you dare feel fucking sorry for me, because you know where I'll head the second you walk out this door?" I steel myself, preparing for the final drop of the axe and the look on his face that will surely haunt me the minute it's done its damage.

"Don't do this." He shakes his head, wiping a hand over his jaw. His eyes are pleading, like he knows what I'm about to say. "Goddamn it, don't do it—"

"I'll head to a man named Christian Walker, Ryder. One of the many married men I've had affairs with. I'll sleep with him, and I won't think twice about getting into his bed. Because that's what I'm destined to be."

"Stop it," he seethes, his jaw working and nostrils flaring.

Lifting my chin, I step closer and bring us nose to nose. My tone drops, flat and hard as ice. "I will always be the other woman. Don't ever forget that."

"No." He grips the side of my face, his lids filling with unshed, angry tears.

"There is no saving me, there is no future for us, and leaving is the smartest thing you will ever do." I don't know how I've mustered up the strength to say the words, and I know they're striking where it hurts. But the pain they're delivering will be nothing compared to what might happen if he sticks around.

"This won't work," he chokes out. "Go ahead. Give me all you've got. Rip my fucking heart out if that's what you need to do. But it won't change this. I love you and I know you love me." He presses his nose against mine, his head cocking slightly as he sears me with sharp daggers. "And you can't run from it, Elise Duchamp."

With that, he releases me and walks out, and a part of

me leaves with him. I may never get that part back. But he's wrong. I can run from it. And I will.

CHAPTER 14

My long white gown sparkles as I descend the wide, luxurious staircase. It's embedded with tiny rhinestones—possibly real diamonds, for all I know, I didn't buy it—and scoops low at the small of my back. A matching fur shawl drapes over my shoulders and I'm gripping my clutch at my side, scanning the ballroom for him. My pressed blonde waves sit softly at my shoulders, caressing my skin like silk, and my black and silver masquerade mask shimmers beneath the dim, romantic lighting. It's just wide enough to conceal the tops of my cheekbones, providing a glimpse of my gaze through the eye cut-out slits.

Couples are dancing below while champagne and Christmas themed hors d'oeuvres are served on ornate silver platters. I descend slowly, watching the event unfold in slow motion. A sea of evening gowns and tuxes rolls before me, casting me in a hypnotic spell. Everything about tonight holds me in a daze, but it's a much needed distraction from the hellish work week I've had.

Natalie and I resumed shifts together as if nothing ever happened. It should have been a relief, to be able to go to work and carry on with my job in peace, but the fact that she was acting so indifferent rattled me to the core. We kept our distance from one another and barely spoke unless it was work related, but it was her eyes that said so much. They were empty and cold, as if I were a complete stranger. That made me more uncomfortable than any dirty look or angry remark ever could. She's made her position clear. I am dead to her.

When I reach the bottom of the staircase, a set of flawless, shiny teeth flashes at me surrounded by sharp black and white—an equally flawless tuxedo. It's tailored for a king, and Christian wears it like one.

"There you are," he smiles brightly, offering me his arm. His face is concealed by a black masquerade mask, but I can see his eyes travel down my body as he devours every inch of me. "I can't get over how stunning you are tonight. Where have you been, Beautiful? You keep slipping away from me."

"Just needed to make a few phone calls," I lie, plastering on a small smile. I've been sneaking out to smoke, a nasty new habit I've recently picked up. I've made it a point to bring a bottle of body mist along to dilute the smell because Christian hates cigarette smoke, and I'm hoping that at the rate I'm downing glasses of champagne, the smell of the booze will drown out any remaining nicotine on my breath.

Christian's eyes rake up and down and he licks his

lips before leaning in to speak in my ear. "You must be hungry. I know I am. Come with me." He sidles up to my side and my arm wraps around his, allowing him to lead the way. Gotan Project's "Época" croons in the background and I notice the chandelier lighting is beginning to look a little fuzzy. I stumble slightly, wobbling in my heels, and Christian's arm tightens, providing me a steady weight to lean on to. "Easy there," he chuckles softly, in that smooth, sensual tone I know so well.

He watches me collect myself and then guides me through the sea of guests, to the edge of the ballroom. He directs us around a corner and down a hall, leading me further down a narrower hallway that leads to a private office space of some sort. Before I can ask where he's taking me, I'm thrust up against the wall and my thigh is lifted around his hip. One of his hands glides up the daring slit of my gown, grasping at the top of my thigh, while the other goes for his bow tie, frantically working to loosen it. "I can't wait a second longer," he breathes, smothering me in the heat of a kiss. "I need to feel you."

I gasp as his fingers breach my panty line, turning my head to the side to breathe. He attacks my neck with his tongue and teeth, and I bite back a groan. Not because I don't want any passerby to hear me, but because I don't want him to hear me. I don't want him to know he's affecting me. I don't want to give him any more encouragement than I already have, but it's too late and there's no undoing what I've done.

Sadly, my body has always been a slave to him, and

my consumption of champagne is only aiding my traitorous flesh. I let him nibble at my neck, let him stroke me until I'm wet against his hand, but that feeling comes over me again and I have to beg him to stop.

"What is it, baby?" He pulls back a hair, dazed but full of determination to make sure I'm okay. "Have I hurt you?"

"God no," I pant, straightening myself against the wall, bringing my palms flat against the cool wallpaper. "It's just strange. Tonight I feel like…"

"Feel like what?"

"As if someone's watching us."

Christian grins, all wicked and dashing, his eyes flicking up to scan the hallway ceiling. "Well, I don't doubt there are security cameras around. You've never had a problem with exhibitionism before. Is my girl suddenly afraid of giving someone a little show?" He snickers, and his eyes glint with delight. "I still have that video, you know. The one Chad and his friends filmed of us—"

"No," I stop him, bringing my hand up to kill that memory. The way he calls me his girl makes my stomach churn. I struggle to bury the endearment. "I'm serious, Christian. Like we're being followed or something." I haven't been able to shake the feeling since we arrived at the ball—another reason I've been sneaking out for cigarette breaks. The persistent inkling has been following me around all evening, and I'm not sure what to make of it other than perhaps I want to be seen. Perhaps I want to be sought out.

But I only want to be found by one person, and even if he truly is seeking me out, I wouldn't know what to say to him. I've made my choice. This is final.

"Okay, I think someone's had enough champagne for the evening," Christian says, bending to kiss me on the forehead. "I say we take this back to my place."

I don't think that's the source of my intuition, but I agree, anyway. I have had a lot to drink tonight, and it's probably wise to head home for the evening. "Okay," I sigh, combing my fingers through my hair as Christian leads me down the hallway, back out to the main corridor. We round the same corner we passed before, and a chill crawls down my spine, pricking lightly as it slithers along each ridge.

"Elise?" Christian's voice makes me jump. "Are you coming?"

I realize I've stopped cold, like a rabbit honing in on the sound of a predator. Christian's arm is still snugly around my waist, his eyes searching mine curiously. "Yes, sorry." He tightens his hold on me and gently guides me forward. We disappear through the lobby doors and wait for the valet to bring Christian's car around. The feeling slips away as we wait, and some of the tension leaks from my shoulders. Maybe the champagne really has been going to my head.

***

Christian's house is cool and dark when we step

through the front door. A single porch light illuminates the front hall, creating a bare glow on the dark wood floors.

"Head upstairs, baby. I'll bring us some water." He gives me his million dollar smile and slips out of his tux jacket, loosening his tie. He strolls away toward the kitchen and the downstairs glows brighter when he flicks on the kitchen lights. I start up the stairs, stretching my neck and back, my feet aching from my heels. I go to reach for them as I reach the top of the stairwell but stop myself. Christian will want me to leave them on.

A pool of cool moonlight bathes the master bedroom as I enter, pouring in through the opened curtains. My shoulders tense at the doorway, my gaze landing on the plush armchair in the corner of the room near the dresser. It's nestled to the left of the window, where a sliver of moonlight casts a faint spotlight over its silhouette. A shadow covers the chair, the pale blue light illuminating only half of its form.

My hand slowly extends to the wall, searching for the light switch.

"Don't," a voice says, sharp and short.

I freeze. Icy daggers scrape down my back.

"Not yet," the woman's voice warns. Fear sinks its fangs into me and my lungs seize up, my hand hovering just below the light switch. "Wait for him."

I swallow and the sound is audible in the quiet room, making the silence even more razor sharp. A soft rustling sounds from behind me in the hall. Christian is approaching, humming to himself.

"Elise? Are you up here, baby? I brought you some water. I don't want you to have a headache in the morning from all that champagne." He strolls up behind me, nearly bumping into my back. "Hey," he laughs, resting his hand on my hip. "What are you doing up here in the dark?" His arm extends behind me, flipping on the light switch, and my eyes are glued to the armchair, unblinking and filled with dread.

"Hello honey," the woman says, her voice dripping with disdain. It's not just any woman. It's the woman in all of Christian's picture frames. The woman he told me he was leaving—who he swore was no longer in his life. I've worn her silk pink bathrobe and tried on her Jimmy Choos. Kylie, his wife.

The fact that she's sitting there elegantly, with her legs crossed and arms draped naturally on the armrests, is not nearly as alarming as what is gripped tightly in her right hand.

A gun.

A shiny revolver that looks much too large to be held with her dainty fingers.

"Kylie," Christian chokes, his body stringing tightly against my back, "my God, what are you doing?"

Kylie's bobbed blonde do skims her shoulders, her sleek pencil skirt hugging her lean, shapely legs. She smiles like a serpent, her eyes rife with a million conflicting emotions. I notice a slight tremble in her grip, where her fingers brush lightly against the cylinder of the gun. Her eyes might be welling with tears, hardened from anger and hurt, but one thing is clear and cannot be mistaken.

They are unstable.

My head is lead on my neck but my gaze darts around the room, searching for signs of booze or pills—anything that might explain her alarming behavior. I see nothing, only a woman scorned and a weapon in hand, aimed right at Christian and me.

"All evening you've been so attentive," Kylie says. "So careful with her. My God," she chokes, her voice cracking, "you can't keep your hands off of her."

"Kylie, let's talk about this. We can talk about this. Elise, give us a minute, will you?"

"Don't you dare move," Kylie snaps, suddenly sitting up to bring her posture straighter. Her hand rises with the movement, bringing the gun higher. "Please, don't let me interrupt your lovely evening. Do carry on." She juts her head to the side, gesturing to the bed. The gun sways in her hand, following the movement. "I'm sure it will be quite the show."

"Kylie," Christian speaks up, gently raising one hand to plead with her. "Please, put that down and come speak with me. You don't have to do this. It's not necessary."

"Not necessary?" She laughs, a dry, biting laugh, and it grates straight down to my toes. "Oh, you mean like flaunting her around at that ball of yours tonight? Or nearly fucking her like a cheap hooker in an alleyway down a secluded hall? Or how about bringing her to our home—like you have so many times before—to tell her more lies? To tell me more lies? Is any of that *necessary*?"

My heart constricts, my lungs nearly imploding. The haunted look in her eyes isn't just anger. It's more than hurt, more than betrayal. It's 100 percent vengeful.

"I haven't lied to you, Kylie," Christian speaks cautiously, his hand still raised in defense. He holds my glass of water in the other, and there's no masking the tremor in his fingers. "You know that things have been over. It was mutual. You agreed. I don't know what's going on. I don't understand this—" he carefully gestures to the gun, "whatever you're doing. But I want to help you. Let me help you. We can put this behind us. There's no need for anyone to get hurt."

"Oh, we're way past that, honey. Help? Hurt? Are you kidding? The damage is done, Christian." She rises from the chair fluidly, remaining if front of it, raising her arm to aim the gun at my chest. Christian carefully shifts to the side, stepping next to me to place himself in the line of fire.

"How noble of you," Kylie hisses. "And water, too? To make sure she doesn't get a headache? So kind and considerate of you, *darling*."

Beads of sweat tickle my forehead and I can't swallow. The tears burn my throat, spilling slowly from my ducts like quiet raindrops.

"Why are you doing this?" Christian asks. "Why now? Help me understand, Kylie. It's never too late for help. We can repair this, we can find a way."

"Why now?" she scoffs, shaking her head. "Why *now*?" she repeats, making a move for the dresser for the television remote. Christian's shoulder bumps mine as he flinches, causing me to gasp. The sound of the television flicking on jolts my nerves like static electricity. "Let me enlighten you."

In seconds, the DVD player clicks on and an image of me and Christian having sex in his office chair appears. We're not alone. There's low chatter mixing with our moans, and two of Christian's friends are seated on the edge of the desk, watching us. One of them turns back to glance at the camera with a wink, and my stomach rolls. My eyes squeeze shut.

I know what's coming next.

Just like I know the camera man. Chad, another one of Christian's friends. I know everything that happened in that room that night because I was a willing participant, and seeing it unfold on the TV before Kylie sends bile rushing up my throat. My brain rejects this reality. This can't be happening. Isn't happening. Not fucking happening.

"Kylie, stop it," Christian demands, his chest heaving. His breathing is growing frantic, and I'm suddenly afraid I might pass out before Kylie kills me. I might not even get to say any last words, because I'll be out cold on the carpet. These images, my dirtiest of sins, might be the very last images I ever see. "Turn this off. Don't do this."

"I found a copy of this in with my DVDs. You know, when I began moving some of my stuff out. As you can imagine, it was quite the shocker. Not that your little girlfriend here is a filthy whore, of course." She fixes hard eyes on me. I can see her hatred through my tears. "That much I knew. But the fact that you were willing to share her like that, with Chad and Brent and...Carl, was it?" She looks to the ceiling, as if recalling the memory. "My, my." She tsks and shakes her head. "For such a dominant, possessive man as you, I must say I'm stunned. Seemed they enjoyed themselves, feasting on your girlfriend, here. How generous of you."

"That's enough," Christian steps forward, moving for the TV, but Kylie beats him to it, leveling the gun with his chest.

"Christian," I manage to whisper, terrified for this man, this man I have no right to hold any claim to.

He retreats, raising his hands, and I hear a sharp sob break from his chest. As he backs away and returns to my side, I sneak a peek at him. His eyes are filled to the brim with fear, just as potent as my own, and I realize right then that he has no hope of talking Kylie down. Not now. Kylie's wild eyes glisten as she grins wider. She doesn't pry her eyes from Christian as she clicks a button on the remote, killing the video footage.

"Oh thank God," I cry, clutching my chest. "Please, Kylie, I'm begging you. I'm sorry. I'm so sorry—"

"Resorting to begging so soon?" she cracks, her eyebrows lifting. "What a shame. I thought you two would do me the honor of giving me a little show first. What do ya say? For old time's sake?" She laughs erratically, waving the gun toward the bed. "Go on."

"Please, no. Oh my God, please no." I beg again, my chest constricting with each syllable. My plea only amuses her more.

"Both of you on the bed. Take your clothes off. Move!" She walks to the edge of the bed, her hand shaking uncontrollably now. "Even better, I'll make a little home movie of my own, how does that sound? I bet your friends will love it, Christian."

"Oh Jesus, please God," Christian grinds out, dissolving into sobs. "Kylie, no. No, no, no."

"Calling on a lifeline now, are you? Isn't that funny." Keeping the gun trained on us, she reaches down for a box at the end of the bed, retrieving a small digital camera.

"You'll go to jail. You'll lose everything. Everything, do you hear me?"

"Shut up," Kylie quips, turning the camera on. "Suddenly you care about what happens to me? Suddenly you're crying out for God to save you? I won't say it again. On the bed. Now!" Her shrill voice sends me jumping, stumbling over to the edge of the bed. My shaky fingers begin to fumble with my gown zipper, but I can't feel a thing. Christian moves next to me slowly, our eyes locking.

"Ah, there we go," Kylie sings, grinning with satisfaction at the camera. "Now Elise, you're on top. Go on. Your favorite position." My entire body quakes as my gown slides down my flesh. I feel Kylie's crazed eyes flare as my bare skin is displayed before her. Christian's unsteady hands are still working on his pants, but he hasn't taken his eyes off of mine. He's telling me something—what, I don't know. I stare right back, willing him to do something, to say something, but all I see is pure, helpless terror.

A vague echo bounces in the back of my skull, wondering if he ever knew his wife was capable of such horror. If he ever knew, even a little, way deep down, that she was sick. Maybe she was never sick. Maybe he's terrified because this is the first glimpse he's ever seen of this unsteady, reckless side.

Maybe I made her sick, just like my mother's cancer.

"Sit down on the edge, Christian," Kylie commands the minute he's nude. He complies, and I see the desperation, the pause in each step he takes. "Now you, Elise. On his lap." A hard wail rocks me as I step in front of him. My body is on autopilot, because I sure as hell am not telling it what to do. Somehow, my panties fall to my feet and my quivering, naked body is crawling onto Christian's lap. Goosebumps spread like wildfire as I grip his shoulders for support. He's mumbling incoherently. I make out a few sorrys. He's saying them over and over again, as if they can somehow save us from what is about to happen.

Kylie's suddenly gone quiet, and I feel her presence looming at my side. The camera is staring me in the face, her gun inches from my head. Time stops and I see flashes of everything, a myriad of images that take my breath away.

Christmas morning when I was three years old.

My first puppy.

My mom and dad kissing in the audience of my ballet recital.

Faces of people I've met over the years. Some I remember, many I don't.

The Eiffel Tower.

Sunny glimpses of L.A., oleander blooming.

My mother laughing, my mother crying.

My father yelling.

Tee.

Jay.

Art, ink, and blood.

Ryder.

Ryder.

Ryder.

The camera drops to the carpet with a thud and the barrage of images rush to a stop. Cold metal presses against the side of my forehead and I suck in a final sharp breath, whispering, "I'm sorry," and "I love you," to no one in particular. I love life, even though I fucked mine up. I hope that counts for something.

I wait for the bang. I wait for darkness, for someone on the other side. Instead I get a "click."

Click, click, click.

Kylie's finger is pumping the trigger, stunning Christian and me still. Warm wetness spreads beneath me. I'm not sure if it's from me or Christian. A beat passes and Kylie laughs, dropping the gun at her feet. Her hand snakes into her skirt pocket and retrieves a fistful of bullets. Her palm flattens as she shows them to us, then lets them tumble to the floor. "Don't flatter yourselves," she murmurs. "I'd never throw my life away over garbage like you." She wipes her palms together as if brushing away dust and grime and strolls unevenly across the bedroom. She disappears out the door and a shudder of aftershock rocks my body before I fall and collapse next to Christian. I slide down, slipping on the floor, one arm draped over the edge of the bed, fingers clinging to the bedspread.

A door slams downstairs, and a muffled thumping pounds relentlessly in my ears, against my temples. I shut my eyes and pray for the numbness to swallow me whole.

***

My body sways gently. Weightlessly. The back of my neck aches, as do my knees. Suddenly my head and back make contact with something soft and comforting. There's an exchange of voices, a jingling of keys. A door shuts and the voices stop. I think one of them was Christian's. Something warm, gentle, and rough skims my forehead, replaced by something cool and damp. The softness I'm resting on dips at my side, and I think Christian's back.

"Elise," a voice whispers, quiet and soothing. My eyelashes flutter, looking for his face. The voice is familiar, but it's not Christian. "Can you hear me?"

"Yes," I mouth, unsure if the sound came out. "Christian?"

"Christian left."

"Left?"

"I'm here for you. You're not alone. It's okay."

My mouth is dry, voice gravelly as I fight to open my eyes. "Ryder?" My vision blurs, then comes into focus, and I see his face: unshaven, handsome, no dimples. "What's going on? What are you doing here?"

He brushes my hair back and removes the cold dampness from my forehead. He sets the washcloth on the bedside, next to my dream jar. Thank God, I'm in my bedroom. And Ryder's here. My stomach churns and I groan.

Oh God, Ryder's *here.*

"Christian said you've been calling out for me. He called me."

"Am I hurt?" My hand lazily slides up to cup the back of my head, searching for an injury.

"No, you're okay. You're safe. You've just been sleeping. I think the shock..." He swallows and takes my hand. "You've just been in shock."

"Christian called you? How..."

"Your cellphone. I guess when you kept asking for me, he scrolled through your contacts to get a hold of me."

Christian spoke to Ryder. Ryder spoke to Christian.

They met. I'm not sure this night could get any worse.

"Is he hurt?"

"No, he's okay, too. He went to the police. He's going to pursue a restraining order." As my vision continues to clear, bringing his rugged, weary face into view, I shift to sit up. My back hits the headboard and I flinch. "Easy. Just take it easy."

"I can't believe you came for me."

He averts his eyes and grinds his jaw, reaching for the washcloth. He fidgets with it, folding it open and closed. "I was worried."

The night's traumatic events slowly begin to unravel in my mind, turning and rolling as they feed me the memories. As groggy as my head is, as weak as I am, there is so much I want to say to Ryder. I want to tell him that he was the last thing I saw before Kylie pulled the trigger. That all I could think about was being loved by him and how seeing his face over and over made me want to give him that love in return. But reality looms, grim and defeating.

I burned him and returned to Christian Walker.

"It's more than typical daddy issues," I say instead.

Ryder's head lifts and his gaze floats to mine. "What?"

"That day, I said I had typical daddy issues. That you wouldn't want to hear those things. But what I didn't say is that it is more than that, and the issues are far from typical." Ryder's eyes are intent and unmoving, fixed on me like I might disappear if he blinks. My throat feels like sandpiper, the coarseness painful, but I continue anyway. "The way he treated my mother…it was abhorrent. He never hit her, not once. But the things he said…"

"Elise, you don't have to do this now."

My hand inches out to seek his. My fingers graze the cool cloth that rests in his fist. "He was a nasty drunk. Thought about raping me once. Never said it aloud. Didn't need to. I knew what he was thinking, could feel his thoughts all over me, like spiders crawling. I'd always been scared of him—of his words. Never scared like that. Not until that night."

Ryder releases the washcloth and squeezes my hand. He listens.

"I watched my mother jump through hoops, constantly seek my father's approval, right up until she died. It was always so sad…so sick. They were both sick, in different ways. It used to confuse me. I used to be angry because I didn't understand it. But one day it just all… clicked."

Ryder shifts and the mattress dips at my side. His eyes are heavy as stone. "What did?"

"That fighting it was useless. Accepting it was the only option. They were broken. I was a product of that dysfunction. There was no use trying to change what I was. That's an uphill battle. It's exhausting."

"Elise, you're not your parents."

"But I am," I say, sitting up farther, letting my head roll back on the headboard. "There's no use denying what you are. The best thing you can do is accept it. Own it. At least then, you know your place in the world."

"Your place?" Ryder squints, shaking his head softly. "Elise, your place in the world is what you *tell* yourself it is. You make that decision."

"And I have. Don't you get it?"

"No. No, I don't."

"I made the decision to let all of that define me. Somewhere along the way…I stopped swimming up the current. I'm a crutch, Ryder. For people like Christian." A shadow passes over Ryder's expression, shielding him in pain. It passes, but I don't pretend to miss how Christian's name affects him. "For men like Nate. People who don't want to commit to definition. Who want to live a lie. They find me, I find them…because they need someone like me."

"Someone like you?"

I lean forward, threading my fingers tighter with his. "Someone disposable. Someone who *knows* she's disposable." My lips press together as I swallow, holding his gaze. "My parents didn't do this to me, Ryder. My mother's cancer, the abuse, none of that is responsible. I chose this all on my own."

"But it affected you. All of it did. It's fucked up. Life is fucked up. It plays a role in who we become. You're right, though." He reaches up and skims my lips. "You've made your choices."

My chest cracks, and I feel something for the first time since I've woken up. "Do you still believe I can change?"

Ryder's eyes turn glassy. He holds my stare. "Quand

on veut, on peut."

The ink on my hips seems to come alive, tickling my skin. I want to crush my mouth to his, want to beg for forgiveness and tell him to make me his girl. I want to be his something.

"Ryder?" I whisper. "You said you'd never just drive away. Is that still true?"

A muscle along his jawline pops and he leans forward, planting a kiss on my temple. "Sometimes you have to just drive away. Get some more rest. I have to get going." The strange mixture of hope and fear melts from my expression, and my eyes drop to the blanket. Ryder stands and pulls at it, lifting it up to my chin, carefully tucking me in. "You're safe now. If you need something…just call Jay. He knows you're not feeling well. I didn't give him any details, don't worry. He thinks it has something to do with you and Natalie arguing."

"Okay," I croak out. "Thank you."

He nods once and turns for the bedroom door, stopping just before he exits. "There's something on the kitchen counter for you. For later. Goodbye, Elise."

He disappears and an aching breath shudders through me. My world crumbles at my feet, imploding beneath me until there's nothing left but soot and dirt and the residue of his words, sticking to my skin. I have no idea where to go from here. How to recover from the event at Christian's that nearly cost me my life. But I do know one thing for certain, just as my mom said I would, when the time came.

I know I am in love with Ryder Jacobson. And it's too little, too late.

CHAPTER 15

Some of the strength returns to my limbs. I pull myself out of bed and step into the shower, letting the hot water wash away my sins. I made sure to lock the bathroom door behind me. Paranoia eats away at my insides, and it sinks in then that I might carry the consequences of last night with me for the rest of my life. I rest my forehead on the tile wall and close my eyes as the water beats at my back. I wince when I hear the clicking of the trigger. It echoes in my mind, haunting me like restless ghouls in a graveyard.

Drying off, I decide to wander out to the kitchen to make some hot tea. It's too soon to even think about returning to work, but I need to at least call Jay and touch base. He needs to know he can depend on me. I refuse to disappoint Jay any more than I already have.

Feeling fresher and more alert, I wrap myself in my soft terrycloth bathrobe and make my way into the kitchen for the first time since Ryder left. I'd dozed off afterward, content to just block the world out for a while.

Between the trauma and Ryder's visit, I must've been wiped out, because I'd slept through the night. When I see what's sitting near the kitchen counter, I stop in my tracks.

Stevie.

Ryder's telescope, the one he and his friends all chipped in to pay for, propped up on its stand. A bright yellow tag hangs from it and I move forward. My fingers latch onto the yellow tag and flip it over, exposing the text.

Some of the best things in life are free, it says.

I smile wryly and stare at the card for a moment, scanning the text over and over again, trying to understand why he would give me something that means so much to him, let alone means so much to his friends at the campground.

A small wooden box sitting on the edge of the counter catches my eye and I make a move toward it. I feel along the edges, getting a closer look at the design. It's not faux wood. It's real. Carved by hand and hollowed out. It even smells good. I reach over the counter and turn on the kitchen light. An image of a tree, similar to Ryder's tattoo design, is carved on the top lid with my name etched beneath. I feel the beveled words, letting the roughness prick at the pads of my fingers.

I hold my breath and open the box.

A sticky note is attached to a wrinkled red envelope, boasting the same handwriting as Stevie's yellow tag. It reads:

Some of the best things in life cost money, too. But they're worth every penny. P.S. It's already been cleared with Jay.

Curiosity burns as I release the sticky note and spot the candy cane label beneath it, addressed to me. I recognize the envelope now, and it makes me even more eager to see what's inside. Quickly opening the back flap, I pull out a long, rectangular ticket. My hands begin to shake as my name comes into view and I register the airline name running along the top. Those aren't the most important details, though.

The destination is Paris, France. Charles de Gaulle International Airport (CDG). The flight leaves three days from now and returns to Seattle-Tacoma International Airport seven days later. My hand cups my mouth and wetness sneaks up on my lids. I glance back to the bedroom, my gaze landing on my dream jar. There's certainly enough there to pay for a hotel stay. Enough for food. I'll have to be thrifty, but I can swing it. This is what I've wanted. This is what I've been waiting for. This is my dream. This is everything.

But it's from Ryder.

I broke his heart, then trampled on it. He met Christian. He knows about Nate. He knows about everything. There are no more secrets, no more barriers between us. Nothing that protects him from the ugly truth. Accepting his love is frivolous enough. How will I ever accept this on top of that luxury? And how did he pay for this? Airfare to Europe is a fortune, and while I know Ryder isn't broke, he's certainly not raking in the dough. He lives in a tent six months out of the year, for crying out loud. Granted, that's by choice, but this…this is too much.

I ditch my internal debate and dash for the bedroom, slipping on some clean clothes. I don't bother checking my reflection in the mirror. My wet hair is tied back and will give me a chill when I step out into the December air, and my eyes are probably swollen and puffy from crying, but I don't care. I hightail it out the door and jump in my car.

***

When I arrive at Stella's, I'm surprised to see that Jay isn't wiping down tables or greeting customers. He isn't anywhere in sight, in fact, but I know he's here. He's here almost every morning around this time, and his car's parked out front. Instead I see Natalie waiting on a section near the breakfast bar. She looks up as she takes a table's order, eyeing me for a moment. Just as quickly, she averts her eyes and resumes scribbling on her notepad.

"Brad," I say, zipping to the other end of the restaurant, "is Jay back there?" I nod to the kitchen, where Brad has just come from. He's carrying two plates of French toast and looking pretty ragged.

"Hey babe," he shakes his head as if trying to wake himself up, "nope, not in the kitchen. Maybe he stepped out for a few."

"His car's here."

"Huh." Brad serves the plates to his customers with a tired smile and turns back to me. "A smoke break, maybe? I haven't seen him since I clocked in. Try his office."

I thank him and begin to race on by, but he stops me. "Hey, you doing okay? Jay mentioned you weren't feeling good or something." He lowers his chin and his tone follows. "Things cool with you and Natalie? I mean, after…ya know." The customers he's just served suddenly turn eyes on me, sneering like they know exactly what Brad is referring to.

They probably do.

"God, you too?" I ask in a harsh whisper. "I don't have time for this." I spin around toward the kitchen and he jogs after me.

"Elise," he begs, "come on, everyone knows now. I'm just asking if you're okay, that's all."

"I'm fine, thank you."

"Are you really?" Something in his tone makes me stop. I slowly turn to face him and he almost runs into me. "Just because we quit hooking up doesn't mean I quit caring, you know. We've known each other a long time."

Sighing and biting my lip, I gently touch his shoulder. "I know. Thanks. I'll be okay, really. But I really need to speak to Jay. It's important."

"Do your thing, girl. We'll talk later."

I nod and hurry into the kitchen, dodging the cooks and other waiters as I make my way to Jay's office. Plates pass over my head while arms extend to reach for them, and billows of steam fill the air. Bacon sizzles and pots and pans clang, causing me to jump as I pass by. Even the cooks' voices make me flinch. They're louder, with more bite, more bass. Every sound seems to jump out and brush my skin.

It takes me a few seconds to register that I'm standing in front of Jay's office door. It's down the hall from the kitchen. It's closed.

Unusual.

I snap out of the funk I'm in, breaking the hypersensitive bubble I've slipped into, and raise my hand to knock.

"Yes?" Jay's voice calls out from the other side. I let myself in, swinging the door open with a deep breath. There's a woman sitting in the chair across from his desk, the back of her head to me.

"Oh, sorry," I mumble. "Didn't realize you were meeting with someone. I can come back."

Jay's face falls when he sees me. He scratches under his chin and shifts in his seat, eyes bouncing between me and the woman he sits across from. She doesn't turn to look at me, but I notice the tension in her shoulders and arms. Her hands grip the armrests, fingers clenching the black plastic.

"Uh, hon, now's not really a good time. It would be best if you came back later."

"Okay, when's a good time? Because it's really important. It's about Ryder and whatever you arranged with him."

"Give me another hour or so." His gaze flicks forward again and then back to me, his expression grim. I bristle, not used to seeing Jay so uncomfortable.

"No," the woman's voice interjects. Her back stiffens and she pries her hands from the chair armrests. Jay quickly stands and shoves his hands in his pockets, panic flushing his face.

"Elise," he quips, "you should really go."

The woman stands with him and carefully steps away from the chair, then turns to face me. My heart lurches against my ribcage when I come face to face with Tim's fiancée.

"Cheryl." Jay hurries around the desk. "Please, don't."

"Don't worry," she sneers, sizing me up. "I'm leaving. I have nothing more to say to you. But *you*," she cuts me a glare and takes a step forward, lifting her chin, "I have a few things to say to you."

"Cheryl," Jay continues to plead, "I'm begging you. Not here. Come on, this isn't the place."

"Oh really? Do tell me where the *place* is, Jay. Tell me when it's a good time to tell this bitch exactly what I think of her."

My palms begin to sweat and the room starts to spin. I don't know what Cheryl's doing here, talking to Jay about me and Tim. Jay mentioned Cheryl knew Tim was unfaithful, but why this? Why now?

"We've discussed this," he speaks sternly, nervously tapping his legs through his pant pockets. "You knew Tim was running around."

"I demand you let her go."

"What?" I pipe up, looking to Jay. "Please Jay, you can't—"

"Cheryl, you're out of line and that's an irrational demand." Jay starts for the door and I step aside, clearing the way. He holds it open, gesturing for Cheryl to leave. "If you're going to cause a scene, then I need you to leave. Do not do this here. Not in my restaurant."

"Irrational?" she scoffs, brows reaching sky high. "What's irrational is that you're keeping this slut employed when you know damn well she's been having an affair with your brother."

"I cannot fire an employee based on that accusation." He grinds his teeth and looks down. "This is inappropriate and I won't allow you to insult her under my roof, do you hear me?"

I want to speak up, want to say that I'm standing right here and I hate that they're talking about me like I'm not right in front of them, but I hold my tongue. I respect Jay and I know it's not my place.

"I'm sorry," I say quietly. It's the only safe thing to say, even though I know Cheryl will only reject it and that it will anger her more.

"Wow." She tightens her purse strap on her shoulder. "You're sorry. She's sorry," she waves to me and looks to Jay. "Accusation? It's a fact, Jay. And you're defending her. We are family."

"*Were* family," Jay corrects her, lifting his gaze to hers. "That's enough, Cheryl. It's over."

“You’re right,” Cheryl nods, moving to stand in front of me. My muscles twitch as her presence hovers, but I don’t avoid her stare. I look right into her eyes. I owe her that much. A sharp sting spreads across my cheek as she brings her hand up to slap me. She finishes off her retaliation by spitting in my face. “How’s that for appropriate?” She storms past us and out the office door and Jay sighs, handing me a tissue box from the top of the filing cabinet.

“Don’t worry about it,” I murmur, taking the box. He shuts the door and gestures for me to sit as I wipe at my face with a tissue.

“I don’t care what you did, she has no right to treat you like that.” His voice is sullen, and I can’t help but ache at his words. Why couldn’t he be my father? Why couldn’t there be more like him?

“I deserved it, Jay. It is what it is.”

He tinkers with his pen holder for a second, then meets my eyes. “Well, she’s leaving him. Finally.”

“I’m sorry.”

“Yeah, you said that.”

“Look, I know I put you in a tough position here. Sincerely, I apologize. I’m…defective, or something. But you already know that.” My gaze drops and I pick at a small tear at the knee of my jeans. How in the hell do I broach the conversation I came to have with him after this?

“You’re here about the trip to France.”

I lift my head.

"Go on, say what you came to say."

"I don't expect you to actually give me that time off. Especially not after..." I shrug a shoulder. "I just wanted to know if this was for real. Ryder really came to you about this?"

He nods stoically. "He arranged everything."

"And you agreed?"

"Of course I did. The kid is crazy about you."

"You just like him because he bribes you with presents and swaps cute puppy stories." A small smile tickles the corner of my mouth, even though I know it's still too soon to lighten the mood. I can't help it, though. Jay is such a softie.

"Maybe." He arches a brow, his expression unflinching. "I also like him because he's real. Honest. Unlike all the other schmucks you seem to run around with."

I shift in my seat. "Yeah, well..."

He holds up a hand and shuts his eyes. "I'm not about to lecture you on your choice in men, hon. Been there, done that, right?" His eyes open and narrow on me intently, the cogs in his mind working. "I am, however, going to tell you to take Ryder's gift. And mine." Rolling his chair backward, he swivels and dips into the desk drawer, pulling out a white envelope.

"What's this?"

"Just open it."

I don't hesitate, swiftly ripping at the flap. "A reservation?" I ask, studying the piece of paper.

"Consider it a Christmas bonus."

"*What?*" My eyes bulge as I take in the hotel reservation. It's for six nights at the Villa Beaumarchais Hotel in Paris. "How in the world did you pay for this? Jay, this is too much. I couldn't possibly accept—"

"You can, and you will. Shelley, Ryder and I all chipped in to make it happen. It's a done deal."

"But who will cover for me while I'm gone? This had to cost a fortune. I can't even…Jay, I just can't take this." I don't want to offend him; I certainly don't want to hurt his pride. But the reality is he and his wife Shelley live a modest life, and it's Christmas time. This kind of financial gift had to have been a heavy burden—much heavier of a burden than Jay is letting on. Not to mention he's giving it to someone like me. Has he lost his mind?

"Elise, you're sucking the joy from the whole gift-giving thing. Accept it and be happy, will you, hon?"

"Happy?" I scoff, standing to my feet. "Happy doesn't even begin to describe what I'm feeling right now." A myriad of emotions barrels through me. My face is growing hot and tears are burning my throat. "Why on Earth would you do something like this for me?"

"Because I care for you, hon. We care for you. Love you."

"I don't deserve this." I set the envelope on the edge of the desk, slowly backing away. My hands are shaking and my skin is crawling. "I don't deserve any of this, Jay. God, if you only knew."

Jay suddenly stands and moves swiftly to my side, smacking his hand on the desk to swipe up the tickets and hotel reservation. The papers crumple and he grabs my fist, handing them to me. His nostrils flare and eyes flash with persistence. "You're taking this," he demands, closing my hand around them. "You can't accept it? Guess what, Elise? That's not our problem. That's yours. And the only way you're going to figure out how to accept it is to march back home, look in the goddamn mirror, and see what we see. Take a good, hard, long look."

"Jay, I—"

"Go!" he shouts, waving to the door. "I don't want to see your face at this restaurant until you return from France, you hear me?"

My mouth is agape, my mind is scattered. I blink, my eyes dropping to the gift in my hands. It's heavy as lead and sweet as sunshine. I pivot and slowly turn away, the papers sticking to my sweaty palms. Jay doesn't say another word. His chair squeaks as he sits back down. I hear the shuffle of paper and the rattle of his pen holder as he clears his throat. I look back over my shoulder as I open the door, lips still parted, thirsty for words. Nothing quenches them. I steel myself and walk out, hurrying back through the bustling kitchen and out to my car. I start the engine, but I'm stuck staring at the steering wheel. Jay and Ryder's gift sits on my lap, and my hands are limp at my sides.

I don't want to go home.

My phone blips and I fish it from my bag, finding a text from Christian. He's just checking to see how I'm doing. I should be asking how he's doing. I should call him, but I can't. All I can think about is the generous, completely unwarranted gesture resting on my lap right now. All I can think about are Ryder's words to me last night. Jay's words, back in his office. Cheryl's confrontation, Natalie's cold shoulder, and even the horror of my interaction with Kylie are steam rolled by the overwhelming swell of my heart.

My hand snaps forward and I shift into reverse. I'm in tunnel vision as I pull out of Stella's parking lot and on to the main road to head toward Ryder's cabin. I'm not sure if he works today or if he's even home, but I know I need to see him. I can't call first. This isn't a conversation to have on the phone, and besides, words still fail me.

It's not long before I'm rolling up to Ryder's cabin. I park next to his Jeep and hurry up to the front door, nervous energy rocking through me like a tumultuous storm. I fidget with my car keys as I knock, fidget with my hair and scarf. I shift from right foot to left, willing him to answer the door before I chew my bottom lip off. Voices murmur from inside, and I turn to where our cars are parked, looking for another vehicle. He must have company, but I don't see another car.

The door finally swings open and a pretty blonde answers, looking frustrated. "Yes?" Her lips are pursed tight and her jaw is stern, her eyes studying me from top to bottom. They do a quick sweep and settle on my stunned gaze. I glance behind her, searching for Ryder.

"Um, hi. I was wondering if Ryder's home?"

"He is. And you are?"

"I'm…I'm Elise. A friend."

"Elise," she says my name like she's tasting it. "I don't think Ryder's mentioned you."

"Sorry, I didn't catch your name." My fingers grip my purse strap, and my keys cut into my palm. There is a small, colored tattoo just beneath her ear. It's ugly as sin, and I doubt it's the only one on her body. There are probably more. In unmentionable places.

"I'm Lauren. Ryder's fiancée."

My heart stalls and I stop breathing. Words stutter from my lips, but they're unintelligible. I try again, pushing them out carefully. "I'm sorry, his…fiancée?"

"*Mmhmm*," she says matter-of-factly, extending her hand to show me her ring. It's small and elegant. Something Ryder would pick out. After she shows me the ring, she cups her belly, and it's then that my gaze drops to the round bump she's sporting.

Air bleeds from my lungs.

My mind rejects the sight before me. Everything turns hazy, turning my world upside down. This isn't real. There's no way in hell. "And you're expecting?" I breathe, feeling my face pale.

"We are." She smiles sweetly, but it's fake. False to the core. "It's cold out here. Would you like to come in? Ryder will be right out. He just stepped into the bedroom to make a phone call."

"No," I mumble, backing away from the door. "That's okay. Thanks."

"I insist." Her fake smile brightens and she widens the

door, beckoning me to step inside. My heart, my mind, and the adrenaline pumping through my veins compel me to dash for my car and peel out of there as fast as fucking possible. To never come back. I start to listen to those instincts, turning on my heel.

"Really, it's okay. I have to get going." I only make it two steps before Ryder's calling out to me, joining Lauren at the door.

"Elise," he greets me cautiously, and when I bring my gaze to his, I see the fear lurking in his irises, just like it's simmering in mine. Only his is a different brand of fear. His is swimming in guilt, and mine…mine is drowning in dread. "Come in, will you?"

"I don't think that's a good idea."

"I think it's a great idea," Lauren quips, turning for the kitchen. Her gaze rolls to Ryder and she smirks as she passes him. "I love to meet Ryder's friends."

"Elise," Ryder says sternly, voice almost a whisper. "I can explain. Please, come in."

My heart is still thumping wildly in my chest and my brain is playing tug-of-war with my emotions. Part of me wants to flee, to run as fast as humanly possible from this crime scene—that is exactly what this will be if I stay here a second longer.

But another part, one I want to banish to some deep, dark place, wants to walk through that door, to hear what Ryder has to say.

"Only for a second," I agree, taking a wary step inside. Ryder hurries to the kitchen, where Lauren is transferring freshly baked cookies from a pan to a Christmas dish. My stomach churns. Here she is, Ryder's ex-turned-fiancée, baking cookies and playing house.

"I'm going to take Duke for a walk," Ryder says to Lauren. "Come with us?" he asks when he returns to meet me near the front door. He looks at me expectantly, but I can't bring myself to move an inch. I'm engulfed in disbelief, staring at the apron wrapped around Lauren's waist and the way she's made herself right at home in Ryder's cabin. There are interior decorating and parenting magazines fanned out on the coffee table, and little feminine touches everywhere. Flowers on the table. Floral throw pillows on the couch that certainly weren't there the last time I was here. A soon-to-be wife's fingerprints at every turn.

I nod gravely and step back outside while Ryder calls for Duke. Lauren pours coffee in the kitchen, her gaze moving to mine as she watches Ryder join me. "Don't be long, you two," she sings. "I'd hate for your coffee to get cold."

"Be right back," Ryder says, shutting the door behind us. Duke trots past us and begins down the dirt driveway. The second we're alone, Ryder grabs my hand and leads me after Duke, ushering me away from the cabin.

"Don't you touch me!" I burst out, yanking my hand from him. I walk briskly after Duke and Ryder follows, his words spilling in a rush.

"Elise, slow down. Just listen to me."

"Start talking, Ryder."

"How are you feeling?"

"How am I feeling?"

"Yeah, since last night."

I whirl around and go toe-to-toe with him, shoving his chest hard. His heels kick up dirt as they slide into the ground. "You son of a bitch!"

"I'm not marrying her, Elise. I know how this looks, but it's not what you think."

"She's wearing a fucking ring, Ryder! You picked it out, didn't you? Say it. I want to hear you say it!"

"Yes, alright! I bought the ring. But it was years ago. I proposed back when we were together. She wanted to think about it. She eventually turned me down. I didn't ask for it back."

"Why is she wearing it now if you're not marrying her? And she's pregnant?" I screech, giving him another shove. "She's fucking *pregnant*? You lying, hypocritical son of a bitch!"

He grapples with my wrists as I beat at his chest. "The baby's not mine. Stop it, Elise."

"Don't tell me what to fucking do! Why? Tell me why you gave me this gift? What was it all for then, huh? Tell me why!" I keep pounding into his chest, tears scorching my face. My vision is distorted, but I can see so many things pass over his hardened gaze.

"Because I love you. You know that. Calm the hell down, damn it!" He catches one of my wrists and juts his head back to keep his face away from my fists.

"How long have you been engaged? I deserve to

know!"

"Oh, yeah?" He catches my wrist and presses it against the other behind my back, holding me at arm's length. "Just like I deserve to know how many times you've fucked Christian Walker since you kicked me out of your place that day? You don't offer me any goddamn courtesies. What makes you think I owe you one now, huh?"

"You bastard." I shake my head, cutting him with a searing glare. My face is drenched and my chest is heaving. "I didn't touch Christian while I was with you. And even if I did, I tried to tell you. I tried to fucking tell you! I'm not girlfriend material. I don't make promises because I know I can't fucking keep them. But you!" I explode into another fit of fury, wiggling against his hold, trying desperately to break my wrists free. "All that bullshit you spewed to me. I believed you! I actually believed you."

"I never lied to you. Not once did I tell you something false."

"Oh, no? What does failing to tell me you're engaged classify as, huh? It's not your baby? Are you kidding me? What, did she just miraculously get knocked up? Did that ring just accidentally slide on to her fucking finger?"

"She showed up on my doorstep wanting to talk. She's pregnant with some other dude's kid. He doesn't want the baby. I couldn't turn her away."

"No, so you just propose to her instead? Invite her in and say, 'Sure, move in to my fucking *house*?'" I groan in frustration and give up fighting his hold, glaring up at him through the tears.

"I didn't propose to her. She was wearing the ring when she showed up. She's going through a hard time. She's been rethinking everything lately. What happened to us, how she turned me down years ago…all of it. The asshole that knocked her up took off and she's lost right now. Confused. She was looking for…comfort. That's all."

"She wants you back." The words come out almost petulantly, and I hate the sound.

"Yes. But she doesn't have me." His hand slides behind my back and grasps at one of my wrists. He brings my hand around and presses it against his beating heart. "You do. Did. Still do."

"She's living with you. How could you…" My lip quivers and I look away, knowing damn well I'm the hypocrite, here. Ryder's right. I've been fucking Christian Walker. Practically living at his place. I can't process any of this. There's no absorbing the harsh reality that is staring me in the face. "Have you been sleeping with her?" Stupid question, I know. But my words asked no permission from my brain or mouth.

Ryder looks away, his grip hardening on my hand, saying nothing but saying everything. I feel his heart thrash harder against his chest. Those rich, soulful eyes are unwavering and tormented, and nothing makes my stomach ache more. "Why are you here, Elise?"

I rip my hand from his chest and stumble back,

panting as I work to drag in deep breaths. "It doesn't matter anymore. None of it does."

"Why are you so angry about finding Lauren here? Come on, I want to hear you say it."

"There's nothing to say. It's too late. I'm too goddamn late."

"It's never too late. Say it!"

"Because I'm fucking jealous, alright? Are you happy?" My feet make a kick-start, darting around him, but he jumps in front of me. I veer to the right and he matches my move, blocking me off from each direction.

"Why are you jealous?"

"Get out of my way, Ryder."

"No. Tell me why you're jealous."

"Because I want you, you know that!"

"Nuh-uh. Wanting me isn't enough. Wrong answer, Elise. Try again."

I can't handle looking into his eyes. They're wild and on fire and they're not mine. None of him is mine. He belongs to Lauren now. "Let me go, Ryder!"

"Not until I hear the truth. I want to hear it straight from your mouth."

"I love you!" The affirmation bursts from my lips like sharp firecrackers. I hear Duke bark in the background but it's a muffled sound, muted by the potency of my words. "I love you, okay? Fuck! Is that enough for you?"

Ryder stills and I'm finally able to pass him. I beeline it for my car but the gentle touch of his hand on mine stops me. His fingers slowly lace through mine. I can't turn around. I can't look at him. If I do, what I see will level me.

"Elise," he says quietly, moving to step around me. When he aligns himself in front of me and peers down into my eyes, my heart implodes. I was right.

There's nothing but love there.

"You're not the other woman, here. You're *the* woman." He gives me a small, careful smile, and those dimples peek out from their hiding place. I missed them. I missed him.

I love him.

"Come here," he whispers, pulling me flush against him. His lips come down and taste mine, kissing tenderly at first in a soft exploration. I collapse against him and his arms close around me, lifting me up and off the ground. My legs curl around his waist and hook at the ankles, and I breathe him in. I want to drown in him.

"What about Lauren?" I ask, gasping for breath.

"I'll take care of it, I promise."

"But you—"

"I haven't been sleeping with her."

"You haven't?" I want to lash out again, want to yell at him for not telling me the first time around, but I know that he was just giving me a taste of my own medicine. And I of all people know what it's like to want to hurt someone because you're hurting.

He nips my lip and brushes his nose against mine, holding me against his firm body. "No. She knows I'm not interested in getting back together. She knows where

I stand. She's hopeful. Persistent. But she knows."

"You can't just kick her out. Not when she's alone and pregnant and scared." I can't believe the words are coming out of my mouth, but it must be proof that God gave me a heart. It must be in there, somewhere. It's bleeding for Ryder, after all.

Of course I want him to kick the bitch out. She had her chance. She turned him down and tossed him out like trash, incapable of seeing what kind of man he is. The good kind. The strong kind. Loyal and sincere. A rock.

She blew that chance, and I'll be damned if I stand around and let her move in and try to stake her claim on him again. Not now. Not when I know I have his heart. Not when I know my place in his life and what he is willing to do to give me his.

Holy shit, I have Ryder Jacobson's heart.

"Where do we go from here?" I ask. "What do we do?"

"We start over."

"There's no starting over. I can't take back the things I've done. Lauren's in your kitchen right now."

"I never said we erase the past. What's done is done. But we can change direction. Can you do that? Do you want that?"

"Yes. God, yes."

"Then let's do it."

I study the lines of his face, wonder if all he's saying is possible. It has to be. If I didn't believe it was, I would have never showed up here like this in the first place.

"I can go to France with you," his voice breaks my train of thought. "It's just what we need. Think about it. Think about what it could mean."

"What?"

"We can go together. We should just leave. Get away. Work all this shit out, you and me."

"What about your job? What about Duke? How the hell would you pay for it? I have some money saved, but I don't know if it's enough to cover everything—"

"I've never asked my parents for a damn thing," he says, his eager knuckles massaging my shoulders. "I can ask them for this. They'd help me, no questions asked. I can talk to my boss and tell him there's been an emergency. I can ask for leave. If he fires me, fuck it. I can be a maintenance grunt anywhere. This is my priority. You. Us. Right now."

I stare at him hard, my head spinning at how quickly this whole thing took a turn. Just minutes ago I was standing in his home, speaking to Lauren. His ex. His faux fiancée.

His replacement.

I lick my lips and kiss him once more, then let my legs slide down his body until my feet hit the ground. I blink. "I love you, Ryder. But I think…" My hands drop from his shoulders and fall to my sides. "I need to be my something."

"Be your something?" His brows pinch and he studies my face.

"Before I can be yours."

Understanding smoothes out his forehead and his eyes go soft, all warm and melting. It turns me to mush.

"I need to see what you see. What Jay sees. What Tee saw. I don't want to just love you. I want to give you everything…give you all of me. What you deserve. But I can't do that. Not yet. I'm beyond grateful for the plane ticket. I'll never be able to express what it means to me. But I need to go to France by myself." I watch him warily for a moment, hoping I haven't stuck another dagger in his heart. His lips part slightly, a small smile tipping them up. He slowly bends forward and presses a kiss to my forehead, letting an arm fold casually over my shoulder. He lassoes me back in to an embrace and sighs heavily into my hair.

"You go be your something, baby," he says, the tone rolling through me like hot, oozing caramel. "When you get back, you can be mine."

My arms shoot forward and wrap tightly around his neck, my face burrowing into his throat, just beneath his chin. His scruff scrapes at my forehead and I memorize the sensation. I'll miss it, but it will be here waiting for me when I come home. I don't know how, but I realize that I suddenly trust that implicitly.

"Thank you," I whisper, tilting my head to drop a soft kiss on his throat.

"Through hardships to the stars." His breath tickles my skin and I step back, glancing over at the cabin, deciding at that moment to let all of my worries about

Lauren dissolve. I have to let them go. I have to do this. What choice do I have? Duke's paws pad in the distance as he trots back toward us. It's time to leave.

I'm most definitely headed for the stars.

CHAPTER 16

My short, choppy blonde cut brushes my shoulders as I tuck it behind my ears. It's uneven and wild, a spontaneous, thoughtless labor of love. A snap decision made the moment I arrived at my hotel room in the Marais. There I lost myself in the Musée Carnavalet, and found myself in the eclectic crackle of rue Oberkampf. It was a Christmas unlike any other. One that turned my soul inside out and my mind upside down. I was no longer Elise Duchamp, notorious, antisocial home wrecker.

Not in Paris, anyway.

Only one thing was missing. A tatted-up, rugged bibliophile with dimples that could kill and eyes that could look right through you.

Sea-Tac airport greets me and I slide into a cab the second I dart away from baggage claim. I direct the driver to my apartment, telling him to take his time getting to Gig Harbor. I don't mind spending the extra cash for a longer ride home. I have a lot to process, and even though I'm immediately immersed in my familiar environment, everything feels distant and foreign, as if Seattle is an untouched destination on my itinerary. The sights on I-5 whiz past as we head closer to Tacoma, light dancing against a dark sky. I still see the bustling night life of rue Oberkampf, can picture the sparkling outline of the Eiffel Tower. It's all there, right here.

At home.

I tip the driver generously when we reach my place, and he helps me unload my luggage before waving me off. My apartment smells stale, like dead air riddled with the faint scent of gingerbread cookies—the ones I baked just before I left for Paris. I flick the light on and sink into the couch cushions, my hand still loosely wrapped around my suitcase handle. I stare blankly into the dim light of the living room, a sad yet sated smile drifting over my lips. It's funny how home can even smell funny when you're away for only seven days.

How will I ever explain to Ryder what his gift means to me?

I sigh and stand, wandering over to the kitchen counter.

There is no explaining it to him. Or to anyone, for that matter. Some adventures are only understood in the spirit—your spirit, the one who experienced them. But I can show him. With words and with honesty. For once, honesty.

And maybe, just maybe, a few others will consider that honesty. Maybe they'll catch a glimpse of the new Elise Duchamp. I'm still me. I'm still broken, but I'm mending. A few days away from home didn't wash away all of my sins. It didn't miraculously heal me from years of hurt, and it won't make the long road ahead any easier.

But it did give me hope, and with time, it will give me peace.

I still can't make up for the things I've done. For the way I've hurt people. I know the words I wrote in Paris benefit me more than any of them, easing a weight I've been carrying for far too long, but there's still a part of me that wishes they'll hear my sincerity, the delicate turning of a leaf.

The Gig Harbor Weekly glares up at me from the counter, its ink fresh and pages crisp. I haven't touched this issue, but I know what's inside. Ryder promised he'd drop off a copy the second it released, so it would be waiting for me when I got home. My fingers graze the edges for a moment and I step away, ready to call it a night. Jet lag will hit me with a vengeance tomorrow morning, and I know I need to rest up and brace myself for the transition I'm about to face. I have no idea what to expect. How I'll be received by the people I left here in Washington.

I only know I have a different reflection.

Unraveling my scarf and slipping out of my coat and tall black boots, I drag my feet into the bedroom and collapse onto the bed, falling fast asleep the second my head relaxes into the cool pillows.

I see stars as I drift off, bright and twinkling and close enough to touch.

***

The familiar jingle of the bells on Stella's front door warms my ears. It feels good to be home. I grip a trusty cup of coffee in one hand, struggling with the door. My brain is foggy, but the aroma of French toast and frying bacon slams into me as I step inside, snapping my senses into high alert. The breakfast crowd is bustling, as usual, and the second the door closes behind me, a quiet hush falls all around me, sets of curious eyes landing on me from every direction. Soft whispers erupt from left to right, and I look down, hurrying to make my way toward the kitchen.

I feel Natalie and Brad's eyes on me as I pass by their sections, but I don't look up, just keep moving. Brad says hey, but it's strangely weak and hesitant—a tone I've never come to expect from him. I wave half-heartedly in his direction and slip through the kitchen doorway, weaving around the kitchen craziness. I'm equally relieved and panicked when I approach Jay's office.

The door is wide open, and he's sitting at his desk, thumbing through The Weekly.

My lungs contract, my mind telling my body to push the air in and out, in and out. I clear my throat, adjusting my purse on my shoulder. "Hey, Jay," I say, fiddling with the lid of my coffee cup. I'm not sure what I expect. Maybe a 'hey hon, how've you been?' and that friendly smile of his, or maybe some typical questions about the trip.

I definitely don't expect to see what I'm looking at right now.

Jay's gaze lifts from the newspaper and lands on me, still with stunned wonder. His jaw is lightly slack and he swallows, eyes finally dropping to the Sorry Secrets column before him. They study the column for a moment, and each second is stretched out, never ending.

"It's good to see you," he says, his voice dry with grit. His mouth closes and eyes glaze over with choked-back emotion, so strong it nearly knocks the wind out of me. The expression tears me wide open, and all I can think of is rushing around his desk to give him a hug. That's all I want from him right now. A big, daddy-like, teddy bear hug that I know he knows how to give. I've seen him give it to his children and to his wife. I know he possesses something that I've never known but yearn for more than anything in the world.

Well, almost anything. Ryder's hugs are pretty fucking perfect.

But I remain still, gripping my coffee cup for dear life, and wait.

His eyes narrow and he sniffles, straightening up and shaking off the softie vibe that gives his heart away. He's suddenly all square shoulders and earnest face, strong and unyielding, like the dependable man I've come to know. "Your hair's different."

"It is."

"Did you get in a fight with your scissors?" A smirk

creeps up.

"Something like that." It's true, I botched the job. But my hotel room had the most stunning antique vanity. It practically shimmered against the cracked damask wallpaper. Its mirror taunted me, highlighting my long, blonde locks. As soon as I stepped into the room, I dropped my bags, moved toward it, took one look at myself, and grabbed a pair of scissors from the dresser drawer.

The rest was history.

"Looks good, hon."

"Really?"

"Really." He leans back in his chair and a squeak fills the air, creaking with his weight. "You've done a lot of surprising things. I gotta say, this one tops them all." He taps the newspaper and his brows rise.

"You know me," I smile, feeling a bit less uneasy, "always dramatic."

"Oh yes," he laughs lightly, "always."

"I hoped it would all blow over by now."

"This?" he pipes up, pointing to the paper. "Hon, this is all the town will talk about for weeks. Maybe months. Shit, years. But I guess you knew that."

"Yeah. Guess so." I specifically chose to write it all down while I was in Paris and e-mail the submission before I came home, just in time for the next issue run. I had plenty of time on the plane ride overseas to think about what I wanted to say. By the time I actually sat to write it down, the words just poured out. There was no controlling the flood. "Sorry if it…caused any commotion here for you."

He laughs again. It's not quite as jovial this time. "That's putting it mildly."

Shit.

"Elise." He leans forward to find my eyes, which are everywhere but on him now. "I'm only teasing you, hon. You're worried about the commotion it's causing me? All I give a damn about is what you're about to walk into out there. You've got a real set of brass balls, let me tell you."

A huff of laughter bursts from my lips, a mixture of nervous energy and genuine amusement at his way with words. "Jay."

"I'm just sayin', hon. You do. More than any man I know. Hell, more than me, that's for sure."

"Um…thanks, I guess?"

He shakes his head and chuckles, finally standing to meet me at full height. I seem to shrink as he rises, restraining my need to bound over to him and ask him for that hug.

There's no need to.

He moseys at first, hands in pockets as he saunters around the desk toward me. He stops in front of me and lifts his chin, staring down with proud eyes. A father's eyes. Not my own, but they're more than enough. Then his arms wrap around me and I freefall, plummet into this man's affection. The kind I have only ever imagined. It's not like Ryder's love. It's different altogether, and I don't know if it's because it's happening right now, right when I need it—when I've needed it all along—or because I understand now.

Because I see what he sees.

A girl who fucked up. A girl who made careless choices—choices she'll never regret, but consequences she'd never wish upon anyone—and who needed something unconditional. Something safe, something strong. A girl who did not kill her mother. A girl who was not rotten, only broken, like the world she and so many women are forced to walk in. A cruel world. Perfectly imperfect, just like Ryder Jacobson.

My something.

Wetness leaks from my eyelids and Jay holds me tighter, shushing me quietly, his body stern yet comforting. Everything in me lapses into something fluid, something uncontrollable. Sparks fly and sunshine floods my chest like butterflies fluttering for escape. My arm lifts and hooks under his, my hand latching onto the back of his shoulder. We stand there like that, with the office door wide open, for I don't know how long. This moment is infinite.

"How about we go for a ride?" he asks, pulling back slightly to peer down at me. A sob escapes me when I look up, never wanting to let go of this man.

"You guys are busy. You sure you can leave right now?"

"I've been holed up in this office since the crack of dawn. I need some air. Besides, these guys can hold the fort down for a day. They've managed before." He smiles and pats my cheek, moving to grab his coat. He leads me out of his office and through the kitchen, back out into the restaurant, where I'm just as much of a spectacle as I was when I first walked in. This time, as we stroll past each table, I force my gaze up, meeting each stare.

"Elise," Natalie's voice calls out to me. I stop and turn to find her at a table to the right, pouring coffee for a customer. "So you finally made it to Paris, huh?"

My gaze darts to Jay's for a second and he nods subtly, telling me it's okay. "Yeah, finally," I say carefully, looking back at Natalie. That same guarded look I've come to know since our fallout holds her expression hostage, but her eyes say something else.

"Good for you." She smiles. It's still careful, still void of trust, but it's kind and genuine, and that's everything to me.

"Thanks. It was amazing."

"Maybe you can show me pictures sometime."

I begin to stutter, but quickly correct myself. "I'd like that. Sure. Any time."

She nods and holds my gaze for a moment, then resumes pouring coffee and chatting with her customers. Jay and I take that as our cue, wandering out to the parking lot.

"My car or yours?" I ask.

"Mine. You'll have a ride back."

Excitement unfurls in my gut, and I climb into his passenger seat, praying my mind will calm down long enough to focus. I need to breathe, need to get it together, but all I can think about is seeing his face. What it'll do to me when I breathe him in, feel his lips on mine.

Jay pays me a knowing side glance as he drives us toward South Bend, and I just grin like the nervous fool I am. We roll up to Ryder's cabin just before 11 a.m. We bounce around as the rocky dirt drive welcomes us, pulling us into the woods' rustic magic. Duke's distinctive bark echoes in the distance when I step out of the car. I straighten my coat and comb fingers through my hair, looking for any signs of Lauren. Nothing so far, but I haven't been inside yet.

"She's not here," Jay says, reading my mind. "Long gone, right before you left for Paris."

"Good." I vaguely wonder how she made out, having to head back out into the harsh world with a bun in the oven, knowing she lost Ryder Jacobson. Losing him can't feel good. I would know.

Duke's bark grows closer. His dark shadow comes bounding from around the back of the cabin, heading straight for us. Laughter follows his mad dash, and the sound sends heat straight down my spine, stopping in my toes.

And there he is.

Striding casually behind Duke, appearing from around back, with all that easy grace I love. Broad shoulders, every-man smile, that imperfect tooth, and a five-o-clock shadow that male models kill for. The rest of his art is covered in denim jeans and a hunter green sweater. He's carrying a pile of firewood, his breath visible as he tells Duke to settle down. I pat Duke on the head, but I can't take my eyes off his owner. He's my owner, too.

I hope he still wants to be.

Ryder meets my gaze as he walks closer. He slows in his tracks, his grin slowly growing as he drinks me in.

"Let me get that for you." Jay strolls up to him, taking the firewood off of his hands. He calls out to Duke and Duke trots up to his side to follow him toward the house. "I'll give you two kids a minute."

Ryder glances briefly in Jay's direction, a fleeting look of gratitude, but his eyes are all on me, every inch, every crevice. With the way he's looking at me, we're going to need a hell of a lot more than a minute.

I shiver as the harsh winter wind whips at my cheeks, but the sting of the cold disappears when Ryder moves in.

"I'm surprised you came back," he says, brushing his hands on his pants.

Disappointment rattles through me, my heart crashing to a ravine in my chest. "You are? I thought…I mean, I thought I made it clear that I—"

"From Paris, Elise." He smirks and steps closer, his presence intoxicating. "I was afraid once you got there, you'd never want to come home."

Relief breezes through me just as fast as panic sought to sink me. "Oh," I laugh, biting my lip.

"How does it feel? Being a celebrity now and all." His lips swish to the side playfully and he freezes when the tips of his boots hit mine. We both just stand there, staring. Waiting.

"I didn't mean to single anyone out," I clear my throat, averting my eyes, "I just had to get some of that off my chest. You know, purge."

"They say confession frees the soul."

"Guess that's true."

A quiet gasp escapes me when he reaches up to smooth his cold, rough fingers over my cheek. They travel along the edge of my earlobe and thread through my hair. His eyes follow their trail, taking in my shorter, edgier hair style. "I like," he says softly, low and smooth, just like the glide of his fingers. "It suits you."

I lean into his touch, closing my eyes. "Me, too."

"I like this more." His lips suddenly touch mine, pressing lightly, his tongue gliding along my lower lip, seeking entrance. I exhale into the kiss, giving him an immediate green light. I open and accept him, letting the reeling force overtake me. His kiss reaches deep, slow and sensual, careful yet firm—a Ryder Jacobson kiss. The one I've been waiting for.

And then I can't wait a second longer.

My hands land on his chest and slide upward, looping around his neck. He cups my face, staggering forward, his mouth turning desperate. Our hot breaths plume in the winter air, our cold lips warming as the kiss turns hard and urgent. He palms the small of my back, smoothing his hand over my ass to pull me against him.

"Hey baby," he murmurs. "I'm glad you're home."

"Ryder?"

"Yeah?"

"I hope you have strawberry ice cream in the house."

His breath tickles my face. "Oh, I stocked up last night."

"Are you always so prepared?"

"Always."

"And patient?"

He laughs and nibbles along my lower lip, sending me a subtle but very pointed rock of his hips. Right here, in the middle of the forest, in broad daylight. With the closest thing I have to a father within viewing distance. "Not always."

"We better get inside."

"Why Elise Duchamp, are you suddenly turning shy on me?"

"Oh, just get moving, Jacobson." I raise a brow and begin tugging on his hand, leading us toward the cabin. Surprise widens those dimples and color spreads over my cheeks. The truth is I do feel shy. Like all of the lights have been turned on and I'm standing naked in the middle of the forest, everything on full display.

I blame it on Paris.

When we step inside, we find Jay tending to the fire while Duke gobbles away at his food bowl, slurping up every last piece of kibble. Jay grunts as he rises, planting his hands on his hips as he assesses the fire.

"I think that'll do," he says with a nod. "Nice and toasty."

"Thanks, man." Ryder slips out of his coat and makes

a move for the kitchen. I scan the cabin, relieved to see all of Lauren's touches are gone. It's Ryder's place again. "Hey, I have a few more books for you to take home. Right there, on the top shelf. The ones you asked about." Ryder points to the chestnut bookshelf near the fireplace while he collects some spoons and bowls.

"Ah, yes," Jay says, reaching for the bag of paperbacks. "Thanks, Kid."

"Care to stay for some ice cream?"

"Ice cream? In this weather? It's not even noon."

"No better time." Ryder sends me a sly glance. "We have strawberry."

"Thanks, but I'll pass. Gotta get back to the restaurant. Just wanted to swing by and bring you your girl, here." He walks over to Ryder and claps him on the shoulder. "Take good care of her, you hear?"

"You have my word." They exchange looks and Jay nods, holding Ryder's gaze for a long moment. He finally waves to us both and strolls to the door.

"Strawberry ice cream in December," he mumbles, shaking his head.

"We have warm brownies, too," Ryder drawls, just as Jay reaches the door knob. He pauses, looking tempted, but groans and pats his belly on a exhale.

"Better not," he says. "Don't want to fatten myself up for the Mrs. You two enjoy your sweets. Behave now, lovebirds."

"We'll try," I smile coyly, joining him at the door. I walk him out to his car and tell him to drive safely, my heart lurching as I watch him drive away. One love of my life on his way out, another on his way in.

I look back at the cabin.

Ryder's silhouette is visible through the frosty windows. An orange glow pools from the fireplace, casting it in soft light. I could stand here, just like this, watching him while I freeze to death. But I want to be bathed in that light with him.

And I want the sweets he's preparing for us.

"There she is," he says, when I come up behind him, resting my cheek on his back. My arms encase him, hands planting firmly on his chest. He's scooping the strawberry ice cream over the warm brownies, which smell divine.

"My three favorite things, all under one roof." I kiss his shoulder, watching him work.

He glances behind him, eyeing me. "Well, did you read it? I left the copy in your kitchen."

"I wrote it. I already know what it says."

"Then why did you want the copy?"

"Just thought I should have it. I'll read it someday, I'm sure."

He sets a spoon down and slowly turns, leaning back against the counter. "Move in with me."

My lips part and eyes widen. "Yeah?"

"Definitely."

"Did everything go okay with Lauren?" I still don't like saying her name. I'm sure it has the same effect on me that Christian's name has on Ryder. Well, maybe not to the same degree, but it's unpleasant all the same.

"It's all settled. There's nothing to worry about. She's my past, you're my future." He lifts my hand and kisses my knuckle. "Simple."

"But the baby…how did she take it?"

"Elise, it's over. I promise, it's okay. Lauren's a strong girl. She'll make it on her own. It wouldn't have worked out. I couldn't give her what she wanted."

"Well, I could get used to this place," I say, looking around wistfully. "What'll we do when Richard needs it back? Go back to the campground?"

"We'll figure it out. Maybe we can get a place of our own. Do a little traveling."

"Yes."

"Yes, you'll move in?"

"Yes to it all." I slouch forward, leaning against him. "Yes to everything, as long as it's with you."

A quiet intake of breath parts his delicious lips, and I inhale, spoiling myself. Rich tree bark and cinnamon spice, all musky and earthen.

Perfect.

"I'm going to make you happy, baby." His eyes flare with determination, and he spins around to grab the bowls, leading us to the sofa. It feels like it was ages ago when I sat on this couch, in front of this fire, with Ryder spooning me cool strawberry cream. We feed one another leisurely, wordlessly. When we're done, I tell him all about my adventures in Paris.

How I got lost in Montmartre.

Made friends in Au Levain du Marais, the most charming boulangerie.

Discovered some of the best vintage shopping and marveled at the Louvre.

Sipped a cup of sweet and spicy mulled wine at the Champs-Élysées Christmas market.

Bought a chic chapeau at Le Bon Marché.

Gawked at Notre-Dame.

Missed him.

Missed him a lot.

"Any word from him?" Ryder changes the subject, after I've indulged him in my travel details. He looks down, pushing his spoon around in the empty ice cream bowl.

"I haven't spoken to Christian, Ryder. Not since that night. He's texted me to ask how I'm doing and I've let him know I'm okay. That's all, I swear."

"I believe you."

"Do you?"

"Yes." His gaze lifts to mine and his jaw flexes. "I do." He rubs my knee and stands, collecting my empty bowl. "I'm going to run us a hot bath. You relax. I'll come get you when it's ready."

"*Mmmm*, sounds perfect." I tilt my head and close my eyes. I love his tub. It's an old, clunky, antique piece of junk, with clawed feet and a squeaky faucet, but it's clean and functional, and when I'm sharing it with Ryder, all is right in the world.

He deposits our dishes in the sink and starts for

the bathroom, disappearing and leaving me with the crackling fire. Duke chews contently on a bone, lounging comfortably on his bed, enjoying the warmth. I sigh and shift forward, rummaging around the coffee table for something to read. This is the perfect afternoon for a hot bath with my man and a good book.

Luckily, I'm in the right place.

Ryder has books sprawled everywhere. There are various timeworn paperbacks, hard cover editions of older classics, and the latest contemporaries, strewn over the table, covering magazines and coasters. I fumble through the selection, stilling when I uncover a copy of The Gig Harbor Weekly. It's the latest one, hidden underneath a pile of woodshop magazines. There's a page flagged at the corner, and I don't have to guess which one it is.

Glancing over the back of the couch, I search for Ryder. The water is running in the bathroom and he's humming an Eddie Vedder song.

On a long exhale, I open the paper to the flagged page. My curiosity fuels me to look. To see what I already know is there.

Sorry Secrets, Issue 53, December 2013
A Letter to My Lovers and their Lovers

If you're reading this, you know who you are. You know who I am. I'll cut straight to the chase.

I'm Elise Duchamp, and this is my confession.

To all of the men I've slept with—if you were taken, I'm sorry. I didn't give a shit about you or your wives, girlfriends, whatever. You didn't either, but that's okay. That's your dirt, not mine. I'm responsible for my dirt and my dirt alone.

To all of the women I've hurt—if I've slept with your man, I'm sorry. I know that sounds weak and shallow, but it's all I can say. Nothing else I could say would convince you of my sincerity, would it?

Yeah, didn't think so. It wouldn't convince me, either.

To my lovers' lovers: I've spent the past few years seeking solace in your man's arms. If you noticed your perfume bottle was lighter, your sheets were rumpled, or your closet was raided, that was me. I sought peace, validation, and distraction, and more shit that I might never fully understand in your bed. With your property. Nothing excuses it and I'd be lying if I said I regretted what I've done. I don't. I don't regret any of it, because I wouldn't be where I am right now if I hadn't made the choices I made. I stand by them, as wrong as they were.

This confession's for you.

I see now that I disrespected myself just as much, if not more than I disrespected all of you. In light of this epiphany, I have a few questions for you. Do you know the man you sleep next to at night? Do you really want to? Or are you content not knowing the person you give yourself to, day after day? Are you willing to settle?

Because I was.

Now, I'm not so sure why I saw any value in that. I think I got the short end of the stick. Just like you. I've been the other woman, but you've been the woman. The keeper. And yet here you are, reading this column. Does that sit well with you? That you got the short end, just like me? That in essence, you're really no better than me?

Now hold up, before you get pissed and start spouting off the obvious: you aren't like me, because you don't have affairs with unavailable men. Or hell, maybe you do. I wouldn't know. And many of you don't even know your man's been screwing around with someone like me. But I'm here to tell you, he has. Bottom line is you're no better than me if you find out and do nothing about it.

No, it doesn't make you a whore like me. It doesn't make you a bad person or a pathetic woman. But it does make you a pawn. A pawn in a game that only ends one way. You're too goddamn beautiful, too goddamn smart, and too goddamn good for a life like that—wise words from a wise man in my life. You know why they're wise words?

'Cause they're true.

Life's too short, and love's too good to pass up for some sham deal. You don't think there's something better out there? You're wrong. I know because I found it—the real stuff—and I'm the last person on the damn planet who deserves it. If the universe can hand me some, it sure as hell can hand some to you. Besides, it's not a matter of deserving. It's a matter of respect. Unconditional grace.

I'm no great philosopher. I know my advice means jack to you. But I know what it means to be a pawn. And I don't want to be one anymore. I hope you don't, either.

Yeah, yeah. Get to the point, right?

Just hang on. Here it comes.

Be exceptional. Be your something. 'Cause you're all you've got. And until you have that, you've got nothing. Look in the mirror. Take a hard, long look. I hope you see what I see. Please accept my sincerest apologies for the hurt I've caused, for everyone—everything—my choices have affected. This part's for me. I win here, not you. I know that. But I choose to own that truth.

Know why?

Because I'm exceptional. Because I'm something. Because I'm loved. And guess what?

You are, too.

My gaze lingers on the last line of the entry, my concentration breaking when I feel Ryder's presence loom from behind. His hand clamps down firmly on my shoulder. I close the paper and turn to look up at him.

"You ready for that bath?" he asks, gracing me with that soft, gentle smile of his—the one I will never get enough of.

"Yeah," I smile back, cupping my hand over his knuckle where it rests on my shoulder, "I'm ready."

"After you, baby."

I stand and lead the way to the bathroom, Ryder on my heels and freedom in my soul. Tonight the stars will be abundant, and my heart will be full.

THE END

EPILOGUE

ELISE
24 YEARS OLD

My comb hits the glass table top, my reflection smooth and glossy in the mirror. My long pressed waves are ready, my ruby red lipstick popping against my pale, luminous complexion. Gold, Art Deco style chandelier earrings drip from my lobes to the tops of my shoulders. I tap them, watching them shimmy and sparkle in the bedroom light, my eyes moving to the shadow that appears behind me, distracting me from my own reflection.

I look at Ryder, our gazes meeting in the mirror.

"Don't you look dapper," I say, absorbing every mouthwatering inch of him. He's dressed from head to toe in a black and white tux, and I know what dressing like this means to him. He isn't a fan of swapping out his flannels and blue jeans for such snazzy attire, but he's doing this for me.

This is my night.

"We're going to be late, baby," he says, tugging at his bow tie with that crooked smile of his. His five o'clock shadow is still intact, just more tailored than usual. "Don't tell me all of this debonair stuff is going to go to waste."

"Oh, it won't." I smile flirtatiously over my shoulder. "I'll enjoy stripping it all off of you when we get home."

He comes up behind me, his calloused hands moving to my shoulders. They massage lightly, bringing me right home. This is my favorite place. "And I'll enjoy peeling you out of this dress," he whispers, leaning down to speak into my ear, leaving shivers in his wake.

"How's the article coming?"

"Good, I think." He kisses my temple and straightens up, continuing to rub my neck. "I wasn't crazy about this one, but it had real potential."

"*Hhhm*." I nod and move to stand from the vanity stool, reaching for my black gloves. My mother is no longer here to slide them on for me, but I'm okay with that, even though I miss her. I put them on myself, feeling a small grin creep up. Ryder's the official book reviewer for The Gig Harbor Weekly—the paper's latest addition to their film and literature critic section. He's been with the paper for a year now, but this is his chance to write his own piece on a regular basis. No more Mr. Fix-It How-To columns. Not that he minded those, but this is his heart. His voice. I couldn't be more proud of him. "And Duke's new toy box?" I ask next, knowing he must be close to finishing the new chest. Duke's toys have taken over the living room, and Ryder jumped at the opportunity to carve him a new chest, just so the pup could have a place for his slobbery, frumpy play things.

This man and his dog. I fucking love it. I love him.

"It's coming along," he replies with pride. I can tell. His fingers are raw and rough, skin broken around the nails. I finish slipping on the gloves and then take one of his hands, bringing his thumb to my lip to bite it, holding it loosely between my teeth. I meet his eyes, enjoying the flash of desire that flickers there. I bite down softly and suck, not giving a damn that I've just smudged my fresh lipstick. "Elise," he warns.

"I know, I know. We're going to be late," I mumble around his finger. I release him and dab at my mouth with a handkerchief, correcting the smudges. "Shall we?"

"We shall." He holds out his arm and I link mine through it, strolling with him through the bedroom doorway. We make sure Duke is situated before we exit the cabin, tossing him a few treats and pampering him with some rubs behind the ears. The air is warmer now, the sting of winter long gone. Still, I slip on my black shrug, and my shoulders thank me. Ryder helps me into the Jeep and then we're off, heading northward to the bay.

Tonight *Les Trois Enfants* is holding a gala to celebrate the induction of their new assistant director.

Me.

Over the past year, the tiny private school has flourished, and I've been there to witness the magic. At first, as a student. Within a few months, I landed a tutoring position for students studying the beginner level, and the owners were so impressed by my commitment to the organization and my passion for the language that they eventually asked me to come on board as a more integral part of the team. I accepted, of course, although it wasn't easy giving Jay my notice at Stella's.

The school might be small and tight knit, but its sense of community is its advantage. It offers an intimate learning environment, like studying with family, and word of mouth about that very appeal has traveled far beyond the borders of Pierce County. Children, college students, and parents of all ages now seek enrollment from all over the Tacoma and Seattle areas, some even making the trek to the school each week all the way from Skagit county.

When we arrive at the gala, Ryder and I greet my co-workers and the many students and supporters who chose to come out tonight in honor of the school's new chapter. There's lots of kissing on the cheeks, many congratulations, and all kinds of talk about when the next group trip to France will take place. We're thinking in the fall, which works well for Ryder and me. We've been itching to do some traveling. Especially Ryder. He gets restless if we don't explore every now and then.

I'm summoned to the podium on a modest platform that overlooks the dining room. As I take my place, I'm met with elegant, sweeping views of the vast picture windows lining the backdrop of the restaurant. They showcase Puget Sound, a sunset wide and glistening. I look out at the audience, my gaze scanning each table, each face, until I find them. Ryder and Jay. My men.

Jay is seated with Shelley and his children, his face proud and rife with excitement. Ryder sits back casually, one leg propped over the other, an arm resting on his lap. His eyes don't leave mine. I square my shoulders and take a deep breath, adjusting the microphone. The sea of faces I see is staggering. Some I know—some intimately—and others are there in spirit. Like Tee. Like my mom. My father, too. Even he has a place in this.

As I open my mouth to greet everyone, I pause, feeling a veil of awareness cascade over me, like the finest silk. A playful tinge colors Ryder's lips, and a spark ignites over my skin, from hip to hip, ink to ink.

My name is Elise Duchamp. I'm 24 years old. Lover, fighter, cageless bird. An unwavering force.

That is something I know how to be.

A Preservation Series
Companion Novel

Available Now

ABOUT THE AUTHOR

Rachael Wade is the Amazon bestselling author of THE PRESERVATION SERIES, LOVE AND RELATIVITY, and the upcoming New Adult sci-fi series, THE KEEPERS TRILOGY. When she's not writing, she's busy going to concerts, watching too many movies, and learning how to protect animals and the environment. She's an avid Brandi Carlile fan and loves all things Tim Burton. Visit her at RachaelWade.com and LightsOnLove.com, and come chat with her on Twitter @RachaelWade.